THE TROJAN HORSE

"Again and again I charged that wall, always driving the corner of the box against one particular block of stone. And when I was staggering with weariness, I noted with a leap of joy that the two blocks below it had given about an inch at the point where they met each other. The light of the torch was becoming so feeble that as often as not I had been driving the corner of the box against these, instead of against the stone above. The discovery gave me strength. A few more charges and I saw the blocks above and below were caving in. Again and again I charged that wall, making a din like a blacksmith's forge. And after every blow I found the blocks had given ground. At first it was only an inch. Then it was two and three, and at last as much as six, with all the blocks to the floor moved slightly inwards."

'this novel seems to combine the breathlessness and hair-raising properties of earlier works with a more sustained and less episodic interest. Here is as exciting an Odyssey as ever kept a man awake . . .' FINANCIAL NEWS

'For sheer excitement Hammond Innes will be hard to beat.' *Daphne du Maurier*, OBSERVER

First published 1940
First issued in Fontana Books 1960
Eleventh Impression February 1971

TO

MY FATHER

© Hammond Innes 1940
Printed in Great Britain
Collins Clear-Type Press
London and Glasgow

HAMMOND INNES

The
Trojan Horse

Collins
FONTANA BOOKS

CONTENTS

Chapter One

THE FACE FROM THE BARBICAN

I READ the writing on the back of the visiting card and then turned it over and looked at the name. Paul Severin, 155 Neath Street, Swansea. It seemed familiar. I looked once more at the writing on the back. " As a criminal court barrister you will know my name," it ran. " You will, therefore, realise how urgent it is that I should see you." The initials P. S. followed. Paul Severin—Swansea. The name and the place went hand-in-hand in my memory.

And then suddenly I knew, and I told my clerk to get me the file of the *Daily Express*. It seemed incredible. Yet it was not altogether unnatural. I had specialised in the defence of criminals, and some success with what had been considered doomed men had given me a certain reputation. But it offended my sense of decorum, mainly, I think, because no one—least of all a barrister—likes to have his conscience set a problem.

When my clerk returned with the file, he said, " Won't you see him, Mr. Kilmartin? He seems very excited. It was all I could do to prevent him from coming right in after me."

" In a minute, Hopkins," I said. " In a minute." I took the file from him and put it down on my desk. " What does he look like, Hopkins?" I asked, as I scanned the pages of recent issues, working backwards.

" He's a rather short gentleman, on the plump side. His face is pale and a bit unshaven-looking, and his nose is—well, he looks to me a bit Semitic, as you might say, Mr. Kilmartin. He's wearing a bowler hat and glasses."

" What else, Hopkins?" I asked.

" An old brown suit and a dark blue overcoat. They're both very dirty."

" He doesn't sound very attractive."

" No, he looks a proper old money-bags. I don't think he's English."

" His name certainly isn't," I said. Then I found what I

7

had been looking for, and knew that I was right. Mr. Paul
Severin was wanted for murder. I dismissed my clerk and
told him I would ring when I was ready to see my visitor.
There was the story right in the middle of the front page.
As my eye glanced down the column, it all came back to me,
and there was a photograph of a tubby little Jew, untidily
dressed, with a straggly tuft of a beard that gave him the
appearance of a rather elderly goat. He wore no glasses,
and even in the photograph his eyes were the central feature
of the man, large and widely set under the big domelike
forehead with its thick black eyebrows. The caption over
the photograph was, " This is Paul Severin. The Police
Want Him."

I glanced at the date—February 2. He had been at large
for just on a fortnight. It seemed a long time for a man of
such unusual appearance. My eye strayed back to the story.
Generally speaking, murders in war-time are not regarded as
particularly good copy. For one thing, they make macabre
reading for all those whose loved ones are daily facing
death, and for another, war makes life suddenly cheap and a
reader automatically wonders what all the fuss is about over
one more person killed. But some murders can stir the
imagination even in war-time, and this was one of them.

It was the cold-blooded ruthlessness of it that made it
front-page news. There had even been half a column of it in
The Times and I remembered that it had been the subject of
a leader in the Herald on the demoralising effect of war.

I turned to the issue of February 1, which gave the story
of the actual murder on an inside page. Then I went over to
my file of The Times and in the issue for that date found, as
I had thought, half a column, giving the bald facts of the
case. I went quickly through this to refresh my memory.
Paul Severin's real name was Franz Schmidt. An Austrian
Jew, he had fled to England after the Anschluss on a false
passport. He had gone to Wales and established contact
with his wife's family, who had a small stamping works just
outside Swansea. Though his wife was dead, these people
appeared to have gone out of their way to help him. They
had allowed him the use of a small workshop at their works,
so that he could continue experiments that he had been
engaged upon in Austria—he was an engineer. They had

found him inexpensive lodgings in the better quarter of the town and had done everything to make him feel at home. And then, when the money that he had managed to get out of Austria was exhausted, they had taken him and his daughter into their own house and had financed his experiments.

That was the background against which the murder had been committed. It was the kindness and generosity of this Welsh family to a refugee that made it so horrible. The head of the family was Evan Llewellin, the brother of Schmidt's wife. The rest of the household was composed of Llewellin's wife and mother. Evan Llewellin appeared to have been the generous one. The elder Mrs. Llewellin had told reporters that she had always distrusted Schmidt, had distrusted the use of another name, and had suspected that her daughter had not really died of pneumonia. Schmidt, she told them, had had a strong influence over her son from the start. He was always asking him for more money for his experiments and she said that much of the capital of the Llewellin family had been sunk in this way.

The murder itself was unusual and macabre. Evan Llewellin's body had been discovered by the works foreman in the main stamping-room. An automatic drill had pierced his skull and, transfixed like an entomological specimen, his body was bent rigid over the machine. It was a peculiar way to kill a man, and one that would only appeal to an engineer who understood how to work the machines. It appeared that both Llewellin and Schmidt had been working late. When the police had arrived, the light was still on in Llewellin's office and the plans for certain stampings for aircraft gun-mountings at which he had been working were still lying on his desk. Schmidt had not returned that night, and, in fact, had not been seen again. The safe had been opened and, on the evidence of the foreman, more than £1,000 in cash, representing a week's wages for the workmen, had been taken.

The case seemed clear enough. I turned back to my desk and my eye fell on the telephone. I hesitated. I had no doubt of the reason that Schmidt had come to see me. But I had never yet defended anyone whom I had believed guilty of premeditated cold-blooded murder. Frankly, I did not want to see the man. My imagination, always a little too vivid, could picture so clearly that wretch who had befriended him, transfixed by one of his own machine tools, and I had a horrible sense of revulsion at the thought of meeting Franz Schmidt face to face. I took a step towards the phone, my mind made up.

At that moment there came the sound of a scuffle from the outer office and the door of my room burst open to admit an elderly Jew in a bowler hat. Behind him I had a glimpse of an outraged Hopkins, murmuring explanations. "I must apologise for intruding upon you like this, Mr. Kilmartin." The man spoke English in a quite pleasant tone. For a second that sense of revulsion gripped me—revulsion tinged almost with fear. And then the mood passed and suddenly I saw, standing on my warm red Axminster, not a cold-blooded murderer, but a dirty, friendless old man who had been hunted by the police for two weeks. I remembered that no man should be judged before he has been heard in his own defence. Clearly he had come to me to say what he had to say, and I knew that I had no right to hand him over to the police unheard.

"That's all right, Hopkins," I said. And as the door closed, I waved my visitor to the chair on the other side of my desk.

As he came forward he took off his hat and his glasses. I paused in the act of sitting down and glanced at the photograph that stared up at me from the *Daily Express* file. There was no doubt about the identity of my visitor. All he lacked was a beard.

"I see you recognise me," he said, as he sat down opposite me. His eyes held mine. They were large and dark and strangely bright. He looked like a dealer in second-hand clothes, with his sallow face blued about the jowl by the stubbly growth that had once been his beard, and his ill-fitting clothes. But, looking into those dark eyes, I saw only the intelligence of the man. Behind this nondescript exterior was a great brain and I began to have a horrible doubt. Yet when he spoke he seemed sane enough. He apologised again for forcing his way into my room. His voice was soft and musical and very quaint, with its accent coloured by Austrian and Welsh and the usual handicap of people of his race. "I feared," he explained, " that your natural instinct as a citizen might override adherence to the code of your profession. I hope you will accept my apology."

I nodded. I took out my case and lit a cigarette. I could feel his eyes watching me.

" I am accused of a particularly callous and brutal crime," he went on. " If I had done it, I could have expected mercy from no one. I trust you will pardon me for fearing that you might be over-hasty in your judgment. I have a particular reason for not wishing to fall into the hands of the police yet. I have come to you because I must confide in someone—in someone upon whose discretion I can rely. It had to be someone, moreover, whose opinion carried some weight in official quarters."

At that I stopped him. " Even if you were to convince me that you are innocent of this crime," I said, " it is not in my power to persuade the police—nothing short of a direct alibi will do that."

He shook his head slowly and his rather full lips twitched into a wry smile. " That is not the reason I came to see you," he said. " Though I shall hope that, if the time comes, you will agree to defend me. No, I came here because, having followed your cases closely—in my leisure hours I have been something of a student of criminology—I considered you to be a man of sufficient discrimination to know the truth when you heard it. I considered you also a man of great determination—more, of great tenacity—once convinced of the justice of a cause. The obstinate tenacity of your nature is the secret of your success at the bar. You will pardon this analysis of your career. I was endeavouring to explain why I had come to you. I have a story to tell that few men would believe, very few indeed, coming as it does from the lips of a man who is supposed to have committed a particularly brutal murder. But you have had great experience of criminals and some understanding of murderers. If you do not believe me, no one will. But I feel that, if I can convince you, there will be one man of unimpeachable honesty who will not rest until he has exposed the cancerous growth that is bedded deep in the heart of this great country."

Towards the end he had grown somewhat excited and I was conscious all the time of those dark bright eyes fixed

unblinkingly upon me. "You speak in riddles," I said.
"Perhaps you will be a little more explicit."

Then he told me his story. It was a strange fantastic tale.
And when he left me I could not decide whether it was the
story of a madman, or the truth. It had to be one or the
other, for I was convinced that it was the truth as far as he
saw it. But whether the strain of the last few years had
snapped a great brain or whether all that he told me had
actually happened, I could not decide. But this much I knew.
It was not so strange or fantastic a story that it could not
have happened. And whilst logic rejected it as the tale of a
man whose brain had become unbalanced, my knowledge of
psychology argued that the quiet, straightforward manner in
which he had told it to me was proof of its reality.

It had not been just the story of the murder. It had been
his whole life-story. Sitting there in the chair opposite my
desk, with the firelight playing on his face, he had been
sufficiently convincing for me to agree not to tell the police
anything for a week, when he would come and see me again.

But it was the end of his story that had weakened my faith
in the rest. He had risen to go. And his voice became
suddenly excited and his eyes blazed with the light of the
fire in them. " If I shouldn't come to you next Monday," he
said, " will you go round to my lodgings and take the face
from the barbican? You are clever. You will understand.
The clue is cones of runnel." After the quiet matter-of-fact
way he had told me his strange but consistent story, this
departure into the melodramatic came as something of a
shock.

I told him so and he smiled that rather wry tired smile
and said, " I don't believe you will think so next Monday. I
have a feeling that I shall not see you again."

" But when the police catch you, I will come and see you,
and we will arrange about your defence."

He shrugged his shoulders. " Maybe," he said. " It is
good of you. But it is not the police I fear. When I told
you there was someone else after the plans beside the Calboyd
Diesel Company, I meant it. Germany wants them too. They
discovered I was not dead and what Fritz Thessen had told
them whetted their appetites. But if I told you who their
agents in this country were, you would laugh at me and I

should be discredited in your eyes. But when I am dead, you will know it, and then you will know who murdered my friend Llewellin. Good-bye, Mr. Kilmartin." He held out his hand and, as I shook it, he said, " I cannot thank you enough for listening to me so patiently. I shall hope to see you next Monday. If not, I have your promise to go round to my lodgings?"

His face was perfectly serious. I nodded. I could do nothing else. His grip on my hand tightened. " I think you will find it is not a case for the police—at first." Then he fished in his pocket and pulled out an envelope. ": That is a letter for my daughter, Freya, when you find her. The address of my lodgings is written in the corner." He put it down on my desk and, replacing his glasses and picking up his bowler hat, turned and went out of my office.

I sat down and tried to puzzle it out over a cup of tea. The man's story was convincing, at any rate in part. I couldn't believe he was a murderer. His point about Evan Llewellin being a bigger and younger man than himself, and the impossibility of his having held him under the drill with one hand while he operated it with the other, was sound enough. And yet it was fantastic. All that about Nazi agents after his Diesel engine plans and the murder being a frame-up to get him out of the way. If they had wanted him out of the way and were prepared to kill a man to achieve their ends, it would surely have been much simpler and much surer to have killed him? Who was he suspecting of being a Nazi agent that I should just laugh at the accusation? And all that rigmarole about how the Calboyd Diesel Company had queered his pitch at the Air Ministry by saying they had tested his engine and considered him a crank. The story was real enough to him. Of that I was certain. But he saw events with a distorted mind. Up to the time of his escape from the concentration camp the story was certainly accurate, but the rest, though based on truth, seemed to have been coloured by an unbalanced mind. God knows what he had suffered in that concentration camp! He had not gone into details about those two months. But, judging by what I had heard of other such camps, it would have been sufficient to affect the balance of a sensitive and brilliant mind.

But then there was that point about Llewellin being

stronger than he. On a sudden impulse I picked up the phone and asked my typist to try and get me Inspector Crisham at the Yard. Crisham was in and knew enough about the case to answer my query. " We realised that difficulty," he said. " But the men were on friendly terms and it wouldn't have been impossible for Schmidt to get Llewellin to bend down to examine something under the drill. Part of a gun-mounting was found under it. More probably Llewellin bent down to adjust something and Schmidt seized his opportunity and pulled the drill lever over. What's your interest in the case?" I explained hastily that it had interested me and I wanted to clear up a point that had been worrying me. I rang off before he could ask any more questions.

Well, that disposed of that difficulty. I was a fool not to have thought of it for myself. The more I thought about it, the less I liked it. I could picture that long low-ceilinged stamping-shop just as Schmidt had described it to me only a few minutes ago. It would be littered with machine tools, and there would be odd lengths and shapes of metal lying on the oil-soaked floor, and it would echo to the hollow sound of footsteps as Schmidt came up from his own work-shop to accompany Llewellin home. And Llewellin would show Schmidt the gun-mounting he had been working on. Perhaps it was complete save for one or two more drill-holes and he had brought it over to the drill, switched the machine on and then bent down to adjust the position of the mounting. And Schmidt, standing beside him, short of cash and wondering about the future, yet knowing there was a whole week's pay in the safe and the key in Llewellin's pocket, had decided to kill him on the spur of the moment, as he saw the man's dark head come directly beneath the re-volving point of the drill. That must be how it had happened. And I was the only person who knew where Schmidt was. I looked down at the envelope on my desk. The name of Freya Schmidt stared up at me, written in that neat scholarly hand. And in the top right-hand corner was his address—209 Greek Street, London, W.1. I had only to ring Crisham and give him that address and Schmidt would be safely behind bars by the evening.

Even now I am surprised that I did not. It wasn't the fact that I had promised to wait until next Monday before doing anvthing that stopped me. If I had thought the man was dangerous, I should not have hesitated. I think it was that letter to his daughter. I felt I ought to trace her first, or at least try to prove to my own satisfaction whether Schmidt's story was true. I could not help remembering that he had convinced me at the time. It was only the melodramatic close to the interview that had cast doubt upon the rest of the story. I ought to try to prove it one way or the other. But how could I? That was the extraordinary part about his story. He had not offered me an alibi or anything concrete like that. His story was that he had come into the stamping-shop, seen Llewellin's body, had gone into the office and seen the safe open and with no money in it, and had known at once that he had been framed.

I lit a cigarette and tried to think it out. Then I picked up the letter and ran my pencil round under the flap. Inside was a single sheet of paper. I glanced through it and then put it back in the envelope and resealed the flap. An affectionate farewell from a man to his daughter. The phrases run in my memory now, and whenever I think of them I have a sense of guilt at having intruded upon something very precious to two people who had suffered much and loved each other greatly. Short though it was, the letter said everything there was to be said, and the words remain with me as something very beautiful. The man's sense of impending death showed quite clearly between the lines. He did not fear death. But he feared for his daughter's safety in the face of a danger that, reading the letter, I could not believe was unreal. This fear showed in the postscript which read, " The man with whom I have left this letter is Mr. Andrew Kilmartin. He knows my story and will have all the information that up to the time of my death I had obtained concerning Them. He will advise you. But until They have been unmasked, promise me to give up the work and disappear. I shall not rest happy if I think you are in danger."

To read that letter was to feel that he had found it necessary to return to my chambers to bind a wavering man to his promise. How could I ring Crisham after reading that letter? It was not the letter of a madman—or was it? That beauty, that sincerity might all come of madness. I had seen cases like that before. If only he had told me where I could get hold of Freya Schmidt. She held the truth of the matter. But he had told me nothing to guide my next step except that melodramatic stuff about taking the face from the barbican and the clue being the cones of runnel.

At that moment my clerk came in to inform me that the court had just phoned him to say that the case of Rex v. Lady Palmer would be heard the next day, instead of on Thursday. It was a dangerous driving case, and though I did not imagine it would take long, it was one of those troublesome briefs that take a lot of preparing. The change of date made it imperative that I should get down to it right away. I decided to do nothing about Schmidt for the moment. I had given my word and there was that letter. I was convinced that he was not dangerous.

I spent most of the following day in the court and returned to find that I had been briefed at the last moment for a drug peddling case due to be heard at the Old Bailey on Thursday, the K. C. who had originally been briefed for the case having suddenly joined the Ministry of Supply. This rush of work gave me little time to consider the case of Franz Schmidt. But I was able to make one inquiry. On the Wednesday night I dropped into the Clachan, which is quite close to my rooms in the Temple. I had a drink with one or two of the Fleet Street boys whom I knew and was introduced to a fellow in the Press Section of the Air Ministry. On the off-chance that he might be able to find out something, I asked him to see if the contracts branch of the Air Ministry knew anything about a man called Franz Schmidt or Paul Severin, and if so, whether they had approached the Calboyd Diesel Company and been told that he was a crank. " Oh, you're expecting to be briefed, are you?" he said. Then he turned to the others and said, " There's a wee bit news for you, boys —Mr. Kilmartin to defend Franz Schmidt."

I shrugged my shoulders. " I don't think so," I said. " I'm just interested, that's all." My tone was final and they accepted it that way. But the fellow phoned me on Friday morning, just as I was leaving for the court, to tell me that I was quite correct. A Paul Severin had approached the Air Ministry in July, 1939, with the request that they test for aircraft use a Diesel engine he had produced. He explained that it was much lighter than any at present in existence as a result of the use of a special alloy he had discovered. He was very secretive about the alloy and was full of conditions as to how they should test it. He wouldn't let the engine out of his sight. The Air Ministry had then got on to Calboyds', who handled all their Diesel engine experiments, and had asked them what they knew of Severin. They had replied that he had already approached them and that they had tested the engine. The metal he had used was a well-known durable alloy and it had not, in their opinion, been sufficiently strong to stand up to the pressure it would have to bear. They had described him as a crank who was a little unbalanced.

Well, that was one part of his story corroborated. But was his interpretation of it right? His point had been that here was a big industrial firm queering his pitch in an effort to force him to sell the plans and the secret of the alloy to them outright. But supposing Calboyds' summing up had been right? I had no time to go into the matter more closely, and I decided to wait till Monday. If he didn't turn up then, it was a case for the police.

I completed the drug case on Monday morning and returned to my chambers somewhat dispirited. The case had been hopeless from the start, and as briefs had been much fewer since the outbreak of war, I liked to be successful with those I did obtain. Schmidt had not called. I went out and had lunch at Simpson's in the Strand as an antidote to depression. I did not return to my chambers until past three. Schmidt had still not arrived. I sat in my office and smoked a cigar. The brief spell of work had exhausted itself. I had not a single case in prospect. I found myself involuntarily listening for the sound of someone entering the outer office. I had tea. There was still no sign of Schmidt. I let Hopkins and the typist go. There was nothing for them to do.

By five o'clock I was no longer waiting impatiently for him to come. I knew he would not come and I was wondering what I was to do. The most obvious course was to get in touch with the police. But I remembered his words about not finding it a case for the police at first. And there was that letter. The man had seemed so certain that he was going to die. I owed it to him to go round to his digs and make a few inquiries. Nevertheless, it was a police affair. I ought at least to get Crisham to come along with me. I rose from my chair by the fire and crossed to the phone. I hesitated on the point of lifting the receiver. That stuff about the face from the barbican and the clue being the cones of runnel. I could hear Crisham's soft sardonic chuckle. He was a hard-headed man, who believed in facts—and nothing else. He'd come, of course, but he'd say at once that the man was mad, and his only interest would be to trace Schmidt's whereabouts.

I went over to the door instead and got my hat and coat. My mind made up now, I hurried out of my chambers and up Middle Temple Lane and hailed a taxi in Fleet Street. We ran through a darkened Strand and by the way of St. Martin's Lane to Cambridge Circus. I was deposited outside a derelict-looking house practically opposite the stage door of the London Casino. It had once been a shop, but the windows were boarded up and the place had a shut look. I paid off my taxi and then flashed my torch on to the door. The figures 209 showed black against the cracked green paint, and below was a little sign which said "Isaac Leinster, Bespoke Tailor." I found an electric bell, that had lost its covering, and rang. No sound came from the other side of the door. I waited, and then rang again. No one answered. I knocked on the door. Then I stepped back and looked up. The aged brick face of the house towered above me, blank and sheer.

I played my torch over the door again, looking for another bell to ring, and I saw that it was not quite shut. I pressed against it, and it opened. I went in and found myself in a bare passage, with two dustbins in it, leading to uncarpeted stairs. I hesitated. I was not over keen on walking into a house in Greek Street that I did not know. But in the end I climbed the stairs and on the first floor I found a door with "Isaac Leinster" on it, and there was a line of light showing beneath.

I knocked and heard feet shuffling across bare floorboards. The door swung open and a small man with thick lips and a bald head stared at me out of little beady eyes. "Vat is it you vant?" he asked.

"I'm sorry to bother you," I said, "but I'm looking for a friend of mine who lives here."

" Vat is 'is nime?"

I hesitated. What was his name? He surely wouldn't have given it as Severin? Then in a flash I remembered what he had told me about his parentage. " Mr. Frank Smith," I said and I began to describe him.

The other held up his hand. " I know. But Mr. Smith is not 'ere now. 'E 'as'ad an accident and is in 'ospital."

" Which hospital?" I asked.

He shrugged his shoulders. " 'Ow do I know?" he complained. " A gent goms 'ere on Thursday, says 'e ees from the 'ospital and can 'e 'ave Mr. Smeeth's clothes. Vat do you vant?"

" Well," I said, " I left some rather important scientific papers with him. He promised to let me have them back by last Friday and I've got to give a talk on them to-morrow evening."

He looked me up and down, and then said, " Vell, you'd best go up and look for them. Another three days and you'd 'ave been too late. 'Is rent ees due on Thursday and I'll 'ave to clear all 'is junk out. You'll find the door open. It's right at the top." And with that he closed the door.

I went on up the stairs and eventually came to the top landing from which a wooden staircase, obviously put in at a later date, rose sharply to a green-painted door. I climbed this and knocked at the door. There was no answer, so I pulled the string of the latch and went into what was apparently a pent-house. I switched on the light. It was a largish room, the ceiling sloped to a skylight, which was boarded up because of the black-out. It had probably been built as a studio, for there were glimmerings of the artistic in its construction that were noticeably absent from the rest of the house.

The furniture appeared to be the sweepings of the second-hand market. There was a double bed in the corner under the window, all brass and cast-iron, two old kitchen chairs, an uncomfortable-looking Victorian arm-chair, complete with a very dirty antimacassar, a dresser of plain wood and a little mahogany table that had been good, but was now split right down the centre. In the far corner was a sink, half-filled with dirty dishes. The place was indescribably filthy and very untidy. There were crumbs all over the floor where vermin had got at a loaf, which lay crumbling on the table.

I looked round in some bewilderment. " Go round to my lodgings and take the face from the barbican," Schmidt had said. A barbican was the outer defences of a castle. How could there be a barbican in this hovel? There weren't any pictures and there was nothing that looked remotely like a barbican. I couldn't even see a face anywhere. A sense of frustration seized me. I had been so busy recently that I had not bothered to think out the significance of Schmidt's words. Or were they just the ravings of an unbalanced brain?

I went over to the dresser and pulled out one of the drawers. There were clothes in it and some handkerchiefs that were clean and had the ironing creases in them, though they were jumbled up with the rest. I tried the next drawer, and here again clean clothes had been jumbled up in an untidy heap. The man from the hospital must have been in a hurry in his search for the right clothes. But why should he have been in such a hurry?

I turned and looked at the room again. It was untidy, but the untidiness was methodical. The bedclothes were all bunched up and loose where the mattress had been flung back, the tattered linoleum was bent up all round the walls and the books in the little bookcase by the fireplace were not all the right way up. The room was not untidy because it had been lived in. It was untidy because someone had searched it thoroughly.

A little pile of books on the floor caught my eye because on the back of one of them I noticed a woman's face and it had suddenly given me an idea. I went forward and picked it up. It was an Ethel M. Dell. I knelt down and went slowly through the bookcase. On the second shelf, in a batch of five that had been put back upside down, I found what I was looking for. It was a recently purchased thriller and on the jacket was a man's face framed in a barbican. It was called *The Face from the Barbican* and was by Mitchel Cleaver. I stood up and flicked through the pages. But there was no letter there, nothing written. I felt disappointed. Then I began to consider what Schmidt had meant by the cones of runnel. I thought it possible that it might be the title of another book.

As I bent down to run through the bottom shelf, I heard

the sound of a door closing and was immediately conscious of the house that lurked in the dark below me. I stood up and went to the door. All was silent as the grave. Then suddenly a stair creaked, and then another. I heard the creak of the banisters and, in the silence, I could hear a man's deep breathing on the staircase below me. I thought of the man who had searched the room before me. Had he been looking for what I had found?

I switched off the light and waited. There was no place to hide. I could hear the man's breathing quite plainly now as he climbed to the landing immediately below me. Had they been watching the house or was it one of the people who lived there? Why had Schmidt been so certain he would die? The man reached the landing, and I sensed him turn towards the last flight. I braced myself. By lifting myself on the banisters I could use my feet.

" Is any vun there?" It was the voice of the Jewish tailor. A sense of relief flooded through me. "Yes, I'm just coming down," I said, and switched on my torch. He was standing on the landing below with his hairless head craned up towards me.

"Did you get vat you vanted?" he asked.

"Yes, thanks," I said, as I came down the stairs. "I've taken the papers and also a book I lent him."

He nodded. "If you see 'im, tell 'im I vill 'ave to let the room on Thursday unless 'e pays me the next week's rent. A man 'as got to live, yes? But I vill keep 'is things in my shop vor a week, tell 'im. I do not vish to be 'ard."

I thanked him and hurried on down the stairs.

Chapter Two

THE MESSAGE COMES AND GOES

By THE time I had reached the bottom of the stairs I was almost running. I had my torch, but outside that reassuring beam the house pressed about me, dark and silent. The blank doorways on the landings seemed to crowd forward to watch me pass, shadows leapt back as I flashed my torch and the walls threw the sound of my footsteps back at me as though, hurry as I might, I should never leave the house. It was a childish fancy. But a strange house is like that. So long as you ignore it, it will take no notice of you. But once you become aware of it, it closes round you, colouring your imagination with its own atmosphere. This house was unfriendly, and it was with a sense of relief that I pulled open the door and went out into Greek Street.

But even in the street, I could not shake off that feeling of being watched. It was very dark and the houses rose on either side, blanklike walls. I sensed rather than saw the movement of people about me. They were vague shadows, distinguishable only by the flicker of a torch until they appeared suddenly in the light of my own torch, passed me and were swallowed by the darkness again. A woman's voice spoke to me and for a moment I saw white, red-lipped features at my side as she shone her torch on her face. And all the time I was walking towards Shaftesbury Avenue, I had that sense of being watched. It was as though I were being followed.

I became so certain of this that I turned sharp left towards Charing Cross Road and slipped into the doorway of a tobacconist. Several figures passed along the pavement. None of them were anxiously peering ahead or hurrying as though to catch someone up. Mentally I pulled myself together. The house and my discovery that Schmidt's rooms had been searched had obviously got on my nerves. I began to think of food, and decided on Genaros on the other side of Charing Cross Road.

I left the shelter of the tobacconist's and continued along the pavement. As I came out into Charing Cross Road, I was checked by a flood of people crossing my path. They had been held up by a car and had just crossed the road. And as I slowed up, a man, hurrying in the direction of Cambridge Circus, cannoned into me. I only just managed to keep my feet and I felt the book slide from underneath my arm. I made a wild clutch at it and it fell to the ground. " I'm so sorry," a voice said. A torch was flicked on to the book where it lay, face up on the muddy pavement, and the man bent quickly down to retrieve it. I saw a hand dart into the beam of the torch as I dived for the book. The white line of a scar showed across the knuckles. The fingers were almost closing on it when the feet of the passers-by suddenly swung closer and a foot kicked against it, sliding it towards me across the pavement. In an instant my hand had closed on it.

I straightened myself, the blood drumming in my ears. The man said, " So sorry, I'm afraid it's got dirty." I swung my torch up towards him, but he had disappeared into the crowd. The incident left me with an uneasy feeling. Either I was being a fool or else the man who had searched Schmidt's digs had failed to find what he had known to be there, and had waited to see if anyone would come to show him what it was. I hurried across Charing Cross Road and into New Compton Street. I remembered how the Jew, Isaac Leinster, had hesitated at the foot of the stairs leading up to Schmidt's room whilst I stood waiting for him at the top. I remembered, too, how he had come up the stairs from his own room so quietly that it was his breathing and not his footsteps that I had heard. Small though he was, he was a heavy man and the stairs were uncarpeted. And there was the unfriendly watchfulness of the house as I had left it. Had that all been imagination?

I turned into the entrance to Genaros and in the warm friendliness of the place my fears melted away. As I ordered my dinner, I thought of a time when I had been scared on Dartmoor for no earthly reason. Anything can seem curious if your senses are keyed up to misinterpretation. I chose my dinner carefully. Then, having wiped the dirt off the back of the book, I opened it and began to look through it for some mark that would indicate what I was expected to find.

There was nothing. The pages were as virgin as they had been when Schmidt had bought the book, though soiled on the outer edges where it had fallen on the pavement. There were no pencil marks, and though I searched diligently through it from cover to cover, whilst at the same time attempting to deal adequately with the courses as they were laid before me, I could see no signs of any markings or pinpricks under selected words. At the end were several blank pages, but there was not a mark on them. By the time I had reached the sweet, I had decided that the only thing to do was to read the book through. There must be some clue in the writing. I turned to the chapter headings and glanced through them to see whether they suggested anything. One called *Cranston Develops the Message* seemed promising.

I had finished the zabaglione and, having ordered a Grand Marnier with my coffee and lit a cigarette, I settled down to discover what it was Schmidt had wanted me to find in the book. Of its kind, it was good, and though I had dipped into it near the middle, I was soon absorbed in the search of a representative of M.I.5, called Cranston, for a message he was certain had been left for him by one Barry Hanson, who had been murdered. The only clue Cranston had was given him in a telephone conversation he had had with his friend a few days previously. Hanson had told him he was on to something pretty big and that, if he should get snuffed out, Cranston would find all the details in the Figurehead of the Orient. Barry Hanson had been duly snuffed out and Cranston had trotted round to his digs to seek out the Figurehead of the Orient. And this was where I began to see a similarity between my own experiences and Cranston's. Of course, Cranston was on the point of leaving Hanson's digs without having found what he wanted, when suddenly he caught sight of a book called *The Figurehead of the Orient*. He looked through it, and there were blank pages at the end. He took it back to M.I.5 and had the blank pages placed under a mercury vapour light. The message, which was written in a solution of anthracene and was invisible to the naked eye, then became fluorescent and it was possible to photograph it. It was all about a secret organisation headed by a personage described as the Face from the Barbican.

I put the book down and found that my coffee had grown cold. I sipped slowly at my liqueur and then, after marking the passage with my pencil, turned to the end of the book. The blank pages stared up at me, innocent of any mark. Was it conceivable that, if they were placed under a mercury vapour lamp, invisible writing would be revealed? Technically I presumed that it was quite possible. But the whole thing was too absurd. I had that placid feeling of well-being that comes after a good meal. Schmidt had admitted to an interest in criminology. Had his interest taken the form of reading thrillers and detective stories, and then attempting to transmit them into real life? That was the sort of kink a man's brain might take. I might almost have been Cranston. routing around in another fellow's digs with the feeling that I might be murdered at any moment.

I thought of David Shiel, who ran a photographic studio and dark-rooms in Shaftesbury Avenue. It was only a few minutes' walk. And I had a sudden urge to see whether or not Schmidt had gone to the length of actually writing something on those blank pages and, if so, what he had written. I rose and collected my coat and paid the bill. Then, with the book stuffed safely in my overcoat pocket, I went out into New Compton Street and made for Cambridge Circus.

I no longer had a feeling of being followed, but I tried to pretend that I had. My brain was excited and I was reluctant to miss any of the sensation of adventure in following up the clues I had been given.

Five minutes later the aged lift was staggering up with me to the top floor of 495 Shaftesbury Avenue. With the aid of an assistant and a secretary. David carried on a great deal of photographic work from the studio. He went all over the place, taking films as the spirit and the film companies moved him. and in his more prosaic moments he hired out cameras, executed any still work that came his way and let his dark-rooms out to all and sundry. By my sister's marriage into a Border family. he was technically my nephew, but he had never evinced any signs of respect on that account, and he was a friend rather than a relation. Many a cheerful evening I had spent at somewhat Bohemian parties that had spread haphazardly from his rooms to the studio. He rented the entire top floor and lived on the premises, partly because his camera-hire service was a day and night service and partly because it was cheaper and more convenient.

The antiquated lift stopped with a jerk and I stepped out into a bare corridor. At the end was a glass door with " David Shiel's Photographic Centre " painted on it in black, and four empty milk bottles ranged against the wall below it. He answered my ring himself and let out a whoop at the sight of me. " The very man," he said. " Come right in, Andrew. If there's any man I could have wished to see it would have been a lawyer."

" I'm a barrister," I reminded him as he dragged me into the room. He was a great bear of a man with long dark hair and a wide friendly face.

" What the hell's it matter?" he said, as he helped me off with my coat. " You know your legal onions, so to speak, and I want advice. How do you get money out of a company that's less yielding than a stone?" He crossed over to a barrel that was a permanent office fixture and returned with a foaming tankard of beer. " There, drink that and tell me what I do. I've received a red slip from the telephone people. They're going to cut me off if I don't pay them by the 23rd —that's Friday. And these bastards owe me a hundred quid, and they won't pay."

" What's the matter?" I said. " Are you broke?"

He buried his face in his tankard and shrugged his shoulders. " Business is pretty bad and this place eats money, what with the rent and Miriam and the telephone bills. John has joined up—he's under the reserve age, that's one blessing. If I can hold on for another six months, I'll be all right There'll be plenty of work when the American stock is exhausted and it's all-British films. But, in the meantime, I can't carry on without the phone. It makes you curse when you're owed the better part of four hundred pounds and can't get it because people are too bloody lazy to pay up. Meanwhile, I'm short of cash and that means a camera will have to go, and what sort of price will it fetch now? I haven't got a single one out on hire."

I said, " Give me their address and I'll see what I can do. What do they owe you the money for anyway?"

" That's very nice of you, Andrew. I did some film work for them. The company is Calboyds Diesel. I went up to their Oldham works to take shots for publicity purposes. They beat me down to a lousy price as it was."

" Calboyds," I murmured. The hand of Fate, it seemed. Then I said, " Look, David, I want you to do something for me." I pulled *The Face from the Barbican* out of the pocket of my overcoat. " Did you know there was a solution which can be used as an invisible ink and which only becomes visible when placed under a mercury vapour light?"

" Several," was the reply. " But I never heard of them being used as invisible inks. They're of the genus tar and are soluble in benzine. They become fluorescent under an ultra-violet ray."

" And a mercury vapour lamp gives off an ultra-violet ray?" I asked.

" Certainly."

" Then I wonder if you'd mind placing the blank pages at the end of this book under an ultra-violet ray?" I passed the book over to him and he opened it and glanced at the blank pages. Then he looked at me.

" So," he said, " you are the master mind behind the British Secret Service? I always knew you couldn't really be a lawyer. Or perhaps you're a spy? Anyway we can discuss that when we've found what's written in the Book of Books." He drained his tankard. " My God!" he said, as he glanced at the title, " you have a lurid taste in thrillers." Then he glanced across at me. He was suddenly serious. " You really mean there's some writing here?"

I nodded.

He rose to his feet. " Well, we'll soon see if it's one of the benzine solutions," he said, and led me into the largest dark-room.

He soon had the first of the blank pages fixed under the enlarger. Then he switched out the light and turned on the mercury vapour lamp of the enlarger. Instantly, the blank page became covered with parallel luminous lines, as though a snail had drawn itself backwards and forwards across it. " By God, yes," David said, " we've got something here all right." I leaned closer, peering at the page, so that the brightness of it hurt my eyes. I could see that the luminous lines were of writing, but it seemed a jumble of unintelligible letters.

"The first thing to do is to photograph the paper," David announced. "Then we'll be able to see what it's all about."

He got a Leica and set to work. When he had taken photographs of all six of the blank pages, he said, "You go outside and swill some beer. I'm going to develop them now."

I left the dark-room very conscious of his capability at his job. I suppose I had always taken his photographic centre for granted before. I had never been here when he was actually working. My only clear recollection of the man was of him lounging around in the most amazing clothes, drinking vast quantities of beer and telling dirty stories. But I had heard from friends how he had built the business up from nothing, starting with a single camera in a cellar office in Frith Street. I knew, too, that he had decorated the studio himself with the help of an odd carpenter.

It was a big room, running the whole length of the frontage, and it was panelled throughout in a good oak plywood. The dark-rooms were on the inner wall. There were four of them, well appointed, with their own sinks, enlargers, lights and telephones. The place was cluttered with apparatus. I knew, of course, that he must be capable to stand on his own feet in such a precarious profession. It was just that I had not been conscious of it before. I had taken him as I had found him, a good-natured friendly fellow, who led a rather peculiar life and ran a somewhat unusual business.

Now that I had seen him at work, I looked at him from a different angle. He was, as I have said, a great bear of a man. The wide shoulders and the fine head, with its mane of dark hair, made him a striking figure. He wore a pair of old brown corduroys, a dark-green polo sweater and sandals. But though his height and breadth were striking, it was his hands I had noticed. They were fine hands, with long and slender fingers. They were the hands of an artist, but capable hands.

When he had hung the films in the drying cupboard, he came over to where I was sitting, obediently drinking beer. "Now," he said, "whilst that's drying off, perhaps you'll tell me something of what it's all about—or is that a deadly secret?"

"No, it's not altogether a secret," I said. "At any rate, I'll tell you something of what it's about." So I told him that part of Schmidt's story which was directly connected with the book. I did not tell him who my visitor had been. But I told him sufficient to explain the book. And when I had finished, he shook his head and said, "Mon, if I didna ken ye were a guid Scotsman, I'd say ye had been drinking. It all sounds very melodramatic, but at least you've got the writing in the book to prove your story." Then he got up and went over to the drying cupboard and took out the negative. "Now let's have a look at it under the enlarger." He led the way back into the dark-room and closed the door behind us. Then he switched on the enlarger and a square of light was flung on to the printing table. He fitted the end of the negative into the slot below the lens of the instrument and immediately the blurred outline of the photograph appeared on the white paper clamped to the printing table. He manœuvred it into position and then adjusted the enlarger. And suddenly the photograph was in focus and lines of print, written lightly with a pen, showed below it.

But it made no sense at all. The first line ran: SDGME DOLI R BXONSOVCO NGN XCOH BSOH. And the rest of it was the same jumble of meaningless letters. Yet, even in these printed letters, I thought I could discern the neat hand of Schmidt. David shifted the negatives along to the next photograph. They were all much the same as the first, though the last negative was blank and the one before it only two-thirds completed. He ran the whole length of celluloid through the enlarger and in all the five pages, with their lines of closely printed words, there was not one that made sense.

"Your boy friend is either pulling your leg," said David, "or else this is in code. Don't you know something about codes?"

I shook my head. "Not much," I admitted. "But one thing I do know, and that is that, if you don't know the key, a good code takes three to six months' hard work by experts to break down."

"Well, I'll take a print of each one of these, and then we'll see whether we can make anything of it."

But we couldn't. I copied the first few lines of the first

page from the image cast by the light from the enlarger, and
worked on this whilst David took a print of it. But it was no
good. I knew something about the theory of codes and I
tried to break it down by the usual method of picking out
the letters that occurred most frequently and changing them
to the letters most commonly in use. But I had had no
success by the time David had completed the print. I
decided that the clue was probably in the book. I flicked
through the pages to see if at any point the author had given
a method for breaking down a code. Rows of meaningless
capital letters would have stood out quite clearly against the
background of ordinary print. But there was nothing of that
sort and I realised that the only thing to do was to read
through the book. I told David so and he grunted. He was
absorbed, as I had been for the last half-hour, in trying to
work it out for himself.

I read that book through from beginning to end and, in
the whole story, there wasn't a single mention of codes.
When I had finished, I threw it from me in disgust. David
was no longer in the studio and I heard the rattle of tea-cups
in the back premises. The print he had been working on was
lying amongst a heap of old stock and hypo dishes. I lit a
cigarette. A moment later he came in with tea. He glanced
at the book lying sprawled on its side on the couch. " You
don't seem to have been any more successful than I have,"
he said.

" I'm fed up with the thing," I replied savagely.

" Never mind," he said, as he poured me out some tea, " I
gathered you enjoyed the book. Whilst I was working, I
heard several appreciative chuckles."

That was true enough. I had enjoyed the book. But, as so
often happens, the return to reality had produced a mood of
depression. I felt convinced that the supposed code had no
meaning, that Schmidt was mad and had been living melo-
drama in real life. I told David so and he shrugged his
shoulders. " You know best," he said. " But don't you
know anyone who really understands codes? I mean, after
all, we've only been working on this a very short time and
we're not experts. I know something about them, and I
haven't nearly exhausted the possibilities. I tried the Playfair
Code—you know, the one that depends on a key-word and

you put the letters down in fives together with the rest of the alphabet and then work on rectangles. It's one of the few you can't break down by placing the letter that recurs most frequently I tried using The Face from the Barbican as the key-word, but that didn't make much sense. If there is any sense in the words, it must be a code like that. I can't believe a man who was just jotting down meaningless letters would have gone on with it for five whole pages."

"You may be right," I said, "but I'm still fed up with the whole business."

"Well, it's your affair, not mine. But don't you know anyone at the Foreign Office? They have decoding experts."

I stretched myself and clambered stiffly to my feet. "Yes, I suppose it would be worth trying. There's Graham Aitken, he'd be able to get them to have a look at it for me."

"All right then. If not, there's my godfather, Sir Geoffrey Carr, at the Home Office. Anyway, leave the book with me and, if you come round any time after, say, eleven to-morrow, I'll have some good prints for you. I want to retake two of the pages, as they haven't come out very well." He picked the print he had been working on up from the litter in which it lay. "You might like to take this to bed with you. Nothing like sleeping on a puzzle."

I nodded and tucked it into my overcoat pocket. Then I thanked him and said I'd be round some time about eleven. I don't remember leaving the studio. The beer on top of my dinner had made me very sleepy. But the cold air of Shaftesbury Avenue soon woke me up. I decided to walk back to my rooms, and I cut down into Leicester Square, where a nearly full moon sailed serenely over the trees and the dark outline of the Odeon tower.

Back at my rooms in the Temple, I found the walk had driven away my sleepiness. I lay in bed and struggled ceaselessly for the clue to the code. With my sleepiness I found my incredulity had also vanished. I reviewed the whole evening and began to wonder once more whether it had been just an accident that that man had cannoned into me in the Charing Cross Road. But for the chance of a passer-by, his hand would have closed on the book, and I wondered whether he would have given it back to me. My mind drifted back to Schmidt himself and I tried to deduce from what he had told me whether or not he was mad. His story had been convincing and I came back, of course, to the melodramatic close of the interview.

I heard him saying once more, " Will you go round to my lodgings and take *The Face from the Barbican*." Well, there had been nothing phoney about that. *The Face from the Barbican* had been there all right and, what was more, his rooms had been searched. But then Leinster might have searched them for valuables. I was beginning to feel drowsy. My brain, tired with the excitement of the evening, was beginning to think in circles. What had Schmidt said then? " You are clever. You will understand." And then——

Suddenly I was wide awake. I jumped out of bed and hurried into my dressing-gown. I switched on the light and the electric fire and went out into the hall, where my overcoat lay over a chair. I pulled the photograph that David had given me from the pocket and hurried back into my bedroom. Then, huddled over the fire with a pencil and paper, I tried the Playfair Code.

What Schmidt had said was, " The clue is cones of runnel." Why cones of runnel, I did not know. It had always seemed a bit daft and for that reason, probably, had not fixed itself in my memory. But the essence of the Playfair Code was a key-word or words, and here it was. I wrote down CONES and underneath FRUL, which were the letters in " of runnel " which had not already been given in " cones." Then I added A to that line and continued with the letters of the alphabet that had not already been used, setting them down in blocks of five, leaving out Y, which I remembered, was regarded as I. This was the result:

```
C O N E S
F R U L A
B D G H I
J K M P Q
T V W X Z
```

I then jotted down the opening letters of the message in pairs, thus: SD GM ED OL IR BX ON SO VC. Starting at the beginning, I took the rectangle made in the code formed by SD and transposed the vertically opposite letters of the rectangle, getting IO. GM, being in a vertical line, I took the nearest letters to each, making UW, ED made HO, OL made RE, and so on.

The resulting letters I put down without gaps, and not as they had been in the code. The result was: IOUWHOREAD-THESENOT. My excitement was tremendous. Reading Y for I, I found I had got, "You who read these not——"

I then settled down to the job in real earnest, and after half an hour's steady work I had decoded the whole of that first page. I sat back and read through the result.

"You who read these notes," it ran, "must decide for yourself whether or not there is sufficient evidence for the matter to be placed in the hands of the authorities. I fear, however, that I shall not live to complete my case." That, I remembered, was what he had told me last Monday. "I am being watched now and it is only a matter of time. Why did I not go to the authorities myself? I was wanted for murder. If I had gone to them and said the Calboyd Diesel Company is controlled by Germany and the murder was committed by their agents, I should have been considered mad. But day by day I shall add to these notes, and as my inquiries reveal new facts, I shall hope that, by the time this comes into your hands, there will at any rate be sufficient evidence to convince you of my sanity and of the seriousness of the position I have discovered.

"I shall probably have explained to you how I was discredited at the Air Ministry by Calboyds. This should not be difficult to verify. When I tell you that the Diesel engine on which I have been working and which has now reached the stage of final tests is a third of the weight of the ordinary Diesel and develops nearly twice the power of present engines at five hundred revolutions, you will begin to appreciate its importance in war-time. I can confidently state that whichever side first obtains this engine and produces it on a large scale will have air superiority. These claims were presented to the Air Ministry last July. Calboyds told them I was a crank. They had been trying to get me to reveal the secret of the special alloy and the design. Those who control the company wanted the engine for Germany.

"You will say this is fantastic. But I have heard that in

T.T.H.   B

the early summer of this year Britain is going over to Diesel engines on a large scale. The Calboyd factories are being extended for this purpose and two shadow factories are being built for the company. They will be the sole producers and the engines will be of their own design. The design is superior to that used in the Heinkels and Dorniers at the present time. But it is definitely inferior to the engines that are being fitted to the latest German bomber and fighter aircraft, which have not yet taken the air. I believe that an order for ten thousand of their Diesel engines will be given to Calboyds within the next few months. If that order goes through and Calboyds are allowed to start production Britain will be . . ."

I put the paper down. The rest would have to wait till to-morrow when David would have the prints of the remaining pages. But what I had read was enough to set me thinking. The man might be mad, but if Calboyds were really controlled by Germany—— It didn't bear thinking about. One thing I could check up on and that was whether or not Calboyds were to receive a big order for Diesel aero engines. Crabshaw of the Ministry of Supply could tell me that. But it was fantastic. Schmidt was right when he had said he would have been considered mad if he had approached the authorities with a story like that. It was too incredible. Old Calboyd was an industrial figurehead. Supposing I told the story to Crisham or wrote to the Prime Minister? They'd think I was going off my head, even though I had led a perfectly blameless life. And why had Llewellin been murdered? It was stupid to frame a man by murdering another.

I gave it up and went back to bed, putting the photograph and the paper on which I had decoded it in the pocket of my jacket.

My man woke me as usual at eight. I had a shower and, after a hurried breakfast, took a taxi round to David's studio. His secretary, Miriam Chandler, opened the door to me. David I found already at work on some stills. "Have you got the other prints?" I asked. I was eager to decode the rest of the message.

He said, "Sorry, you're a good deal earlier than I expected. The fact is I've got to take them all again. I left that negative on the desk over there. I didn't notice it, but there was a bottle of hydrochloric just by it. I came in this morning to find it tipped on its side. Awful mess. Look at the linoleum there, and the negative of course was completely destroyed. It was that bloody cat, I expect." He indicated a shabby tortoise-shell curled up placidly on the couch. " It keeps the mice down, but it's always upsetting things in the process. I shan't be long though. Give him a cigarette, Miriam, and stroke his fevered brow, he looks as though he's had a bad night. Did you dream of codes and jumbled letters like I did all night?"

" No, I solved it," I said triumphantly.

He swung round from the big sink. " You solved it? Well, grand—good for you. How did you get at it?"

I told him and he cursed me good-humouredly. " Why the hell didn't you say the fellow had said that? May I have a look at it?"

I shook my head. " No," I said. " Wait until you've got the other prints out and I've decoded the rest, then maybe I'll tell you the whole story." I had an idea that his resourcefulness might be an asset if I found it necessary to make further inquiries on my own before handing over to the authorities.

He said, " You're enough to drive a person crazy." Then he went into the big dark-room, taking *The Face from the Barbican* with him. I had suddenly remembered that I had promised to help him extract money from Calboyds, and I asked Miriam to produce the correspondence. When I had run through it, my mind was made up. Providence isn't always kind enough to hand things to you on a platter. This would make a good excuse for going up to Oldham and seeing Calboyds for myself.

David suddenly emerged from the dark-room. " Funny," he said. " These pages seem absolutely blank now."

I crossed the room and went into the dark-room. The blank pages of the book lay under the light, but there was no fluorescence. They were just blank. He turned to another page. It was blank. " Is it the same lamp?" I asked.

" Certainly."

I had a sudden sense of uneasiness, the sort of feeling a man has when he has mislaid a Treasury note and knows it was just plain carelessness. I ripped the book from the stand to which it was clamped. The back of it was smeared with mud, but when I ran through the pages, looking for the passage I had marked, I could not find it. After careful searching through the chapter I knew it to be in, I eventually found the passage. But there was no pencil mark against it.

I turned to David. "This isn't my book," I said.

"Don't be silly," he replied. "It's got *The Face from the Barbican* at the top of every page."

"Yes, but it's not my copy." I explained about the pencil marking and showed him the passage.

"Are you certain?" he asked. "You were awfully sleepy last night."

"Yes, I'm certain all right," I said. "This isn't my copy. And that bottle of hydrochloric wasn't tipped over by the cat. Where did you put the negatives when you went to bed?" I asked him.

He frowned. "I don't know," he said. "Where I found them this morning, I think."

"And what about the hydrochloric—was that just beside them?"

He shook his head. "Honestly, old boy, I don't know." He went to the door of the dark-room. "Miriam," he said, "can you remember whether that bottle of hydrochloric was on the table there last night?"

"I don't know," she replied. "Depends on whether you used it after I'd gone yesterday. I tidied up as usual and left it on the shelf over there, where it belongs."

"And I didn't have it out." He swung round on me. "No, I didn't use it last night. You're right—somebody moved that bottle from the shelf over by the window there and deliberately spilt the contents over those negatives."

Chapter Three

CORNISH PRELUDE

I KNEW where I was then. Schmidt's story, fantastic as it seemed, was true. There was no longer any doubt of that. "How did they get in?" I asked. My voice sounded flat. I was thinking of the four other pages.

"From the roof, I expect," said David. "If you're prepared to take a few risks you can get the whole length of the block." I followed him out into the passage. He opened the door at the end and climbed rough wooden stairs to another door. He turned the key in the lock and we went out on to the roof. Then he bent down and examined the lock on the outside, and I looked across the rooftops to the dome of the Globe Theatre. The roofs were all joined and an agile man could have come from any one of the buildings in the block.

"I thought so," said David. "Look!" I bent down. "See that mark where the metal is bright, on the inside edge of the keyhole? That's where our friends pincers scraped as he grasped the end of the key and turned it." He straightened up. "I expect he came by way of that house with the tall chimneys. It's a brothel. They had a burglary next door a few months back and the police sergeant told me that the burglars probably got on to the roof that way. They couldn't prove anything, of course. The girls aren't going to split. An extra quid or two comes in handy with nothing to do for it but let a fellow on to the roof. Come on, let's go down, and then perhaps you'll tell me something about this business."

When we reached the corridor I said, "Do you mind if we go into your room?" I had decided to tell him the whole story. I had to have someone to argue it out with. For answer he pushed open the door. "Make yourself comfortable," he said. "I'll just tell Miriam to hold the fort." He was back in a moment with two tankards of beer. "Now," he said, as he subsided into an easy-chair and began to fill a

37

big curved briar, " I hope you're going to play ball. Can I see the results of your midnight labours, or is that a deadly secret?"

I said, " I think we'd better take things in their proper order." Then I told him how Schmidt had come to see me on Monday of the previous week and how he had pushed his way into my office just as I was refreshing my memory about the facts of the case. As I sat there, drinking beer and looking out across the chimney pots of Soho, I saw once again that elderly, tired-faced Jew, sitting opposite me across my desk, with the firelight flickering on his lined face. And I heard once again his quiet voice telling me his story.

I told it to David just as he had told it to me. " My father's name was Frederick Smith," he had begun. " Both he and my mother were English—he was a Jew, you understand. Shortly after their marriage, my father went to Austria as an agent for the Western Aluminium and Metal Alloy Company. I was born in Vienna in the winter of 1882. Soon afterwards my father, having bought an interest in a local metal concern, decided to establish himself in Vienna and was naturalised. He became Frederick Schmidt and I, who had been given the name Frank at birth, became, as I am now, Franz Schmidt. My father grew to be quite a big man in the metal business and this influenced me to make engineering my career. After my apprenticeship, I entered my father's business. In the eight years before 1914, I was responsible for the discovery of several durable alloys and travelled all over the world for the group. I spent nearly a year in England, where I met a Welsh girl, and though she was not of my race I married her. I remember my father was furious when he heard, but she was lovely and gay and irresistible. She died four years ago. We had one child, a girl. She was born in 1913. Then came the war. My father sold the business and we went to live in Italy in the days when Italy was still neutral. The war was a great blow to him. He died two years later.

" When the war was over Olwyn and I went back to Vienna. Metal companies were in a terrible state. I bought a good sound business dirt cheap and for four weary years tried to build it up. But it was no good. I had not my father's business acumen and conditions were against me.

After losing practically all the money he had left me, I sold the business for what the buildings and plant would fetch. There followed a very difficult period. You know what Vienna was like after the war, and I hadn't the means to move. But in 1924 I obtained a post at the Metallurgical Institute. The use of a laboratory enabled me to resume my experiments in durable alloys. Within a year I had discovered a hard steel alloy. I sold it to the Fritz Thessen group. They became interested in my experiments and made me free of their laboratories at the M. V. Industriegesellschaft works on the outskirts of Vienna. Then followed the happiest years of my life. I had the work I loved. And I had my family—little Freya was growing up. Vienna, too, was becoming gay again. We never lacked for money. I discovered new alloys and developed them for use in the production, first of car engines, and then of aircraft engines. I spent much time on the Diesel engine. That is important for what follows. I was engrossed in my work and left all my business arrangements to an old friend of mine on the bourse. Politics did not interest me. I lived in a world of my own into which few outside events penetrated. The outside world was of little importance beside my experiments."

He had been staring into the fire and he suddenly turned to me, his face haggard with memories. "Have you ever lived in a world of your own?" he asked. Then he shrugged his shoulders. "Of course you haven't. You're a practical man. A world of your own is all right until that outside world breaks in upon it. Then——" He spread his hands with a lift of the shoulders. "I had had ample warning, but I was too engrossed. There was the Dolfuss murder. And shortly after that, my broker friend called me down to his office and persuaded me to let him place some of my money in England. I knew, of course, that my countrymen were having a difficult time in Germany, but I shrugged my shoulders and said I thought it was unnecessary. And I went back to my work, and the gathering stormclouds passed me by as I pressed forward with experiments on the Diesel engine, in which I had become absorbed.

"Freya was my one interest outside my work. She had passed through the university, a brilliant mathematician with a bent for scientific research. I sent her on to Berlin to continue her studies. Three months later she wrote to me from London, saying she had become the disciple of Professor Greenbaum at the London University. I thought nothing of it at the time. I have never questioned her as to the real reason why she left Berlin. But two months later, in December, 1936, I went home to find that my wife had not returned from a shopping expedition. I rang my friends, the hospitals, and finally the police. I walked the streets, frantic. I can remember that night so well. How I reviled myself for my neglect of her! She had reached a difficult age, yet she never reproached me because my work came first, always."

He became silent for a moment. The room had been getting dark and the firelight flickered on his face, accentuating the deep lines of his forehead and the stubble on his chin. "I hurried from street to street, streets that had been familiar from my boyhood's days, streets that I had shown proudly to her when I had brought her back to the little house in the Grinzingerallee. I questioned countless strangers and every policeman I met, and I resolved to devote less time to my work and more to making her happy, to recapturing the lost spirit of our youth. But my resolutions were useless." He sighed. "I returned home in the early hours of the morning, and a little after six the Bürgerspital phoned me to say that she had been brought in by the police suffering from exposure. When I reached her she was delirious, and in the babble of her delirium I learned that she had been assaulted by a band of Nazis. They had taunted her with being the wife of a Jew. She—she had compared my work with theirs, and one of them had struck her down for daring to uphold science as a greater art than Jew-baiting. Apparently they had feared to leave her there in the street, for the police had found her lying in the backyard of a big apartment house. I stayed on by her bedside and learned how this taunting had become an almost daily occurrence. She had never mentioned it to me. She died that night. Double pneumonia was the cause."

Again he became silent for a moment. Then he turned to me and said, "I am sorry—you must be wondering when I am coming to the point. But I want you to understand, so that you will believe what I am telling you."

I said, "Please go on." It had eased him to tell me the

story, and the insight it gave me into the development of the man's character fascinated me. I pushed my cigarette-case across the desk. He took one automatically. I lit it for him, and he sat there for a moment puffing at it nervously.

"At that time, it seemed that nothing more could touch me," he went on. "Yet it was but the beginning." He tossed the cigarette into the fire. His voice was quite toneless as he said, "I went back to my work with the zest of one who wants to forget. But I was sensitive now to the atmosphere that surrounded me. I was conscious of the growing contempt for my race. I persuaded Freya to stay on in England. She broke the news of Olwyn's death to her family in Swansea and stayed with them for several weeks, writing enthusiastically of their kindness. Then suddenly the M. V. Industriegesellschaft informed me that I could no longer have the use of their laboratories. I was not altogether sorry. Sneers were no longer veiled. From that moment I received no more royalties from the group.

"However, it did not matter. I had plenty of money. I bought a little workshop on the outskirts of Vienna and equipped it with all I needed. And there I settled down to continue my experiments. I lived on the premises and saw scarcely anyone. My Diesel engine experiments were reaching the point at which I could see the possibility of tremendous success. Freya came back for a time and worked with me in the shop. She was enthusiastic. But, though she threw herself wholeheartedly into the work, I could tell she was not happy. She was young and not content, like me, to live the life of a recluse. Vienna was no place for a Jew's daughter and I feared lest she should share her mother's fate. In January, 1938, I persuaded her to return to London, ostensibly to arouse the interest of one of the big British firms in our experiments. Two months later I stood by the roadside and watched the armoured columns of Nazi Germany roll into Vienna. I knew it was time for me to leave.

"But I had left it too late. The frontier was closed. It was impossible to get money out. I waited for ten hours in a queue at the British Embassy. It was no good. They could do nothing. The Nazis were combing Vienna for Jews. In the papers I read of the death of those few of my old friends who had not already fled the country. I went back to my workshop and destroyed the engines I had built. Two days later I was in a newly-constructed concentration camp. I was more fortunate than most. Freya got in touch with Fritz Thessen himself. She gave him some idea of the stage reached in our experiments. In those days he was still a power behind the Nazi Party. He was sufficiently interested to obtain my release. I was sent under escort with three others to Germany. But I was very weak with the beginnings of pneumonia. The effort of marching to the station finished me. In the heat of the carriage I collapsed. And because my release papers had Fritz Thessen's name on them, I was taken to a hospital in Linz, which was the next stop. There my guards left me, as they had to deliver the other prisoners.

"They came back three days later to find that I had died. Two weeks afterwards, still very weak, I crossed the frontier into Switzerland and went to England."

"I don't quite follow," I said.

A ghost of a smile flickered across his lips. "I was lucky, that was all. One of the doctors at the Linz hospital was a friend of mine. I had helped him when he and his wife were in a bad way. A Roumanian happened to die that same night. He was about my build and cultivated a beard. The doctor switched us round and bound my head whilst I grew that." And he pointed to the dark little tuft of beard that showed in the photograph. "I hope they never discovered how I escaped. But for that man I should be working for Germany, and Germany would hold the supremacy in the air." He made this pronouncement quite calmly. It came from his lips as indisputable fact. "The Nazis are more receptive to a new idea than the English. Fritz Thessen would have recognised the value of my work. In this country, the land of my forefathers, I am not recognised. I am hunted down like a criminal for a crime I did not commit. But I should not have been happy in Germany. There would have been no Freya, and life would not have been easy."

I stubbed out my cigarette in the ash-tray at my side and looked across at David, who was reclining full length on his bed, his unlit briar clamped between his teeth. "Well," I said, "that is the story he told me. It's strange enough, but I think it was its strangeness that convinced me more than anything else. It's hardly the sort of story a man would make up—too much detail."

" What about the Diesel engine business?" David asked.

" Yes," I replied, " that's where I wasn't so sure. I thought his brain might have become unbalanced. His claim was extravagant. Yet his daughter, Freya, believed it and on the strength of it Thessen obtained his release from the concentration camp. And when he arrived in England, Schmidt went straight down to Llewellin's place in Swansea. The invitation was due to Freya's conversations with her uncle. Llewellin was apparently enthusiastic. He placed one of his shops at Schmidt's disposal and did everything possible to help him. Schmidt had retained the Roumanian's name, by the way, which was Paul Severin. Freya had also interested Calboyds in his work. But Schmidt would not allow either the metal or the plans to be seen by anyone, and for a time the company lost interest.

" This interest was suddenly revived, however, shortly after inquiries had been made about him by two men, who described themselves as representing the immigration authorities. They approached the elder Mrs. Llewellin, and as she disliked Schmidt and had distrusted him ever since her daughter's death, she told them all she knew. This was in July of last year. By that time Schmidt, working with the money that his broker friend in Vienna had invested in England several years before, had practically completed a new engine. Calboyds approached him and offered to purchase the Diesel design and the secret of the new alloy for a very substantial figure. They also offered him a princely salary for his services. This Schmidt refused, having a very shrewd idea, as he put it, of the value of his discoveries and not wishing to be tied to any one firm. Shortly afterwards his rooms were searched. He carried the secret in his head, however, and the searchers got nothing. But by this time he had begun to realise that the secret of his identity had leaked out, and it was then that he discovered about the visit of the immigration people to old Mrs. Llewellin. He removed the nearly completed engine to a place of safety. In its place he put an old type engine. Two weeks later this engine disappeared overnight. By this time he had approached the Air Ministry, informing them of the probable performance of the engine. But he got the bird. Llewellin was furious and, knowing someone in the Ministry, he learnt the reason. Calboyds had been approached for an opinion and had described Schmidt as a crank. Llewellin then began a long correspondence with the Air Ministry in an effort to obtain a test of the engine. In the meantime, Schmidt's finances were exhausted and Llewellin had taken the pair into his own house, and was financing the work."

I lit another cigarette. " Well, David," I said, " that's his story. He says that he found Llewellin dead, and after going into the office and seeing the safe open he knew he had been framed and got out while the going was good."

" Why should they go to all that trouble to frame him? Why didn't they kill him?"

" That's just what I couldn't understand," I replied. " It was that and the melodramatic manner in which he concluded the interview that made me wonder whether he wasn't a little unbalanced." And I told him word for word what Schmidt had said as he stood up with the firelight blazing in his eyes.

" Cones of runnel," David murmured, and sucked noisily at his pipe. " Those are funny key-words for a code. Perhaps it has a further significance." He heaved himself off the bed and stood up facing me. " The whole thing is damned funny," he said. " I wouldn't believe a word of it, I'd say he was definitely nuts, if I didn't know that I'd been burgled last night and that the book had been replaced by another and the negatives destroyed. Can I have a look at the page we have got decoded?"

I put my hand in the pocket of my jacket. I think I knew what to expect a fraction of a second before my fingers encountered the smooth leather of my wallet. There was nothing else in the pocket. I looked up at David. " We've both been burgled," I said.

" Sure you put it in that pocket? It's not in your rooms anywhere?"

I shook my head. It was no good. I remembered slipping it into the pocket the night before and I had not looked at it since.

" Well, what do we do now—call in the police?" he asked. His tone held a note of sarcasm, and I pictured myself telling the whole thing to Crisham. "I don't think we can very well do that," I said. "Not yet at any rate." And I gave him a brief résumé of the page I had decoded. When I had finished, I said, "Schmidt was right. Just before he went he said he thought I wouldn't find it a case for the police— at first."

David filled his pipe and lit it. He was frowning slightly. "What's this girl Freya like?" He put the question in an abstracted manner. He was thinking of something else.

"I don't know," I replied. "Why do you want to know?"

He swung round on me. "Well, isn't she the clue to the whole thing? Where do you suppose she is?" he asked.

The thought had already occurred to me.

"I've got a hunch that the cones of runnel is not only the clue to the code, but the clue to the hide-out where that Diesel engine is. Somebody's got to get to Freya Schmidt before these lads, whoever they are, discover those key-words." He went over to the phone, which stood on the table by his bedside. "Get me Central 0012, will you, Miriam?" He turned to me. "If we fail here, we'll have to go round to that professor laddie you mentioned."

"Greenbaum?"

"Yes." The phone rang, and he picked up the receiver again. "Is that you, Micky? David Shiel here. Can you let me have a picture of Freya Schmidt? Yes, that's right— the daughter. Oh! They haven't traced her? You think so? Well, maybe you're right. No, a pal of mine on the *Record* just rang me up to see if I could get one for him. Cheerio, old boy." He put the receiver back. "No luck," he said. "The agencies haven't been able to get hold of any photo of her and the police don't seem able to trace her. They think Schmidt may have killed her too. Nice minds these boys have! I suppose Schmidt really is dead? I mean, supposing you wanted someone to take some notice of an invention of yours, wouldn't this be a good way to do it?"

"And what about Llewellin?" I said. "It's no good, David. I've been over the whole business from beginning to end and there's only one conclusion, and that's the one that Schmidt hinted at. Schmidt may or may not be dead. At the moment it's immaterial. Somehow we've got to find that girl."

"You may be right. But I still don't understand that murder. It doesn't make sense. Perhaps you're leaping to conclusions?"

"This sort of game is my job," I said a trifle stiffly.

"What—lucid deduction?" He looked at me quizzically. Then he burst out laughing. "Lucid deduction, my foot! Your job is to make any twelve of your fellow citizens believe anything you want them to believe."

"Maybe," I said, "but this business is serious. From the start there were only two ways of looking at it. Either Schmidt was speaking the truth or else he was mad. After what has happened during the night, I am quite certain he isn't mad. Do you type?" He nodded. "Good!" Then perhaps we could have the typewriter in here. The first thing is to get out a statement, which I can leave at my bank."

"You're going to take it up yourself, are you?" He hesitated. Then he added, "If all Schmidt says is true, this is something pretty big."

"That's why the first essential is to make a statement of what we know."

"Yes, but wouldn't it be better to call in the police?"

I shook my head. "Not yet," I said. "Police investigations can yield nothing in the case of a firm like Calboyds. If we knew what Schmidt had set down in those other four pages, there might be enough evidence to prove something. As it is, I shall have to go ahead on my own."

"But, good God!" he said, "you'll be a marked man from the word Go."

"Perhaps," I said. "But don't forget that, if I disappear, the police will have to take some notice of my statement."

David nodded and fetched the typewriter from the studio. "We'll have a carbon copy," I said, as he settled down in front of it.

It took me over an hour to complete that statement. When it was finished, I signed the carbon and placed it in a foolscap envelope, addressing it to Inspector Crisham. In a covering letter to my bank manager, I told him that it was to be handed to Inspector Crisham in person if at any time more than a week passed without his hearing from me. I emphasised that Crisham was to read it through in his office, and I gave him a detailed description of the Yard man. I was taking no chances. When I had signed this letter and placed it, with the statement, in a larger envelope, I asked David whether he had a back entrance.

"Not that I know of," he replied.

"A fire-escape, then?"

"No, the roof was considered sufficient."

"Of course, the roof. You know the people next door, don't you—the people that were burgled? Will their roof door be unlocked?"

"I shouldn't think so. But they're on the top floor. If I knock on their skylight, I expect they'll come and open it."

"Do you know them well enough to ask them to take this to my bank and keep quiet about it?"

"Well, I don't know them very well, but Harrison seems quite a good sort. I expect he'd do it. You think we're being watched?"

"I'm working on that assumption. And whilst you're doing that, I'm going to make certain, and at the same time ring Crisham." I handed him the envelope. "And don't use this phone again to make any inquiries," I said as he went to the door. "There's just a chance it may have been tapped."

He laughed. "Good God!" he said. "You don't under-rate them."

"No," I said. "I've played this game before. Crooks are one thing, but foreign agents are another, particularly if they're German. Don't forget, I was in the Intelligence in the last war."

"You are old, Father William."

I nodded. I was well aware of the fact. I was not as fast as I used to be at squash. But I was fit enough and I still held down a golf handicap of two. "Maybe," I said. "But age has the compensation of experience. Keep off that phone."

"Very good, sir." He grinned and went out through the door.

I took up the typescript of the statement and placed it in another envelope addressed to Crisham. This I put in my pocket. Then I got my hat and coat and went to the lift. There was no doubt that we were being watched. As I came out into Shaftesbury Avenue I noticed the quickened pace of a sandwich-board man.

I paused for the traffic at Piccadilly Circus and I saw that the man was still on my trail. But after crossing the Circus I lost him. Nevertheless, as I went down Lower Regent Street, I was conscious of being followed. By cutting down Jermyn Street and pausing to look in the window of Simpson's, I was able to identify my follower as a ragged-looking individual wandering along the gutter in search of cigarette ends. I should have taken no notice of him, but as he passed me he looked up and met my eyes. A feeling of awareness passed between us. It was almost embarrassing. He seemed to feel it too, for he mumbled, " Spare a copper, sir." I fished in my pocket and went over to him with two pennies. I put them clumsily into his outstretched hand so that one of them fell on to the pavement. He stooped to pick it up, and I noticed that, though his face was dark with dirt, the back of his neck below the collar was quite clean. I noticed, too, a slight scar on the back of his right hand. It was very small, just a thin line of drawn flesh across the knuckles. But I remembered a hand thrust out into the torchlight as it grabbed at a book.

I crossed the road and cut down Duke of York Street to Pall Mall. In the sanctuary of my club I made my way to the secretary's office. I handed him the envelope and asked him to put it in his safe. " I'll drop you a line or wire you every few days," I said. " If you don't hear from me for a whole week, get Inspector Crisham of the Yard to come round and give him the envelope. He's to read it in your office." Except for a slight lift of the eyebrows, the secretary betrayed no surprise, and I left him to ponder over the peculiarities of members.

I then went to one of the phone-boxes and rang Crisham. I was kept waiting some time, but in the end I got through to him. I told him of the arrangement I had made, but cut short his questions. " One other thing," I said. " You still want Schmidt, I suppose? Well, you can pick up the scent at 209 Greek Street. It's a little stale, perhaps, but he was living there as Frank Smith until about the middle of last week. The owner of the place, one Isaac Leinster, might repay attention." Again I had to curb his curiosity. " And don't try and get in touch with me unless you've found Schmidt," I warned him, and put down the receiver.

Next, I rang up my bank manager. The statement had reached him and had already been placed in the strong-room. My next call was to a big issuing house in the City. Bernard Mallard was an old friend of mine. "Do you know anything about Calboyds?" I asked.

"A certain amount—why?" was the cautious reply.

"I want to know who controls the company," I said.

"No one in particular, as far as I know," he replied.

"My information is to the contrary," I replied.

"Well, I think your information is inaccurate. As a matter of fact, we went into the company's position very closely about three years ago. We were hoping to be able to handle that big issue of theirs. There are a number of nominee holdings, but they're not large. All the big holdings are in the shareholders' own names, and none of them are big enough, singly, to constitute a controlling interest."

"Can you tell me their names?"

"There you've got me, old boy. Calboyd was one, of course. But I can't remember the others and I don't think we kept the details. Better go along to Bush House, if you're really interested."

"I will," I said. "Who handled the issue in the end?"

"Ronald Dorman—and damned badly, too. He put the price too high and got stuck with about seventy per cent of the Ordinary and practically the whole of the Preference."

"He underwrote the issue himself, did he?"

"Yes. There may have been some sub-underwriting, but I fancy the firm were left with the bulk of the issue."

"Where did Dorman get the capital?"

"There you've got me. He was pretty successful in 1935 and '36, don't forget, and he probably had a tidy packet put by. Dorman is supposed to be pretty wealthy." He gave a soft chuckle. "Those who have money can usually find money."

"You mean, he may have had backing?"

"Well, anyway, he covered what he'd underwritten somehow. He must have needed the better part of four millions, so I don't imagine he would have been able to find it all himself."

"Where would he be likely to get it?"

"Now look, Andrew, there's a limit to the questions I can

answer. What's the matter with the fellow? If you're suspecting him of being a racketeer, I warn you, the whole issuing business is a racket. And the whole City for that matter," he added frankly. " Or has he got mixed up in a murder case?"

" He can probably answer that better than I can," I said. " I'm just curious, that's all."

" Well, old boy, if you take my advice, you'll pick Home Rails. Try ' Berwick' Second Prefs. And have a game of golf with me some time."

" I will," I said. " But just now I'm busy. Many thanks for what you've told me." And I rang off, wondering whether or not Bernard Mallard knew who Dorman's backer was.

As I left the club, I saw my friend searching for cigarette ends in the gutter by the R.A.C. I walked leisurely along Pall Mall and jumped a bus as it slowed down to take the corner from the Haymarket. And so to Bush House, where I looked up the shareholders' list of the Calboyd Diesel Company. Of a total issued share capital of £6,500,000, no less than £4,000,000 odd was held by three private persons and Ronald Dorman and Company. I put down their names and their holdings. Ronald Dorman and Company had the biggest holding. Then came a Mr. John Burston of Woodlands, the Butts, Alfriston. Next, Mr. Alfred Cappock, Wendover Hotel, Piccadilly, London, W. And last, Sir James Calboyd, Calboyd House, Stockport, Lancs. Sir James Calboyd was the only big holder who was also a member of the board. Possibly Dorman had nominated a director. That remained to be seen.

I put the paper in my pocket and took a taxi back to David's studio. " Now what the devil have you been up to?" he demanded, as I entered the room. " I was just on the point of sending out a search party."

" I'm sorry," I said, and told him what I had been doing.

" You're certain you were followed?" he asked.

" Absolutely," I said.

" Good! Now we know quite definitely where we are. But what's the point of taking the orginal typescript of your statement down to your club whilst, at the same time, you send the carbon to your bank?"

"They followed me to the club," I explained. "I think they'll guess that the first thing I should do would be either to get in touch with the police or to leave a statement for them in case of accidents. My belief is that they'll burgle the club and, when they find they've got hold of the type-script, they'll not worry so much about the possibility of a duplicate."

He nodded. "My respect for my elderly relative grows hourly," he said. "In the meantime, I haven't been idle. Whilst waiting for friend Harrison to return from the bank, I made free of his phone and tried to find out something about the cones of Runnel. I tried the A.A. first, but drew blank. Then I tried the Ordnance Survey Office. They refused to make an attempt to trace it. So then I went the round of the map-makers. I was convinced that Runnel was either the name of a place or a man."

"Well, did you find out anything or didn't you?" I demanded.

"Not from them," he replied. "But as a last resort, I rang up the Trinity House people. I thought it might be on the coast. Well, it appears there's a Runnel Stone lying about a mile off a point called Polostoc Zawn, near Land's End. It's a submerged rock and Trinity House keep a buoy on it which gives out a mooing sound."

"It's cones of Runnel," I said, "not cow of Runnel."

"Wait a minute," he said, and there was a gleam of excitement in his eyes. "Apparently there's a Board of Trade hut on the point and near this hut are two conical-shaped signs. When they are in line, they give the direction of the Runnel Stone."

I jumped to my feet in my excitement. Cones of Runnel! It sounded right. Or had Schmidt just chosen those two words at random? I couldn't believe that. He was bound to give some clues as to the whereabouts of his daughter and the Diesel engine he had designed. "I think you've got it, David," I said. "Where exactly is this Runnel Stone?"

For answer he took me over to the desk in the corner where a Ward Lock of West Cornwall lay open, the map of the Land's End district spread out. "There you are," he said. "Polostoc Zawn, just west of Porthgwarra." He flicked over the pages. "Here's what Ward Lock says. ' Continuing our walk,'" he read, "' we notice on the higher ground on our left two iron cones, one red and the other black and white. They are beacons, which, when in line, give the direction of a submerged rock, known as the Runnel Stone, on which many good ships have met their fate. It is about a mile off the point. On it is a buoy producing a dismal sound like the mooing of a cow.'"

"Where's the nearest station?" I asked.

"I don't think there's anything nearer than Penzance."

I nodded. "Well, many thanks for your assistance, David. I don't think I have to remind you of the need for silence."

"Here, wait a minute," he said. "You're going to Penzance?" I nodded. "You're not broke by any chance, are you? I mean, I don't expect business is flourishing, but you're still quite well off, aren't you?"

"Yes," I said. "Yes, I think I am."

"Then you can afford to give me a little holiday."

"Listen, David," I said, "this isn't going to be any holiday. Don't forget we're at war. It's difficult to realise it as yet. But we are, and the chances of coming out of this alive may not be great."

He looked at me thoughtfully for a moment. "You're serious, are you?" he said suddenly. Then he laughed. "What do you take me for? I want to see this business through just as much as you do."

I was torn between a desire for his company and a reluctance to endanger anyone else's life. The excitement aroused in me by the initial process of investigation had given place to a mood of depression. As I saw it, this wasn't just a single spy or a single criminal I was up against. It was organised espionage. The organised espionage of a power notorious for its efficiency and ruthlessness. That's the way I looked at it as I stood there in David Shiel's room on the threshold of what now seems like a nightmare. "What is it that attracts you about this business?" I asked. "Is it adventure or Freya Schmidt?"

"A bit of both, I expect," he replied with a grin. "I never could resist the idea of beauty in distress."

"Well, listen to me," I said sharply. "There's no such thing as adventure, except in retrospect. You read stories or hear people talk of adventures. They sound exciting. But the reality is not exciting. There's pain to the body and torture to mind and nerves, and a wretched death for most adventurers. Few come back to tell their stories to excited audiences. Do you really want to pit your brains and your body, with mine, against something that is probably much too big for either of us? As for Freya Schmidt—well, I must say I thought you'd grown out of the adolescent stage. You're romancing about a woman you've never seen just because she's in a tough spot." My shot got home and I saw him flush. "If you ever see her, you'll probably get a shock. Women with men's brains usually dress like men and are altogether terrifying."

"Have it your own way, old boy," he said. "But as long as you've got my fare, I'm coming with you."

I saw that his mind was made up, and I must say that I was glad. I sat down and wrote him out a cheque for fifty pounds. "There," I said, handing it to him, "that's a loan to carry you on. I want you to leave that Calboyd account over till we get back. It'll be a good excuse for us to go up and see them. Now, I suggest we meet in the lounge at Victoria Station at two o'clock. There's a Cornish express that leaves Waterloo at three. Try and shake off any followers, but not too obviously. If by any chance one of us is followed to Victoria we'll still have an hour in which to shake them off between there and Waterloo."

"Good! I'll be there at two, and no followers."

Chapter Four

CONES OF RUNNEL

As soon as we left London we ran into sunshine. It was that bright, rather brittle sunshine that goes with February and an east wind. The sky was a light chilly blue and cloudless, and its colour was reflected in the water, which lay everywhere on the low ground. The fields, as they streamed past, looked sodden, but their green gave promise of a good early bite. As the sun went down, a dull mist spread over the landscape. By the time we ran through Salisbury, with the thin cathedral spire standing like a grey needle out of the gathering gloom, David was dozing in the seat opposite me, his heavy curved pipe lodged in the corner of his mouth. But the rhythmic beat of the wheels had filled me with a wild sense of excitement, and I did not feel like sleep.

Big stations, filled with the noise and bustle of travel, have always thrilled me. A car is a prosaic thing by comparison. Perhaps it is a matter of association. To me, a car is a method of conveying one to the beauties of the country. But a train spells travel. Go to Victoria, Waterloo, Euston— the Continent, the West Country and Scotland come instantly within your grasp. New scenery, adventure, fighting in some remote battle-ground, whatever your soul longs for, the cold ice of the north or the hot sun of the south, is there for the asking if you have money in your pocket. And the incessant clatter of the wheels! It's the pulse of life, the rhythm of adventure. It's the urge that makes children want to play trains. It's the sound that lifts you out of the rut and sets you down in a new world for a week, a month, a lifetime maybe. It brings you to new friends, new loves. It takes you to your death. It takes you to the fear of death. But it is adventure. And listening to the rhythmic beat, the mood of depression that I had felt in David's studio was gone, and I felt elated.

It was dark long before we reached Exeter, and we passed through Okehampton with the tors of Dartmoor etched black and clear against a full moon. It was past midnight before we glimpsed the sea at Marazion and saw St. Michael's Mount rearing its compact defences out of the silvered waters of the Bay. We went to earth for the night in a comfortable little hotel just opposite Penzance Station. My window looked out across the harbour to the moonlit bay. The outline of a destroyer and the complete absence of lights reminded me that the West Country, as well as London, was at war. I felt the presence of the sea, but everything was very still. I had a hot rum and tumbled into bed. But though I knew I was on the threshold of a big and dangerous task, I slept like a log.

I woke to a dismal sea mist and the mournful cry of a fog-horn. "The Runnel Stone," David murmured, as he took the seat opposite me in the breakfast-room. "They may not mean it that way, but it sounds remarkably like a cow."

" Well, I hope to God we haven't been leaping to conclusions," I said. The mist had damped my spirits.

" I'll be damned surprised if there's more than one place in this country that could be described as the Cones of Runnel," he replied. And I had to admit the truth of that. It was an unusual name. And I fell to wondering what Freya would be like and what sort of trouble lay ahead of us.

This sense of trouble ahead persisted against all the arguments of logic. We had not been followed to Penzance—of that I was certain. We had both been followed on leaving our rooms on the previous day, but had both been able to report on meeting at Victoria that we had shaken our followers off. Even so, we had taken elaborate precautions against any possible hangers-on in getting across to Waterloo. But though I sensed trouble ahead, I was not fighting shy of it. There was merely a slight tautness of the nerves, a tautness which I had not experienced since my climbing days. Of one thing I was glad. I had lived soft during recent years, but I had sat loose in my comfort and the wrench of leaving the rut was not severe.

After breakfast we went in search of a car. David took charge of this expedition. He has a flair in these matters. I remember, at one of his parties, hearing a young fellow, who had been told by David where he could pick up a steam-pressure cooker cheap, say, " Anything you want, go and ask old David. He knows so many odd people that he can always tell you exactly where to find anything at a knock-down price." But David also had a sense of atmosphere. He turned down a perfectly good Austin, which was offered us at normal hire rates together with unlimited petrol. " What!" he exclaimed, when I protested that all we wanted was a car to get us over about ten miles of country. " Turn up in an Austin? My dear Andrew, an Austin is essentially a family car. It's not the right background for us at all. Besides, you never know." Well, he was right about that.

Altogether we wasted about an hour wandering round Penzance, but eventually we ran a big Bentley roadster to earth. We heard of it from a back-street garage proprietor and found the owner in dingy lodgings down by the harbour. Neither of us had any doubt about the position. The man was the chauffeur and his master was away. David was not scrupulous, however, and when the fellow suggested a pound a day, he said, " Ten bob—for yourself." The man took the hint, and we left Penzance in style.

The mist had lifted a bit and turned into a downpour, which hit the Bentley in a flurry of wind as soon as we reached open country. We kept to the Land's End road as far as Lower Hendra, where David turned off to St. Buryan. Penzance to Porthgwarra is not more than nine miles, but as soon as we were off the main road, the way became windy and the going slow. Barely two miles short of Land's End, we turned sharp left into a narrow lane up which the Bentley shouldered its way between reeking hedgerows. We climbed steadily and, breasting a hill by a farm, we suddenly came upon open moorland and looked through the driving curtain of rain to the dismal grey of the sea mottled with white-caps.

David slowed the car up as we bore round the shoulder of the hill and took the descent into Porthgwarra. And then simultaneously we cried out and pointed across the valley. Against the rain-drenched background of the hill opposite, the iron cones stood out, sombre and foreboding. They looked like a pair of giant pierrot's hats, one red and the other a black check, set down carelessly upon the headland. And yet they seemed to have grown out of the ground like dragon's teeth rather than to have been set down in that desolate spot.

The valley, into which we were descending, ran practically parallel to the coastline, snaking out into the natural inlet of Porthgwarra at the finish. The seaward side of the valley rose steep and bare to the coastguards' houses and the Board of Trade look-out on the top. Beyond it were the cliffs. They presented an almost solid front stretching to Land's End. These cliffs are regarded by those who know their Cornwall as the grimmest natural battlements in the country.

As we slid quietly round the bend and into the valley, we lost the wind and the sudden stillness was almost eerie. Porthgwarra had scarcely the right to be called a village. It is just a cluster of cottages huddled together for shelter close by the shore. David drew up at the local shop. We got out and stood for a moment, looking at the heaving mass of water that jostled in the inlet. Behind the regular beat and hiss of the waves on the foreshore we heard the dull roar of the Atlantic out beyond the headland. And behind all this cacophony of sound the mournful groan of the Runnel buoy was borne in on the howling wind.

I led the way into the shop. The sharp note of the bell over the door brought an elderly body from the back parlour. "I'm a solicitor," I said. "I'm looking for a young lady who has recently come to live in these parts."

"Ar," she said, and looked me over. "What would 'er name be?"

I said, "Well, that's the trouble. I'm not quite sure. She used to be a Mrs. Freya Williams, but since she divorced her husband I believe she has returned to her maiden name." It was a gross libel on the girl, but I could think of no other satisfactory reason for not being able to give her name.

"Ar, well now, there's Miss Dassent over to Roskestal."

"When did she arrive?"

"That'll be two winters ago now."

"Then that's not the one," I said. "The young lady I want to get in touch with must have arrived only a few months back."

"Ar, well then, it'll be Miss Stephens down at the studio you're wanting mebbe." She thought for a moment, and then turned to the back parlour and called out, "Joe!" A grey-haired man with a dark weather-beaten face and a seaman's jersey emerged. "There's two gentlemen here looking for——"

"Ar, I heard. It'll be Miss Stephens arl right that you'll be looking for," he said to me. "She came here with 'er boat at the end of the tourist season. She's got the studio down afore the beach. Might you be a friend of hers?"

"I have some business to discuss with her," I said.

"Ar, but you'm a lawyer fellow, like?" I nodded, and he spat accurately into the corner behind the counter. "Then it do look as though the Lord 'as sent you. The lass be over in the little cove with two naval men. They want to take her boat, and she'm mighty fond of that boat. You'll mebbe know the rights of the matter. When I left them five minutes back they were still arguing it out and she were getting mighty sore."

"Thanks," I said. "I'll go down and see what I can do."

When we were outside, I said, "Looks as though you were right, David, about the Cones of Runnel."

"What makes you so sure all of a sudden?"

I laughed. "Everything fits so snugly into place," I said, as we went down the road to the beach. "The tripper season ended about the time Schmidt got that engine away from Llewellin's works. And here is this Miss Stephens with a boat. Don't you see—Swansea is on the coast. What better way of hiding a Diesel engine than by putting it into a small yacht."

David nodded thoughtfully. "The reasoning is sound. But what about this requisitioning party? Don't tell me that we've arrived just in the nick of time to save the heroine from having the secret engine stolen from her by her father's enemies."

"I doubt it," I said. "You've got a thriller mentality, David. But stranger coincidences happen in real life. What is more likely is that we have arrived just in time to see the boat requisitioned by the naval authorities. A lot of these small craft are being called in for patrol work just now."

We had reached the beach, but there was no sign of the girl. The foreshore was narrow and the slope to it was paved. On this paved slope lay a few small boats. The studio itself backed on to the shore. The road curved round and finished against a shoulder of rock, and in this rock gaped the mouth of a cave with daylight visible at the other end. I went over to it and entered. It sloped sharply to another beach, and fishermen's nets and other gear were stored against the walls of it.

We went down it and emerged on to the second and smaller beach. Here were more boats and, among them, a motor-cruiser painted white with the name *Sea Spray* in black on the stern. She was a forty-footer, fast-looking, but broad enough in the beam to be handy in a seaway. From beyond the boat came the sound of voices raised in altercation.

We moved nearer. "Look, I've said I'm sorry," came a man's voice. "I'm not responsible for the requisition order I have. I'm merely acting on instructions."

"What if the boat isn't mine?" This was a woman's voice, clear and firm.

"That doesn't make any difference. I've explained that. All I'm concerned about is the boat, not its ownership. Anyway, if the boat isn't yours, what are you worrying about?"

"Well, the boat is mine, but the engine isn't. It's a very costly kind of engine and the person who lent it to me would be most upset if it passed out of my hands with the boat. You'll have to let your order stand over until I've had the engine removed."

There was no doubt in my mind now. I nodded to David and we rounded the stern of the boat to find a young naval lieutenant in the act of clambering on to the yacht. "I'm afraid legally an engine is part of a boat," he was saying. "It wouldn't be much good to us without one, anyway."

He had two sailors with him and he motioned them on board. But it was the girl that riveted my attention. She was dressed in a blue corduroy suit, which, though it had obviously seen a great deal of hard wear, was well enough cut to still look very smart with its navy shirt and red-striped tie. But though her figure was entrancingly neat and boyish, it was her head that inevitably held one's gaze. I think it was the finest head I had ever seen on a woman. The face was oval to the point of the firm chin and framed in black hair brushed sleek to the nape of the neck. The mouth was clearly moulded and full enough to give promise of warmth. The nose was straight and small, with delicately chiselled nostrils, and the thin line of the eyebrows swept upwards over large dark eyes to a high forehead. It is difficult to describe her and at the same time give any idea of the extreme perfection of those features. It was a beauty that took your breath away when you first saw it. It was the nearest I have ever seen in life to the head of Nefertiti.

"Well, you can't take her out in this sea," she said. Two angry spots of colour were showing through the tan of her cheeks.

The lieutenant turned towards the sea and saw us. He was obviously extremely uncomfortable. Looking at the girl, I could appreciate his difficulty. "We'll manage it all right," he said gruffly, and climbed on board.

"Just a minute," I said, as he beckoned the two ratings to join him. He swung round, his face still flushed. "I'm a barrister. Perhaps you would let me have a look at your requisition order?" I turned to the girl. "Miss Freya Schmidt?" I asked quietly, and the look of surprise on her face was unmistakable. She did not deny the name. "My name is Kilmartin," I told her. "Your father asked me to come down here to discuss a little matter of business with you." Her large eyes suddenly seemed to dilate, and I knew that surprise had given place to fear. But I could do nothing to help her.

The lieutenant dropped down on to the beach at my side. He produced an order from the pocket of his greatcoat. As I had expected, it was perfectly in order. "I'm sorry the lady is so upset about it, sir," he said, as I handed it back to him. "But it's nothing to do with me. I'll take every care of it, and if you can get the order rescinded, then it'll be all right. But, however much she objects, I'm afraid I'll have to take it now. Those are my orders." I think he was glad to have a man to deal with.

"Who took out the order, do you know?" I asked.

"Well, the naval authorities at Falmouth made out the order," he said, indicating the signature. "Who actually discovered the boat, I don't know. You see, we've got quite a number of scouts out along the coasts, picking out likely vessels for patrol work. And this is just the sort of craft we want."

"Where are you taking her?" I asked. "I shall want to know where to find her if I can get this order rescinded."

"I doubt whether you'll get it rescinded, sir," he said. "She's a good boat for light patrol work."

"Well, just in case, I'd like to know where I can find her."

"I'm taking her up to the Thames Estuary."

"Whereabouts?"

He glanced at the order again. "Calboyd Diesel Power Boat Yards, Tilbury," he said. He glanced at the graceful lines of the boat. "Maybe they're going to put a powerful engine in her and convert her into a torpedo boat. She's got the lines for it. Have you any objections if I get on with the job now?"

I shrugged my shoulders and looked across at Schmidt's daughter. There was nothing I could do. These were not Calboyds' people. They were naval men. Out of the tail of my eyes I had caught sight of a drifter lying off the inlet, her bows headed into the wind. As no one made any comment, the lieutenant turned and climbed on board the boat.

The girl watched him go with large sombre eyes. I felt she was very near to tears. "This is Evan Llewellin's boat, isn't it?" I asked her.

She nodded.

"And it's fitted with your father's engine?"

Her eyes met mine, and again I noticed that sudden flicker of fear. "What do you know about us?" she asked. "Do you know where my father is?"

For answer I took her father's letter from my pocket and handed it to her. She looked at the writing for a long time, as though trying to pluck up the courage to open it. Then suddenly she made up her mind and ran her finger down the fold of the envelope. She read it through slowly, as though bewildered by it. Then she looked up at me. I saw the tears gathering in her eyes. "Is—he's dead, isn't he?"

"I don't know," I said.

Her long finely-shaped hands were clutched so tight that the nails bit into the flesh. "Pray God he's dead," she whispered. "Oh, God, don't let them torture him." Then suddenly she became aware again of the two of us, standing there. "He has suffered so much and he was such a brilliant man," she explained. She had control of herself now. "Will you come up to the studio? We can talk there."

"This is a friend of mine—Mr. David Shiel," I said. She nodded to David. I think it was the first time she had really become aware of him. "I'll explain how he comes into it with the rest," I said.

She led the way back to the studio. She did not speak, and I left the silence unbroken. She seemed to have withdrawn into herself, as though she wished to be alone with her thoughts. I could do nothing to comfort her.

The studio was a small brick building that did service as a bed-sitting-room cum workshop. There was a friendly coal fire blazing in the grate and a divan bed in the corner. There was a sink near the window and a big serviceable bench littered with tools. The easel and canvases of the owner were stacked behind the door. A kettle was singing in front of the fire and, like a person in a dream, she began to make tea. When this was served, she squatted down on the floor in front of the fire and we drew up two wooden chairs.

Then I told her the story, omitting nothing. She did not once interrupt, and when I had finished she sat silent, seemingly lost in thought. As last she looked up and her eyes travelled from me to David. " You have been very kind, both of you," she said. " It must have seemed a fantastic story and it was kind of you to take my father at his word." She hesitated. Then she said, " Franzie didn't kill Evan Llewellin. He was incapable of hurting anyone. Besides, Evan was the best friend we ever had. It's on his money that I'm living down here."

" Can you add anything to what your father wrote on that first page of the code message?" I asked.

But she shook her head. " Nothing," she said. " In fact, what he wrote there is largely new to me. I was bundled off in the yacht shortly after war broke out. The engine had been installed in it in July. I knew people were after it, and I presumed that it was Calboyds. But I knew nothing about the company being under Nazi control. I don't think my father knew it then. Evan and I brought her here on our own, and then he went back to Swansea. My instructions were to lie low. I got very little news. Every fortnight there was a message from my father in the personal column of the *Daily Telegraph* under Olwyn, my mother's name—that was all. The day after I read about Evan's death there was a little message from my father to say that he was all right and that I was to sit tight here until I heard from him. That was three weeks ago, and not a word since. It's been horrible just sitting here, waiting."

" And what now?" I asked.

" I don't know." Her voice sounded weary and very dejected. " The police must be informed. Oh, God!" she cried, " if only I knew what had happened to him."

" There's more to it than that," I said. " You understand the implication of that part of his message we did decode? Tell me, just how good is this engine?"

A far-away look came into her eyes. " Franzie was a genius," she said. " And that engine is the fruits of his genius." She looked up at me and her voice became suddenly matter-of-fact. "I won't bore you with technical details, but I'm a fairly good engineer, and that engine is something far in advance of anything that has yet been designed. It's not a marine engine, though, geared down as it is in the *Sea Spray*, it gives a pretty amazing performance. It's an aero engine. Do you know anything about the principles of aeronautics? Well, I think you'll understand this. The production of an aero engine that gives a higher speed isn't just a question of increasing the revs. If the propeller goes too fast, it creates a vacuum. You don't necessarily need a high-revving engine. What you need is an engine that is light and yet gives tremendous power behind the swing of the propeller, so that it bites into the air. You follow?" I nodded. "The Diesel engine is, of course, the ideal type of engine for aircraft because it develops great power at relatively slow speeds. The drawback to the Diesel so far has been its weight. The cylinders have to be extremely strong to stand the pressure. So far this has required a heavy weight of metal by comparison with the petrol engine. My father, as he told you, was a specialist in metal alloys. His chief discovery was a new lightweight alloy of unusual strength. The secret of this alloy is still his. Realising where its possibilities lay, he then set to work to modify the Diesel design. Eventually he produced the engine that is now in the *Sea Spray*."

"Won't those naval boys realise that they've got hold of something unusual when they take her out?" David asked.

"No. Whilst I've been here, I have incorporated a little switch valve of which I have the key. The valve, which is now regulating the fuel supply, will keep the engine down to a performance very little different from that of an ordinary Diesel. But a firm like Calboyds will soon discover what is checking the performance and put in a new valve."

"How long will that take?" I asked.

She shrugged her shoulders and poured out some more tea. "I don't know," she replied. "A day—perhaps more."

"And how long to analyse the alloy?"

She looked up quickly and there was something in her eyes that I did not for the moment understand. "Ah, I see what it is," she said. "You are thinking of your country."

" And yours, too," I said. " You were born before the 1915 Act."

" Yes, mine, too," she said. " I'm sorry. I always think of myself as an Austrian. But now—— They might take a week or a month to analyse it—who knows. But if I were in their position, I should take a piece of metal from the engine for analysis, make rough drawings of the design and then try and smuggle the engine itself through to Germany. It would be surprising if both methods failed."

" Agreed," I said. " I think that's what they'll try to do. And that is what we've got to prevent at all costs."

" How?" she asked.

" I don't know yet."

" The police must be told everything," she said, after a moment's pause. " Do you know anyone in the police force?"

" I do," I said. " But it would be folly to try and tell the police at this stage that one of the biggest industrial firms in the country is under Nazi control. Calboyd is a public figure—philanthropist and all that. The police would just laugh at us."

" I don't mind. I must find Franzie. Don't you understand," she cried, turning her big eyes on me appealingly, " these men are fiends. They may be torturing him. Literally torturing him, I mean. You English never can be made to understand that on the Continent people are tortured."

I leaned forward, looking down into her eyes. " Don't you understand, Freya, that you're putting the life of one man before the lives of thousands? If Calboyds are not exposed and this engine gets into Germany, then we lose our superiority in quality as well as in numbers, and if we do that, we lose the war. Will you risk that, even to save your father from torture? He wouldn't. He knew the danger he faced, but he was not prepared to yield that engine, though the offers made him were reasonably good considering the probable alternative."

She put her hands to her eyes. " I can't bear it," she said. " I love him. He's all I've got. Oh, why should I have been given such a choice?" She spoke quietly, as though dulled by the uncertainty.

" There is no choice," I said. " You know that. Would

you set the police to hunt down your father before you've fashioned the means to prove him innocent? Do you want him to hang?" It was a brutal argument, but it was no time for gentle persuasion.

She took it as though it were a challenge, for she raised her head and said, " Yes, of course, you're right. But what can we do? You can't stop them taking the boat, can you?"

"No," I said, " That's where Calboyds have the advantage of us. Until we have sufficient evidence they have the law on their side. And at the same time, their agents will not hesitate, I fancy, to go outside the law."

David laughed. " It seems we get the worst of both worlds, he said. "What do we do about the boat?"

I rose to my feet. Freya's talk of the police had given me an idea. " Where can I phone?" I asked.

" There's a phone over at the shop," Freya said.

" Good! I'll ring Crisham at the Yard and tell him to hold the boat when it arrives at Calboyds' yard."

" But will he?" Freya asked.

" I think so,' I said, " when he hears whose boat it is. I'll also tell him about the engine and Calboyds. He won't believe it, of course, but it'll give him something to chew over." I let myself out and went over to the shop.

The telephone was in the back parlour. I lifted the receiver and waited. But there was no sound from the exchange. I joggled the rest up and down, but the line was completely dead. " Your telephone seems out of order," I told them.

" That it can't be," replied the old man. " I were only using it this morning to ring to Penzance to get the doctor to Mrs. Teale. She's near 'er time, she is." Then he tried, but he got no answer. In the end I went up the road to a little house owned by a young writer, but his phone was also out of order.

I went back to the studio in a very thoughtful frame of mind. And as I walked down the road, the soft chug-chugging of an engine sounded through the noise of the gale, and the *Sea Spray* came into view, battling its way out of the inlet, the naval dinghy trailing at her stern. I could not help admiring the way in which the young lieutenant handled her, for the sea was running very high and he had to take her close in to the rocks. And as she passed out of sight round the eastern headland, I wondered whether or not we should ever see her again. It seemed strange that that little craft should mean so much to two countries in the throes of war. And then I fell to wondering about the phone again. It seemed curious that the line should go out of order just as the boat had been requisitioned.

David turned as I entered the studio. " Did you get him?" he asked.

" No," I said, and explained to them what had happened.

" Funny," said David. He lit a pipe and tossed the match into the fire with a frown on his face. " You know," he said, " if I were on the other side, it might occur to me that the person from whom the boat was requisitioned would make some such move."

" Yes, but we could go into another village," I pointed out.

" Maybe," he said.

" I could walk up to Roskestal or along the cliffs," Freya pointed out.

" The way I look at it is this," David said. " Bona fide naval scouts may have seen the boat and may have got her requisitioned just as they would any other fast craft along the coast. In that case, we have little to fear. On the other hand, the people who want this engine may suddenly have woken up to the fact that Llewellin owned a boat at Swansea and that it was no longer there. They'd have been some time working round the coast, looking for her. When they did find her, what better way of getting her away quietly than by giving the navy the job. And I think the last of these two possibilities is the right one."

" In which case," I asked, " what would you do if you were in their shoes?"

" I should see that the one person who knew the truth about the boat was safely disposed of," was his prompt reply.

" So you'd cut the phone and watch the road to see that she didn't get word to anyone?"

" Precisely."

" But, don't you see, I could walk over to St. Levan or to Porthcurno along the cliffs," Freya pointed out again.

" Yes, but would you arrive?" David asked. " I suggest we stick to the Bentley and make a dash for it."

"But look, this is silly," Freya persisted. "They can't isolate a whole village. Suppose we split up and all go different ways? Anyway, you don't know the phone isn't just an accident. There's quite a gale blowing and the wires may be down somewhere. It has happened before. As for the requisitioning, lots of boats are being requisitioned. It's one of the things I've been dreading. That's why I made that switch valve."

Her point was reasonable. We hadn't been followed from London and it would take them a long time to work out that code and discover that the key-letters CONESFRUL stood for Cones of Runnel. "I think Freya is right," I said. "We're just jumping to conclusions. I suggest we drive into Sennen and I'll phone Crisham from there. If you'll bring a few things with you," I said to Freya, "we can decide on our next move as we go along."

"That seems sensible," she said.

David shrugged his shoulders and relit his pipe. I noticed that his eyes followed Freya as she pulled a little suitcase from beneath the bed and began packing a few things into it. When she had finally closed it, she put on a tight-fitting little cloth cap and a heavy gabardine cape.

Chapter Five

WE TAKE THE OFFENSIVE

FIVE MINUTES later we were in the Bentley and moving up the valley out of Porthgwarra. Surprisingly enough David had insisted on Freya sitting in the back, whilst I went in front with him. He took the long hill slowly, and every now and then he half-leaned out of the window and stared up towards the roadway above the hairpin bend. "Didn't I notice a track running off across the moor at the bend up here when we came down?" he asked.

I didn't remember it, but Freya leaned forward and said, "Yes, it doubles back along the other side of the valley to the coastguards' houses."

"Doesn't it go anywhere else?" he asked.

"Yes, there's a track running away to the right to a farm and back inland to Roskestal. It's terribly bad going."

"Any gates?"

"Several, I think. Why?"

"Oh, nothing. I just like to be sure of the lay of the land." He accelerated slightly as we neared the bend, and as we rounded it I saw the track running steeply down to the head of the valley. As soon as we were round the bend, David slowed up again and we climbed slowly with a fine view down the valley to Porthgwarra. The rain had stopped now and the clouds were thinning as though the sun might break through at any minute.

As we neared the top of the hill, I asked David what the trouble was. The car was barely moving and beginning to pink. "I'm a careful driver, that's all," he said. We crept round the bend which led inland at almost a walking pace. But, even so, I was pitched forward by the suddenness with which David jammed on the brakes. The next second the gears crashed as he put the car into reverse and, with his offside door open, the car shot backwards.

I had a fleeting picture of a big American car drawn up across the road with two men standing on the grass verge. Then my whole attention was riveted to my side of the narrow road, for David, leaning out of his door, was roaring backwards round the bend and down the hill. How he managed it, I don't know. The noise of the engine, grinding away in reverse, was terrific. We must have been doing over thirty. "Hold tight," he said, as we came to the hairpin. the car's wheels suddenly locked over and we took the bend at its steepest point, just as the American car came into sight round the bend at the top of the hill.

Then suddenly we were thrown hard back against our seats and there was a horrible screeching sound as the wheels skidded, fully locked, on the wet tarmac. Our bumpers hit the bank on the outer edge of the bend and immediately the car leapt forward, the engine roaring full out. We slithered round on to the track and took the hill at a fantastic speed. As we neared the bottom, I glanced back just in time to see the American car come on to the track, lurching and swaying like a tank going into action.

"I hope to God the gates are all open," David said be-

tween set teeth, as we took the water-course at the bottom
with a bump that brought the wheels hard up against the
mudguards and caused us to pitch violently.

I said nothing, but I kept my hand on the handle of my
door, ready to jump out if necessary. The track rose steeply
from the water-course until we could see the Board of Trade
hut and the cones away to our left. On either side of us the
sodden heathland stretched away flat to stone walls. The
line of the cliffs could be seen quite clearly with huge
irregularly-shaped stones standing like druidical temples
against the leaden sky.

Ahead of us a stone wall suddenly showed, grey against
the darker heath. It cut right across the track, but the gate
was open and we swept through it at near on fifty. How
David held the car to the track I don't know, for there was
barely a foot to spare on either side and we were bucking
madly in the potholes with yellow muddy water spurting up
from our wheels and blowing across the windshield.

We were hardly through the gateway when Freya reported
that the car behind was also through and gaining on us.
David swore softly and I felt the speed of the Bentley
increase. His face was set and he leaned slightly forward as
though he would thrust his face through the windscreen to
see better. The wheel was like a live thing in his hand and we
pitched from side to side of the track in a most terrifying
manner. "We'll never beat them on this side-track," he said.
"American cars are made for this sort of thing. We're too
tightly sprung. What we need is a nice windy road." Then
he called out over his shoulder, "Are they still gaining on
us?"

"I think we're just about holding the distance," Freya
called back.

It was crazy. We were doing something between fifty and
sixty. I don't think I've ever been so scared in a car in my
life. Every minute I expected the car to leap from the track
and turn over, and all I could do was sit and grip my seat.

David suddenly cried out, "By God, I believe we've got
them now." I glanced at him and, intent though he was on
driving, I could see he was excited. "See that bend ahead?
Isn't that a gateway into a farmyard?"

I peered through the arc of clear windscreen, across which

the wiper flicked rhythmically, and saw the track curving away to the left and then back again to the right in a long sweep. And at the end of that sweep was a farm. The track appeared to bend sharply round the farm between stone walls, and on the bend was the entrance to the farm. A moment later it was lost to sight and there was no possibility of our seeing it again until we were right on top of it, taking the bend.

Freya reported that the American car was drawing up on us again. I saw David steal one quick glance in the driving mirror and the car swayed violently. I gripped my seat in my excitement. We were running between stone walls now on the long bend leading to the farm. I saw the out-houses across the field to our left. I looked round. The car was less than a hundred yards behind us now. The light springing caused the body to sway and bounce far more than our own car, but the wheels were holding the track much better. There was no doubt that it was gaining.

I turned back to find that we were practically on top of the farm buildings. The track straightened up and the bend round the farm showed about fifty yards ahead. "Hold tight," David said. And at the same time I felt the brakes begin to bind. As we took the bend the back wheels began to skid. There was a horrible screeching noise as the rubber cut across the rough metal of the track. The car seemed for a moment completely out of control. The back jarred violently and there was the sound of metal against stone. Then David ground his gears, swung the wheel over the opposite way and we shot into the farmyard. Fortunately it was empty of stock and largely cobbled. David brought the Bentley to a standstill with its nose half-buried in a pile of manure. Then we shot back and came forward with our nose in the gate just in time to see the American car come round the bend, its tyres screeching and the body swaying and dipping.

Whether they saw us or not we didn't have time to tell. David swung the Bentley out of the farmyard as their tail disappeared round the bend, and we went hell-for-leather back down the track. "Nice work!" I said. David grinned. There was the exultation of speed and fine driving in his eyes.

"It'll take them quite a time to stop," he said. "And by the time they've backed to the farmyard to turn, we'll be well on our way."

This was true, for it wasn't until we were actually on the Porthgwarra road again and climbing the hill to Roskestal that Freya reported the car coming through the gate in the stone wall. The rest was easy. We made terrific pace to Penzance and ran up through Redruth and Bodmin to Launceston. There we turned sharp to the north and made for Bideford. At Holsworthy we paused for a late lunch and I phoned Crisham.

My object was to tell him just enough to whet his appetite. Desmond Crisham is one of the bulldog breed. He won't be driven. But he'll follow a clue with all the obstinacy of his type. If I had told him the whole story, I knew well enough he wouldn't have believed me. He's not the sort to believe in fairy stories, unless he's worked them out for himself and then they aren't fairy stories to his way of thinking. I thought that if I could tell him just enough to make him curious he'd make an awful nuisance of himself at the Calboyd Power Boat Yard. But when after nearly half an hour's wait, for I had made it a personal call, I got through to him, he cut me short and said, "I've been trying to get you everywhere. Listen, you were perfectly right about that address you gave me. Franz Schmidt lived there for nearly three weeks. Did you know he was supposed to have had an accident? Oh, you did? Well, why the hell couldn't you have told me? And I suppose you knew that his rooms had been searched?"

"Yes," I said. "I searched them myself. But there was someone before me. He came to get some clothes for Schmidt, who was supposed to be in some hospital."

He took me up on that. "Supposed to be?" he cried, and his voice rose almost to a shout. "Then I suppose you know that he's not in hospital, that he's just vanished?"

"I expected it," I said.

"Look here, Andrew, you and me have got to have a little talk. Can I come round to your rooms?"

"No. I'm speaking from a little place in Devon."

"What the hell are you doing down there? All right, it doesn't matter. Let's get down to business."

"Listen," I said. "I rang you up to tell you something, and this call is costing about two bob a minute."

"Well, damn it, you can afford it, can t you? What were you going to tell me?"

"Just this. Did you know Evan Llewellin kept a motor-cruiser at Swansea?"

"Yes, and it's missing. I've been searching all over the place for it."

"Well, it has just been requisitioned by the naval authorities. It's now on its way to the Calboyd Diesel Power Boat Yards at Tilbury. I think it'll repay investigation. Perhaps I should tell you that Schmidt was a specialist in Diesel engines."

"I know that."

"Did you also know that Calboyds had been after it?"

"How do you know?"

"Never mind that now. And look here, Desmond," I added, "this is entirely between ourselves—about Calboyds, I mean. I've no proof yet. But keep your eyes open and for God's sake don't let them hold that boat of Llewellin's for a moment, or your evidence will be gone."

"What are you talking about?" Crisham's voice sounded exasperated. "Listen, Andrew. Where the devil do you stand in this business? What's your game? Has Schmidt become a client of yours, because, if so, you can set your mind at rest."

"You mean you've discovered that he didn't murder Llewellin?"

"Yes. But it's no thanks to him. Running off like that, the fool nearly ran his head into a noose. It's just a stroke of luck that we've been able to fix him up with an alibi. Just as I thought the case was as clear as daylight, along comes an old scallywag who has been thieving scraps of metal from Llewellin's works. He looked in through the open door of the stamping-shop that night just as two men were coming out of Llewellin's office, and he could see Llewellin's body bent over the drill. He slipped away and nearly ran into Schmidt crossing from his own shed to the stamping-shop."

"Well, that's fine," I said. "And who did murder Llewellin?"

"If I knew, I wouldn't be wrangling over the phone with

you," he said angrily. "What I want to know is where you come in? What do you know of this business? Where's Schmidt? Where is his confounded daughter? And who murdered Llewellin? This case is giving me a pain in the neck and the Commissioner has been leading me a dog's life because—well, I suppose I oughtn't to tell you this—because Evan Llewellin was a secret agent. He covered the Swansea district, and since the beginning of the war he had been particularly helpful to the Ministry of Economic Warfare. Now, for God's sake, tell me what you know."

"All I know is in that statement at my bank, and you'll be able to read it at your leisure when I am no longer of this world. In the meantime, all I can tell you is that Schmidt's daughter is with me now and that Schmidt was framed. Find Schmidt and I think he'll be able to clear up the whole business. But understand this, Desmond," I added, "don't run away with the idea that this business is as simple as murder. It's big. Work in with the Intelligence, and remember particularly what I said about geting hold of that boat and keeping an eye on Calboyds." I cut short his sudden burst of questions by putting down the receiver.

When, over coffee, I told the others what I had said, David's comment was, "Having gone so far, I should have thought it would have been best to tell him the whole thing."

"Listen, David," I said. "If you were an obstinate bull-dog of a policeman, what would you say to that yarn? I've told him enough to make him curious. So long as he's curious, he'll go ferreting around Calboyds, however much of a howl they kick up. He's like that. A little knowledge makes him a dangerous man. Give him the whole thing worked out for him and he won't stir. Don't forget what we're up against. Calboyds isn't some tupenny-ha'penny little concern. It's a big and powerful organisation and there's maybe something even bigger still behind it. If he thought he was on the point of trying to expose Calboyds as a Nazi-controlled company operating in favour of the enemy, he'd fight shy of it. He'd be out of his depth completely. But let him think that he's just investigating a murder that is linked up in some way with a little industrial swindling, and he knows his duty and will do it."

Freya, I could see, was not interested in our conversation.

She was sitting with clasped hands and a smile on her lovely face. "Well, that's one of your father's difficulties over," I said. "Perhaps it's an omen."

"Oh, I hope so," she said. Then suddenly she leaned forward and took my hands. "You've been so kind," she said. It was an impulsive gesture, but something within me seemed to shrink from the touch of her cool fingers. Her big dark eyes were swimming. The boyishness was gone suddenly from her and she was a woman on the verge of tears because she had found friends. She turned to David. The movement was less impulsive and she did not take his hands. "Thank you," she said. "Thank you both. You have given me new heart."

"You've put new heart into me, too," David said with a laugh. But I fancy his eyes were serious. He had come to Cornwall like a romantic schoolboy prepared to fall for the damsel in distress, and the damsel's beauty had exceeded his wildest dreams. Well, I must admit, they made a grand pair. And I wished suddenly that I was younger.

After our coffee we sat and smoked cigarettes and held a council of war. David was all for some desperate attempt to get the boat back. But I said, "No, there's a better way than that—the legal method, which they used. I know Rear-Admiral Sir John Forbes-Pallister. I can get him at the Admiralty and I think he'll be able to get that order rescinded. Another thing, we don't want to make straight for the Calboyd yards by car. We've thrown these boys off our track by swinging north like this out of the direct road route to London. Crisham will look after the boat for a day or two at any rate. And remember this, if we remain on the defensive, we're lost. We've got to attack. And the only place to open an offensive is in the City. The whole thing hinges on this control. I'm certain of that. If we can find out who is really at the back of Calboyds, then we'd be getting somewhere."

"Or if we could find my father," said Freya.

"That's true," I said. "But I think the two go together. Crisham will do his best in the routine manner."

They both agreed with me, so we pushed on to Barnstaple, where we arranged for the car to be driven back to Penzance, and boarded an Ilfracombe-London express. We had dinner on the train and got into Paddington shortly after ten. I took them to a boarding-house in Guilford Street kept by a Mrs. Lawrence. Both my rooms and David's studio were bound to be under observation. Mrs. Lawrence was a Scotswoman married to a Chinaman—a wonderful combination for running a London boarding-house. I had had rooms there in my student days and she was glad to see me again. She looked tired and old, and when I discovered that she could let us have three rooms, I guessed that the war had hit her business badly. She took a fancy to Freya at once and fussed round her like an old hen, whilst her husband came and went with hot-water bottles and tea and his barely intelligible chatter of English.

I had just got into my pyjamas and was sitting in front of the hissing gas-fire in my dressing-gown smoking a pipe and thinking over the situation, when there was a knock at the door and David came in. He also had reached the dressing-gown stage and in his hand he held the evening paper that he had bought at Paddington. " I thought this might interest you." He handed me the paper and pointed to a paragraph on one of the inside pages. It ran:

Sir James Calboyd has been appointed Director of Aero Engine Production. This appointment was announced by the Prime Minister in answer to a question in the House this afternoon.

Sir James Calboyd is the chairman and founder of the Calboyd Diesel Company and the Prime Minister emphasised that the appointment had been made in conformity with the Government's policy of appointing industrial specialists to control industry wherever control has been found necessary.

Sir James is well known as a philanthropist. And it will be remembered that for many years he has been an advocate of the greater use of Diesel engines for aircraft. He has a wide knowledge of the aircraft industry and of aero engine design. It is common knowledge that the Calboyd factories are undergoing rapid expansion and that the output of Diesel engines for our bomber aircraft is being rapidly increased.

I looked across at David, who had pulled up a chair to the fire. "The old boy has a big pull somewhere," I said. "It looks as though friend Schmidt was right about that order."

David nodded. He was smoking a cigarette. "But is he our man?"

"No," I said. I had made up my mind on that point from the start. "Have you ever met him? Well, if you had, I think you would realise where he fits in. He's the unwitting tool behind which the Nazi control can operate without fear of discovery. You have some knowledge of the history of the man—how he built up Calboyds by mating a small engineering business to a little marine yard on the Mersey. He was probably quite a clever engineer, but not brilliant. He succeeded enough to be able to afford to buy other people's brains. Very likely he used German brains. Calboyds has been built up since the last war and German brains were cheaply had in those post-war years. Don't forget, Germany is the home of the Diesel engine. With success, Calboyd emerged as a philanthropist and was seen in the drawing-rooms of Mayfair. Mayfair is not a far cry from the skirts of Government, especially if you have money to spread about. He's a successful but not a brilliant man. And he's solid British—cultivates a military figure and can trace his family back to the Middle Ages. No, he's not our man, David."

"Well, how are we going to find out who is?"

"That is just what I was considering when you came in. We haven't much time. That paragraph about Calboyds proves it—quite apart from the danger of their getting at the boat. And we've got to take the offensive." I took my pouch from the corner of the washhand-stand and began to refill my pipe. "My line of attack is the City. I ought to be able to find someone in that rabbit-warren who can tell me who is at the back of Calboyds. But it may take time. It may be a question of delving into the background of the big shareholders. There's Ronald Dorman and the two others, besides Calboyd—John Burston and Alfred Cappock." I lit my pipe and looked across the flame at David, his big powerful body hunched over the fire. "Somehow," I said, " we've got to trace Schmidt. Alive or dead, I believe he'll prove to be the key to the whole thing."

"I don't follow that at all," David replied. "If he's alive and at liberty, he would have come to see you that Monday."

"I'm not sure about that," I replied. It was a point that I had been turning over in my mind for some time. "I think he knew he'd got me interested. Perhaps that's all he wanted to do. Remember, he was on his own, wanted for murder by the police and by foreign agents for the knowledge he possessed. If I had been in his shoes, I should have looked around for an ally. As a suspected murderer there were not many people open to him. But there was a chance with a man who was accustomed to defending criminals and murderers in the courts. Anyway, that's one way of looking at it, and if I remember rightly it was you who suggested it."

"That's true," David replied. "But don't forget he was expecting the worst. I think it might be safer to work on the assumption that he is either dead or a prisoner. And in either case, I don't see that he's of much use to us."

"Take it at the worst and he's dead," I said. "If we knew where he had been killed and could trace what he had been up to during his stay in London, we should know something. I have an idea he has friends among the refugees in this country. Somewhere he will have left a clue."

David rose to his feet and stretched himself. "Somewhere," he said. "You can't go looking through London for a clue dropped by an elderly Jewish refugee. I'm for bed, and in the morning I'm going to Manchester to see Calboyds about that money they owe me."

So in the morning we each went our ways, he to Euston and I to the City. I left Freya with instructions to stay indoors, and I told Mrs. Lawrence to go out and get her a book and some chocolates.

But by the end of the morning I was tired of pumping friends about Calboyds and was feeling a little light-headed because my curiosity had involved me in a good deal of drinking. About lunch-time I found myself wandering into the City Office of the *Record*. Henderson, the City Editor, I knew through Jim Fisher, Editor of the *Record*. He greeted me like a long-lost friend and hauled me off to lunch with him. He ordered an enormous meal for us both at Pimms and then demanded that I tell him all about the Margesson murder case, which I had completed just before the outbreak of war. " The City is dead, old boy. I'm bored stiff." So I explained to him how I had got the woman off. And in exchange I got nothing out of him except the lunch. " Calboyds, old boy," he said, when I broached the subject. He was already a little drunk. " Been out with Slater and a few of the boys," he explained, " trying to get the low-down on this bullet-proof glass racket like a good little City Editor." He made a wide encircling gesture with his hand. " Calboyds. Now there you've got something. You go in, old boy—make a packet if only this war lasts." He leaned close to me and whispered confidentially in my ear. " There's a big deal on there right now. I have it straight from the jolly old horse himself—you know, old Jimmy Calboyd, monocle and all. He's landing himself a contract for 10,000 of those new Calboyd Dragon engines. He tells me there's nothing to beat 'em —nothing at all. They're the goods, old boy. Absolutely. Knock the bloody Bosche as flat as—as——" He looked round for something to illustrate flatness and then spread his hands in a vague but expressive gesture. " And do you know who gives him the order, Andie, my lad?"

" I'll buy it," I said.

He suddenly laughed. " Why, he does, you old fool—he does. Haven't you read the papers? They've made him Director of Aero Engine Production. Neat—eh? You go and buy as many Calboyds as you can get hold of, old boy. They're offered at around 42s. 6d. this morning. Take my word for it, they're going to a fiver at least."

" Listen," I said. " What I want to know is, who controls the outfit?"

" Why worry about that, old boy? You can't lose on it. I've put my shirt on 'em already."

" Well," I said, " I'm not buying till I know who controls the group."

" What's it matter? Calboyd owns a big interest and Ronald Dorman—you know, the issuing house—got stuck with a lot. God! he must be coining money on them now. Think of it, man! He took up damn' near the whole lot of that Ordinary share issue in 1937 at par—quite apart from the Preferences, that would be a matter of two million shares."

"I know about Dorman," I said. "But do you know anything about a John Burston and an Alfred Cappock?"

"Never heard of them, old boy. They sound like brewers. But look here, why don't you go down and see Sedel? Nice boy, Sedel. Tell you everything."

"Who is Sedel?" I asked.

"Max Sedel? He knows all about Calboyds. Fact is he knows a lot about the aircraft industry. Great lad. Tremendous worker. Come to think of it, it's incredible. The fellow came to this country just after the Reichstag fire business. He was an anti-Nazi. Escaped from Germany. Hadn't a bean. Didn't know the language. Came to us. Began up at the City Office under me. Then gravitated to the Fleet Street end as foreign editor. Now he's free-lancing and making a big income. First-class contacts. Industry is his subject—industry and foreign affairs. Tremendous output even in these times. Why I mention him is he wrote a couple of first-rate feature articles on Calboyds for one of the financial papers. Appeared only the other day. If you like to come back to the office with me, I'll show you the cuttings. But the thing to do is to go down and see Max."

The lunch seemed to sober him up a bit, for by the time we got back to his office he was beginning to think of a lead for the last edition. His secretary broght me the file on Calboyds and I waded through it. There were several articles on the company, mainly from the financial weeklies. But the two by Max Sedel stood out. They gave me a very clear insight into the financial structure and industrial position of the company. It was unmistakably a puff, but it was cleverly done and a wealth of information about the company was included. There was nothing, however, on the subject of control. I decided to go and see Max Sedel.

Following Henderson's instructions, I went down Copthal Avenue and turned into a rather dingy building. H's office was on the first floor—" Max Sedel " was painted on the door and underneath, " Journalist and Publicist." The interior might easily have been mistaken for a stockbroker's office. The walls were surrounded by filing cabinets. There were newspapers and papers everywhere. The room was occupied by two girls—one, I presumed, a plain typist and filing clerk, and the other, who came to find out what I wanted, his secretary.

I sent in my card and was shown into the inner office. Here was some attempt at order, and a cheerful fire burned in the grate. The central feature of the room was a heavy mahogany desk, and behind it was a plump little man with fair hair, little steel-grey eyes and an absurd sort of cavalry moustache. He rose to greet me. The hand he offered me was white and limp, and there was a gold signet ring on the little finger. My first impression of him was not favourable, but when he spoke I realised he had charm. His smile was pleasant and friendly, and there was an air of courtliness in the way he offered me a cigarette—it was almost old-fashioned. But as I lit it, I was conscious of his eyes. He was young, but he was astute. I knew I should have to tread warily.

"I am afraid I am about to waste some of your valuable time," I said. "But I read your two articles on Calboyds. My impression was that you knew your subject. Now, a very old friend of mine has had a lot of money left her and she wants to invest it in the best interests of the nation, without of course losing sight of the object for which one does invest money. My inclination was towards Calboyds. But in this connection a point has arisen which I thought you, with your intimate knowledge of the company, might be able to clear up. I am always very careful about giving advice over investments. Frankly, I don't fancy it much—the responsibility is too great. A thing I always go for in these matters is the management and the control. Are they sound is the question I always ask myself. Now I find that in the case of Calboyds there are four big shareholders—Calboyd himself, two gentlemen who, as far as I know, are completely unknown in the world of finance, and Ronald Dorman, who may be backed by anyone. Who really controls Calboyds?" I don't know why I put the question so bluntly. My intuition told me, regardless of the cautious approach I had originally decided upon, that this was the way to obtain results. As I put the question, I raised my eyes and looked at him.

His cigarette was burning unheeded in his hand and those little steel-grey eyes were fixed on me as though he would seek to know what was going on inside my head. In an instant the tenseness of his body relaxed. But it was an artificial relaxation. He shrugged his shoulders and smiled pleasantly. "I'm afraid you have caught me out, Mr. Kilmartin," he said. "I cannot tell you who controls the company. My concern at the time I was going into its affairs was simply to write it up from the point of view of both the general public and the investor. The question of control does not come within the scope of articles of that sort. Indeed, it would have been impertinent of me to make inquiries."

Was it my imagination, or did I stand thus rebuked? But Sedel rose, smiling and holding out his hand to me, apologising for not having been more helpful.

As I walked down Copthal Avenue to Throgmorton Street, I could not rid myself of the memory of that moment of tension when I had put the question so bluntly. I hesitated in Throgmorton Street and, looking up at the doorway outside which I had stopped, realised that it led to the City Office of the *Record*. On a sudden impulse, I hurried up the stairs and into the office, where I inquired for Mr. Henderson. "Sorry to bother you again," I said, as I was shown into his office, "but I was rather interested in Sedel."

"Yes, he's an interesting person," Henderson replied. His voice was brisk and he seemed to be his old dapper self again. The effect of the drink had apparently been dispersed by work.

"Could you tell me a little more about him?" I asked.

"I don't know that there's really much to tell." He tapped his teeth with a silver pencil, at the same time waving me to a big leather-padded arm-chair. "He came to us in '33 as I told you. He had an introduction from Marburgs to our old man, you know, J. K. The fellow was pushed up here to make himself useful on the foreign side. He learnt quickly. He made good contacts. Believe it or not, within six months he could talk almost faultless English and was writing really good City stuff for us. His vocabulary was not large, but then that soon comes. I think it was in '35 he became foreign editor. He worked that job up to £1,250 a year and then in '37 he chucked it and set up on his own in the City. It seems incredible, doesn't it. He was in the country only four years before he had got so much highly-paid outside work that he could afford to give up a safe four-figure salary. Since then he's written three or four books, mostly on Germany. It's funny. He's terribly fond of Germany. But he hates the régime, curses the people for their folly in submitting to it. As I say, he hates the régime and thinks that it will ruin the country. Yet he thinks Germany will be the centre of the world within the next decade. Anyway, that's what I know of Max Sedel. He's a brilliant man and as a foreigner—he's naturalised of course—but as a foreigner born he's very much at home in the cosmopolitan world of the City. That's where he has the advantage of us English journalists. Here I am, the City Editor of a big evening paper. I know all the heads of British industry, I know the bankers and the stockbrokers, but I don't know the City. It takes a man with a gift for tongues and a queer twist in him somewhere to be able to say he knows the City. But if you know the City, you know the secret of international politics. Everything that happens in Europe is hatched in this Square Mile. But I've drifted away from the point. I merely say that Sedel sees a side of the City that neither I nor any other British journalist ever sees—the side of the underground movement of Big Business through international affairs."

"But I suppose he has the English contacts as well?" I asked.

"You mean firms like Calboyds? Oh, rather. I tell you he's a first-rate journalist and a very clever business man. He's got a lovely place just outside Eastbourne. He's realised something that so few journalists ever realise, and that is that journalism can be the gateway to money. I think you'll find that he'll have bought Calboyds quite heavily. You see, if you know the right people at the right time, you can't help making money."

I thanked him for what he had told me and took my leave. As I passed through the main office I heard a man who was running the tape through his hand exclaim, "Calboyds up another bob." Outside I turned left and walked to the taxi rank in Lothbury. And as I drove down Queen Victoria Street and along the Embankment to Whitehall, I began to consider where to cast about next. The time factor was the trouble. Given time, I might get somewhere. But already I had spent the better part of a day hunting round the City and had achieved nothing. Max Sedel had provided the only real interest of the day. I couldn't help feeling what a useful man he would be to Germany. But though he intrigued me, he had not been able to help me. By the time I arrived at the Admiralty, I had decided that the morning had been wasted and that the only thing to do was to try and get some sort of line on Dorman or the other two big holders. Somewhere there must be a clue to the link-up between Calboyds and Germany.

After a wait of nearly half an hour I was able to have a few words with Forbes-Pallister. I explained to him half the truth—that a friend of mine was working on a new type of Diesel engine and that it was fitted to the boat. He promised to see to it that the order was rescinded. " Don't worry," he said, as he saw me to the door of his office. " I'll fix it for you and I'll give you a ring when it has gone through. What's your number?"

" Terminus 6795," I told him. " If I'm not in, have your people leave a message, would you."

As I walked up Whitehall, considering what line to follow up next, I remembered a fat smiling little man of the name of Evelyn Ward. He was a half-commission man, who was not above a little business blackmail and whom I had got out of a tight corner once. I went into the nearest call-box and looked up his address. Then I crossed the Strand to Duncannon Street and took a bus, for I wanted to think out the position before I reached Ward's office.

Ward specialised in gossip. In good years he made a bit on half-commission. But gossip was his speciality. And he made money out of it. It was not blackmail in the ordinary sense. In the first place, it was never personal gossip that interested him. In the second place, he never demanded money. His knowledge of the shady side of the City was encyclopædic. It had to be. His consumption of liquor must have been colossal, but then so was his girth. His danger lay in the fact that he was popular. He was generally known as The Slug, or Slugsy to those who knew him well. He was a fat genial fellow, with a great moon of a face in which two little eyes twinkled, half-buried in flesh. His chins were a really noble sight, and his head, being to his disgust practically bald, was almost invariably covered by a broad black hat.

His usual line was options. Lounging round the bars, he would pick up a piece of gossip, overhear a scrap of conversation or buy the confidence of a junior clerk with a few drinks. He would then learn all there was to learn about the deal, and in due course he would approach the interested party, suggest that the information he had might be of use to the other side and evince a desire for an option on some of the shares of the company involved. He had explained to me rather ruefully at the time when I was defending him that it never failed to work. On that one occasion, he had failed to check up on his information as thoroughly as he might have done and his proposition had fallen on honest and outraged ears. Nevertheless, he had known enough for me to convince the prosecution that it would be better to settle the matter out of court.

I arrived at a dingy little office at the top of a block in Drapers Gardens to find him out, and was directed to a well-known City club. He came out to meet me, a glass of whisky in his hand and his huge face glistening with sweat. His great podgy hand wrung mine and he took me into the club and bought me a drink. " Now, Mr. Kilmartin," he said, as we sat down at a little table to ourselves, " do you want to know what to put your savings into?" And his face screwed itself up into a great smile.

" No," I said. " I think I know the answer to that. Calboyds is the thing to buy. Am I right?"

" Quite right," he said. " But don't hold for too long."

" Why?" I asked.

He shrugged his wide padded shoulders. " Tell you the truth, I dunno. Just a hunch I got."

" What I want to know," I said, leaning forward and speaking softly, " is who controls Calboyds?"

His eyes seemed to narrow slightly and he pushed his hat farther on to the back of his head. " There you've got me. If I knew, I might make a lot or I might—well, I might not. There's Ronald Dorman, of course. And then there's two other boys by the name of Burston and Cappock. Apart from old Calboyd, they're the big holders."

" I know that," I said. " But who is behind them? Dorman, for instance—did he have enough capital to take up all those shares his firm got stuck with?"

" No, but he had the credit."

" Well, who financed him, then?"

" I dunno. It's the same with the other two. They're just dummies. But who they're playing dummy for I don't know, and between you and me, old man, I'm not at all sure I want to know."

" Why?" I asked.

" Why? Because if I knew, I might be tempted to do something rash. The sort of game I play is all right so long as the people are running a racket. But when it comes to big game like Calboyds—well, I don't interest myself. That time you got me out of that mess scared me plenty and I'm much more cautious now, even though it is getting very difficult to make a living."

" But you must know what the gossip is? I'm not asking for a statement of facts. Who is thought to be behind Dorman?"

" Quite honestly, I don't know," he replied. " But I do know this; Burston didn't make a pile in Mexican oil and Cappock didn't strike lucky in Rhodesia. They were both of them down and out before they returned to England."

" You mean they were both broke? Yet they returned to England and immediately plunged up to the hilt in Calboyds?"

He nodded. " That's about it. Considering what big holdings they have, they don't live over well. Burston has a little place down at Alfriston and Cappock lives quite quietly at a London hotel."

" How do you know all this?" I asked.

His face creased into a smile. " You needn't worry about my source of information. It's all true enough."

" Why didn't you use your knowledge? I should have thought it would have been in your line."

" So did I—at first. But I know which side my bread is buttered."

" How do you mean?"

But he did not answer my question and I saw that his eyes were fixed on the doorway. I turned in my chair and saw the

neat rather podgy figure of Max Sedel entering the room.
Instinctively I turned to conceal my face. But I was not
quick enough. For a second his small steely eyes met mine
and I saw him half-check in his stride. Then, with a brief
nod of recognition, he passed on to the bar.

"My *bête noir*," said Evelyn Ward in a low tone.

"What do you know of him?" I asked.

"He's an adept at my own game. He's in here or one of
the other clubs practically every day, pumping people."
Then he outlined for me Sedel's story, much as Henderson
had told it to me. But he added one point which I thought
significant. "He hates Jews," he said. "That's his weak
point, for he finds it difficult to hide his hatred of them, and
you know how lousy the City is with Jews."

I laughed. "Well, anyway, that's a good sign," I said. "If
the City is full of Jews even when there's a war on, things
can't be so bad." An American once told me that he followed
the migration of the Jew from capital to capital on the
principle that the place the Jews were flocking to was the
place where there was money. The American had been in
London in 1933 and England was the first country to re-
cover from the Great Slump. I began pumping Ward for
more information about the Calboyd control, but either he
knew nothing more, or else he did not want to talk. "Why
don't you go and see Dorman or one of the other two
dummies?" he suggested.

"Not a bad idea," I said, rising to my feet. A frontal
attack might at any rate rattle them.

When I got outside the club, I found it raining. It was
prematurely dark, and the lights blazed in rows in the
windows of the offices on the other side of Threadneedle
Street. It was like the old days before the black-out. Behind
me loomed the bulk of the Royal Exchange, and as I came
out into Threadneedle Street I saw the long façade of the
Bank. Opposite me, dominating the junction of Old Broad
Street and Threadneedle Street, stood the imposing granite
bulk of Marburgs, the big merchant banking house, with its
somewhat indecently blatant sign of an eagle sweeping down
upon its prey blazoned in gold above the massive bronze
doors. I cut down Old Broad Street, past the Stock Exchange,
and into Austin Friars.

Needless to say, I got nothing out of Ronald Dorman. And yet I did not feel that the visit had been wasted. The extraordinary thing was that I felt as though I had been expected. An exquisite young man took my coat and hat, and with the minimum of delay I was ushered into Ronald Dorman's luxurious office. The whole place was ostentatiously sumptuous. From its thick-piled carpets to its heavy gilt-framed pictures, it was designed to impress. " Cigar, Mr. Kilmartin?" A deferential air and a glimpse of white teeth behind the little black moustache was symbolic of the whole atmosphere of debonair success that the man affected. Ronald Dorman spared no pains in the dressing of his window. But it was not only dressing. He was astute. I lit my cigar and then, as I blew out the flame of my match, I said, " Who is behind Calboyds, Mr. Dorman?" I put it quietly, hoping to catch him on the hop.

But he didn't bat an eyelid. " What has that to do with you?" he countered.

In the end I had to be satisfied with the assurance that he was the owner of his own holding. But not before my persistence had rattled him a bit. It wasn't noticeable in his manner. He was charming and very patient with my thirst for knowledge, but I noticed that his long, rather artistic fingers were never still.

Ronald Dorman was my last call of the day, and in the gathering black-out I joined the rush-hour crowd that surged towards the Bank. I found an empty taxi, and within ten minutes was back at my digs. There had been no phone-calls for me, but would I join Miss Smith in her room for tea. I went upstairs to find Freya lounging on her bed, eating crumpets and reading. She seemed glad to see me and thanked me for the chocolates. She jumped up and settled me down in a chair by the gas-fire with tea and a crumpet. " Look," she said, and thrust the morning paper into my hand. " It's down in black and white now for all the world to see."

She was excited, and well she might be, for there in print was what Crisham had told me on the phone the previous day. Franz Schmidt was no longer wanted for murder. But the story explained that the police wanted to discover his whereabouts as they were afraid that he, too, might have suffered harm. " If he's at liberty, I hope he sees it," I said. I carefully refrained from saying " if he is alive."

" Oh, I hope so, too," she said, with a mouth full of crumpet. " Mustn't it feel marvellous, when you've been hunted for three weeks for a murder you didn't commit, suddenly to find that you've been given an alibi."

I was just putting the paper down, when my eye caught sight of a small paragraph farther down in the next column headed: CAR OVER BEACHY HEAD. My eye had caught the name Burston. It was my Burston all right. John S. Burston of Woodlands, the Butts, Alfriston. His car had apparently gone over the cliff near Birling Gap. The paragraph explained that it had been a foggy night and that Burston had been to a party. Coming down the road from Beachy Head to Birling Gap, he had apparently mistaken the road under the Belle Toute and driven straight over the cliff.

Freya sensed my change of mood and asked me what was wrong. There was no point in bringing sudden death into the conversation, so I handed her back the paper and gave an account of my activities during the day. After all, people did get drunk and miss the road. But Beachy Head is associated in my mind with suicides, not accidents. I saw the sheer white cliff under the Belle Toute lighthouse and pictured the wreckage at the foot washed by the chalky sea. Death was so certain that way. And why had Burston been driving along that road at all? He lived at Alfriston. The road to Birling Gap was all right. But to get home, he had to take the track to East Dean. I knew it well. It was a terribly bad surface and not the road one would choose in thick mist.

I suppose my preoccupation was obvious as I ran quickly through the various interviews I had had, for Freya picked up the paper and began searching for the page at which it was folded. And when I had finished she said, " Won t you tell me what is on your mind, Mr. Kilmartin? It was something you saw in the paper, wasn't it?"

I said that it was nothing, just a thought that had crossed my mind. But she was insistent, and in the end I told her. She read the paragraph through, a frown wrinkling her usually smooth brow. Then she looked across at me. " My father once mentioned the name Burston to me," she said

"He was talking to Evan Llewellin, but I happened to be present. They were discussing Calboyds and I remember him saying that he thought Burston the weak link."

"Anything else?" I asked.

But she shook her head. "No, I'm afraid not."

"Look," I said, "are you certain you have told us everything you know? Didn't your father discuss the position with you?"

"Yes, but I don't think he knew much at the time. You see, the engine was transferred to the yacht in July. Two weeks later the old engine in his workshop was stolen. A month later he decided it was no longer safe to keep the *Sea Spray* in Swansea and Evan Llewellin and I ran her round to Porthgwarra. The lease of the studio there had already been taken. I took up residence and have not seen my father since. I am afraid that at the time I went to Porthgwarra he knew very little about the business. The night he mentioned Burston was just before I left. He knew that Calboyds were after his engine, but I don't think he knew anything about the control of Calboyds. In fact, his remarks about Burston being the weak link suggest that he and Evan were just becoming interested in the control."

We were interrupted by a knock at the door. It was Mrs. Lawrence to tell me I was wanted on the phone. When I got downstairs, it was to find that it was Forbes-Pallister himself ringing me. He was very apologetic. "I would like to have helped you in the matter, Kilmartin," he said. "But it's out of my reach. The order emanated from the First Lord and I can, of course, do nothing."

I thanked him and rang off. That was that. Calboyd himself had probably arranged for the order. As I climbed the dark stairs from the basement, a feeling of depression crept over me. I was out of my depth, and I knew it. I could make no headway against an organisation that could call, not only upon the forces of law, but also upon the political heads of the country.

"Bide a moment, Mr. Kilmartin." It was Mrs. Lawrence, speaking from the front door, and I paused on the stairs leading up from the hall. "There's a telegram for you." She brought it to me and I opened it. It was from David to say that he was having an interesting time and had decided to

stay the night. " There's no reply," I said, and thanked her
and went back to Freya's room. She received my information about the boat with dark, troubled eyes. " What do we
do now?" she asked. " I'm tired of sitting cooped up in this
room."

" Then we'll go and have dinner somewhere and then go
to a show," I said. I felt rather guilty at the suggestion, but
as far as I could see there was nothing more to be done, and
she agreed. " To-morrow we will go to Eastbourne," I added.

Chapter Six

DEED-BOXES MAKE GOOD COFFINS

THAT EVENING remains vividly in my memory as a pleasant
oasis. It had something of the quality of the lull before the
storm. I think I was conscious of this at the time. With
the exception of the brief chase by the Cones of Runnel, we
had not crossed swords with the other side. So far it had
been a game of hide-and-seek. But I was not fool enough to
imagine that it would remain just a game. And I think it
was that thought that added an almost unreal beauty to the
evening. I felt an unnatural, almost hysterical gaiety. And
there was Freya. For some reason that was essentially feminine she had brought an evening frock with her. Until then
I had only seen her as a rather boyish creature, striking
enough with her slim figure encased in slacks and her lovely
sleek head. But when she came out of her room on to the
dimly-lit landing in her dark-blue frock, I caught my breath.
The boyishness was gone. Where I had taken her for a girl,
I found a woman. The beauty of her made me wish that I
were younger. I took her hand. " You look lovely," I said.

That was one of the happiest evenings of my life. Freya
was in great spirits. I wished David could have been with us
to see her. But at the same time I was glad he was not. We
had both agreed upon the Palladium and it suited our mood.
And when we came back, she insisted on my paying the taxi
off at the top of Shaftesbury Avenue and walking home the
rest of the way. It was a glorious moonlit night . " This is

the first time I have seen London in a black-out," she said. Her voice was low and almost husky. I looked down at her. She was wearing the heavy gabardine cloak she had worn with her slacks, but it looked different now. It gave her height and poise. And from it rose the perfect oval of her face, pale in the moonlight. She was gazing upwards. "Isn't it marvellous?" she said. "See the way the moon picks out the steeple of that church. You scarcely even notice the moon in peace-time when all the street lights are on."

I laughed. "Wait until you see the black-out on a dark night," I said. "It's not the same at all when you walk down streets that seem like dark clefts. It gives you an unpleasant sense of desolation."

At that she laughed and said, "But I'm seeing it in the moonlight so I can be happy. See how it shows up the Senate House." And we paused to look across the lifeless trees of Russell Square to the tall white block of the University building. As we did so I noticed out of the tail of my eye a car stop by the curb a little way down Southampton Row. I don't know why I suddenly had the feeling that it was following us. But I noticed that no one got out, and as we turned the corner into Guildford Street I saw it on the move again. I drew Freya into the dark doorway of a chemist's shop and waited. The car crawled round the corner. There were two men in front and they were peering through the windscreen. Then the car accelerated and disappeared down the length of Guilford Street. I don't think it was following us, but it had a dampening effect upon our gaiety and it was a sober, rather nervous pair that let themselves into their rooms.

The next morning I was up early and got my car out of its garage in Fetter Lane. Shortly after nine we were on the road. It was a blue-skied, friendly day, warm, with a hint of spring in the air. The drive would have been fun, if we had not both been weighed down with a sense of trouble ahead. When we arrived at Eastbourne I went straight to the office of one of the local newspapers. We were lucky, for the boy who had covered the Burston story was in. I handed him my card. "You may have heard of me," I said.

"Why, yes, of course, sir. You're interested in this business?" he asked.

I told him that I was and that my own view was that it might not be an accident.

At that he said, "Well, I'm glad there's somebody thinks the same way as I do. I had a word with the local inspector, but he pooh-poohed the idea and told me that I was just out for copy. Do you know the Belle Toute?" he asked.

I nodded.

"Then you'll remember the road bends away sharp to the right there. Now the mist was pretty thick, I admit that. But this fellow Burston, who has lived in the neighbourhood for over four years, goes and turns sharp left. It doesn't make sense to me. He may have been drunk, but I don't see why he should be as drunk as all that. The air was cold and raw. It was enough to sober anyone up. And why was he on the Birling Gap road anyway? He came down from Willingdon and he lived at Alfriston. The direct way would have been to go through Old Town and straight up to the hills. Or, if he must go round by the Beachy Head road, he would have turned to the right when he got to the top of the downs and on to the East Dean road. Sedel said he had mentioned something about going over to see a friend at Birling Gap. But it was past midnight, and that's a damned funny time to start making calls, especially on a filthy night like that."

"Sedel?" I said. "Who is Sedel?"

"The fellow at whose house he got drunk. Mind you, I'm not saying he wasn't drunk. From all accounts the fellow has been drinking fairly heavily in recent months."

But I had remembered what Henderson had said about a lovely place just outside Eastbourne. "Is this fellow's name Max Sedel?" I asked.

"Yes, that's right. Free-lance journalist in the City. He was very helpful to the police, I understand. But I didn't get much out of him. I told him I thought it was extraordinary that a man should drive over the cliff like that on a road he must have known like the palm of his hand. But all he said was that a cub reporter trying to make a suicide out of it for the sake of copy wouldn't help a poor fellow much."

"Was he married?" I asked.

"Who—Sedel? Oh, you mean Burston. No—but he had

plenty of friends in the district. A bit of a rough diamond, I gathered."

" Any money troubles?"

" No, not as far as I can gather. He made a pile out in Mexico, I'm told. He'd worked through a lot of it. But the inspector did mention that he had a pretty solid bank balance."

" Did you know that he held a big block of shares in one of our leading industrial companies?"

" No, that's the first I've heard of it."

I nodded and picked up my hat. " If you're interested," I said, " get the list of shareholders of the Calboyd Diesel Company. And then find out who has his holding now." I left him looking rather puzzled and we drove up South Street to the police station.

" Where does this Max Sedel come in?" Freya asked.

" I don't know yet," I replied. as I pulled the car up to the curb. " But I think he comes in somewhere."

We had to wait some time for the inspector who had handled the case. When he came out to see us, I explained to him that I was interested in the case and wanted to ask him a few questions. He had intelligent brown eyes and he looked at me rather closely, I thought, as he told me to go ahead.

" First of all," I said, " are you taking the view that it was an accident?"

At that he smiled and said, " That's rather a leading question, Mr. Kilmartin." He seemed to hesitate. " Are you acting for anyone in this matter?" he asked.

" No," I said, " I can claim no sort of privilege. But I happen to be interested in another matter with which Burston was connected."

" I see." Again he hesitated, and glanced at Freya. I explained that she was also interested in the matter. Then he said, " Well, quite frankly, Mr. Kilmartin, I don't know. It looks like an accident. But it may be suicide—you never know. But, mind you, there's nothing to suggest that it was, and I'm inclined to let well alone."

" There's no question of foul play?" I asked.

" Any reason why there should be?" he asked, and again I was conscious of his eyes watching me closely.

" I just wondered," I said. " It seems strange that a man who had lived four years in the district should turn left instead of right at the one dangerous spot on the whole of the road."

" Yes," he said, fingering his jaw. " Yes, I did consider the idea of foul play. But there was nothing to suggest it. The marks of the car ran straight across the turf. He had no enemies, as far as we can tell, and no fortune that would benefit any relations."

" Had he any relations?" I asked.

" Well, we've unearthed an old aunt up at Sheffield. He was a Yorkshire man, you know. There's no will, so she'll take what the State doesn't."

" Did he leave much?"

" Nothing vast."

" What about his holding in the Calboyd Diesel Company? He owned the better part of a million shares."

" Yes, but he'd been speculating pretty heavily. They were all mortgaged."

" What bank?" I asked.

" It wasn't a bank. It was the Southern Thrift Society."

That was what I had wanted to know. " What about this fellow Sedel?" I asked.

" Seems all right. Burston certainly was drunk. The proprietor of the Wish Tower Splendide himself was at the party and vouches for that. He's one of our councillors. The fellow had been drinking heavily since the outbreak of war. Seems it had got on his nerves."

" Did he go to London much?"

" Occasionally."

" For the day?"

" No, for a night or two usually."

" Where did he stay?"

" His club."

" The name?"

" The Junior First National."

I could see the inspector was getting tired of my questions since they did not appear to help him. I thanked him. But as I took my leave, I suddenly felt a wicked urge and, turning to him, I said, " You know, Inspector, I think you'll find it's murder."

He came after me at that. "Perhaps you'll explain, sir," he said.

But I shook my head and laughed. "There's nothing to explain," I said. "I know no more than you. But that's my view." And I climbed into the car and left him looking very puzzled on the steps of the police station.

After that we drove down to the front and up the twisting road to the downs. It was the first time Freya had seen Beachy Head and she fell immediately in love with the rolling downland country, which looked soft and pleasant in the warm sunshine. From Beachy Head itself the road to Birling Gap snakes down behind the cliffs. Ahead of it stands the old Belle Toute lighthouse and, in that fresh light, it looked very white on its steep knoll. The lighthouse is used as a residence now and a tarmac drive runs down the steep grass slope to join the road at the foot. It is here that the road comes closest to the cliff with only twenty yards or so of flat turf between it and a three-hundred-foot drop. The road swings away sharp to the right to round the Belle Toute hill and drop to Birling Gap, and, as I drew into the car-park, I couldn't for the life of me understand how a man, drunk or sober, could have turned left, instead of right, even in a mist.

We crossed the turf to the cliff edge. The marks of the car's wheels were still faintly visible and the chassis had torn into the edge of the cliff, where it had plunged downwards. Freya held my arm and we walked to the edge. The cliffs of the Seven Sisters away to our left were very white against the blue sky, and gulls circled incessantly with their mournful cries. Down below us the waves washed against the white cliffs, creamy with chalk. We lay down and peered over the edge. Above the creaming waves we caught sight of a car's wheels. I felt Freya's body shudder and I helped her back.

We said nothing as we drove back to Eastbourne. I was busy working out the next move. Freya, I fancy, was thinking of her father. We had a hasty lunch at a hotel on the front and then drove back to town. I returned the car to its garage and, having put Freya on to a trolley-bus in the Gray's Inn Road, I took a bus to Piccadilly Circus and strolled down Lower Regent Street to Pall Mall. I turned in at the Junior First National, and after a little persuasion I was allowed to go through the list of members. Burston's name was there, and a little farther down I saw the name of Cappock. Ronald Dorman's name was also on the list. For a small club I noticed quite a number of famous names, mainly industrial. There was Lord Emsfield and Viscount Chalney, Baron Marburg, Sir Adrian Felphem, a sprinkling of cabinet ministers and one or two newspaper magnates. And among this fine array I noticed the name Sedel—Max Sedel—and looking back I found Sir James Calboyd and those of the other Calboyd directors.

I left the club with the feeling that I was at last getting somewhere. It was not just coincidence that all these people belonged to the same club. Of course, it was possible that they had met as a result of being members. But I was inclined to think that they had met first and that their membership of the same club was designed to allow them to meet without exciting comment. And what about Sedel? Where did he come in?

I found a call-box at the corner of Lower Regent Street and rang up Henderson. "Do you know anything about the Southern Thrift Building Society?" I asked. "Who controls it?"

He said, "Hold on a minute and I'll have a look at Moody's card." After a moment he returned. "Well, I can't say whether anyone in particular controls it, but Ronald Dorman is the chairman." And then he ran through the list of directors, none of whom I knew.

I thanked him and rang off. Ronald Dorman was the chairman and the building society held the whole of Burston's shares in Calboyds. Things seemed to be falling into place. Whilst I was in the booth, I decided to ring up Crisham. As I dialled the Yard number, my next move was slowly taking shape at the back of my mind. My idea was to cause as much trouble for the other side as I could. I was put straight through to Crisham and was just telling him what I thought about the Burston business, when he cut me short. "I've been wanting to speak to you," he said. His voice was sharp, almost imperative, and I realised that he was worried. "First, about that boat of Llewellin's. It arrived at Calboyds' yard just before midday yesterday and we took possession. And a hell of a nuisance it was, because Calboyds were furious and got on to the Admiralty, and before I knew where I was the Chief Commissioner was on to me to know why I had taken such a step. Well, I had my way in the end, though I was told to release it as soon as possible. But—and this is the point—a fire broke out at the Calboyd yard about three this morning. I had two men on guard on the boat, but they considered it their duty to attend the fire. When they came back the boat was gone."

"Gone?" I exclaimed. "My God, Crisham!" I realised the futility of blaming him. "Go on," I said. "I suppose there's no trace of it?"

"None whatever," he replied. "The other thing I want to mention is that your club has been burgled. Amongst other things taken from the safe in the secretary's room is that statement of yours. Look, Andrew," he said, and there was a tone of pleading in his voice, "don't you think you had better come out into the open. What is all this?"

"There's still the statement at my bank," I said.

"I know. But I think it's time you talked. Look, I shall be in this afternoon. If you care to pop round and tell me what you know, I think it'll be good for us both."

I hesitated. The boat was gone. Something had to be done. "All right," I said. "I'll be there in half an hour." And I rang off. My mind was made up. I had got to frighten someone into an admission. I looked up Sedel's number in the directory. I felt tensed up with excitement. But Sedel was out. Well, then, it would have to be Cappock. I jumped into a taxi. "Wendover Hotel," I said.

In a few minutes I was running up the steps of the hotel. "Is Mr. Alfred Cappock in?" I asked. He was and he would see me. I was taken up to a small but pleasantly furnished suite on the third floor overlooking the Green Park. A tall thin man with a slight stoop unfolded himself from an easy-chair drawn up close to the electric fire. He had an almost boyish-looking face, yet the skin was parchment-like and sallow. His eyes were pale and lack-lustre. On a table by his side was a decanter, a soda siphon and two glasses, both of which had been used. He waved me to the chair opposite his and as I sat down I had that peculiar sensation of having been expected that I had experienced in Ronald Dorman's office.

I had no time to waste and came straight to the point. " You are one of four big shareholders in Calboyds," I said. He inclined his head in assent.

" But of those four," I went on, " Sir James Calboyd is the only one who really owns his holding." I was watching him closely. My tone had been matter-of-fact, as though I were merely repeating what was common knowledge. I saw his dull eyes narrow. "Ronald Dorman got his big holding by purposely pitching the price of an issue too high," I told him. " But you and Burston were given yours. Did you know Burston?" I asked.

" Slightly," he said. His voice was soft, and he made no attempt to deny what I had said.

" Of course," I went on, " you were members of the same club. You have read of Burston's death, I suppose."

He nodded. " He had taken to drinking rather too much."

" You've been primed with that." I spoke sharply and leaned slightly forward. It was a technique I had often used when cross-examining doubtful witnesses, and I had the satisfaction of seeing him flinch. " He was on the point of blabbing. He drank because he was scared." I paused, and then said quietly, " He was murdered."

" Oh, but——"

I cut him short. " He was murdered," I repeated. " Yes, murdered—just as you'll be murdered when the time comes."

His pale eyes were a little wider now. But I had no chance to press home my advantage. Out of the tail of my eye I caught a slight movement. And as I turned a soft suave voice said, " I am sorry to break in upon this melodramatic scene, Mr. Kilmartin."

The bedroom door was open and framed in it was the podgy little figure of Max Sedel. A revolver dangled carelessly from his right hand—an ugly little weapon fitted with a silencer—and in the light from the window I saw the gold of his signet ring glitter. " I have been expecting you," he said quite calmly. I met his eyes, and a shiver ran down my spine. They were narrow, steely slits in the puffy flesh of his face, and suddenly I knew what he reminded me of—a stoat.

Sitting in his office, he had seemed to me essentially a sedentary man. I had thought him dangerous, but passively so. I had thought of him as a man who might prove useful to Germany, a man who could obtain valuable information. Now I saw him for what he really was. It showed in his eyes, in the poise of his small plump, almost feminine figure and in the careless way he held the gun. He was a gangster. Not just a common gangster, but that most dangerous of all gangsters, a fanatic with boundless ambition—a little Napoleon.

He picked up the phone and asked for a number. Cappock had risen to his feet. His sallow features seemed a shade paler, and the boyishness had gone from them so that they now looked sharpened and hard. I remained in my chair, my eyes fixed on Sedel. He was swinging the revolver rhythmically to and fro by the trigger-guard, and with the other hand he moved the mouthpiece of the receiver against his fair moustache with a soft caressing movement. Little silky golden hairs marked the line of the razor across his soft white cheeks. At last he got his connection. "We are waiting," was all he said, and replaced the receiver. Then he turned to me. "For a criminal barrister," he said, "you're an incredible fool. Did you imagine that you could go around, openly asking awkward questions, with complete impunity? *Mein Gott*! It is always the same with you stupid English. You never plan ahead. You think you'll always muddle through somehow. Well, this is the end of your muddling. You're through. The whole lot of you are through. In a few months we shall be running everything for you."

"And massacring the people, as you have massacred them in Poland," I said, my tone bitter with contempt.

He laughed. It was a high-pitched sound, something like a giggle. "Maybe," he said. "We don't do things by halves. That's where you people always fall down. You don't plan and you're never thorough. You're too squeamish. If you intend to conquer a race, you must conquer them. And that means that you must ruthlessly subdue them. If you only half do the job, they'll rise against you as soon as your back is turned. But England will not rise again once we have conquered her—never."

"And all this just because you've stolen a Diesel engine from a defenceless old Jew?" I asked.

"Defenceless old Jew!" he exclaimed, and for a moment I thought he would spit on the carpet. "A damned traitorous swine. That engine belongs to the Reich, and back to the Reich it will go."

"And how do you propose to get it there?" I asked scornfully.

He looked at me. "You want to know too much, my friend."

At that I forced a laugh. "You talk of organisation," I said with fine scorn. "You have me at your mercy, yet you're so afraid that I shall escape that you daren't give me even the most obvious information. There's only one way you can get it out of the country, and that is in a neutral ship bound for a neutral port. And that's where you lose. You've no conception of the meaning of contraband control, though you would have if you lived in Germany and faced the pinch with the rest of your country. Germany never had a navy that had the freedom of the seas, so you don't understand the meaning of naval efficiency. You've as much chance of getting that engine through to a neutral country as of flying it there."

I saw the flush spread from his neck to his white cheeks, and I knew I had succeeded. He strode up to me and struck me across the face. I did not move, but sat watching his eyes. "Your navy!" he sneered. "Where does your precious navy look—why, in the hold of a ship. You smug, foolish little lawyer! In three days that engine leaves the country. A day later it will be in Germany. Everything is ready—the materials, the skilled workers, everything. In six months from now our planes will be bombing your towns with impunity."

He was interrupted by a knock at the door. He motioned Cappock to answer it. The man crossed the room. His stoop was very noticeable. He opened the door slightly and peered out. Then he pulled it wide open and two men came in, dressed in a dark-brown livery and carrying a large tin box between them. It was black and had the name A. Cappock painted in white on the lid. It was a deed-box of the type you see trundled in and out of banks in the City. But it was a good deal larger than the ones I was accustomed to seeing.

"Cappock's deed-box and your coffin," Max Sedel told me.

Until that moment, I think the whole scene had appeared somewhat unreal to me. I had seen much of the seamy side of London and other big cities. I knew that strange things happened behind the quiet façade of these places. But those who live in London never fear it. The strange happenings they read of never touch them, never break the daily routine of their lives. My eyes turned to the window. I could see the bare black branches of the trees in the park. Soon they would be green, with the bright fresh green of spring. My heart overflowed with the longing to see that spring green again. The cold wretched winter was a thing of the past. Ahead lay the spring, with promise of new things. And in that moment it was of Freya that I thought. My eyes travelled from Sedel's revolver to the tin box and back again to the revolver. But my brain scarcely registered what my eyes saw, for my mind was occupied with a picture of that oval face, with the slender arch of the eyebrows and wide dark eyes above the finely chiselled nose. I saw down the whole corridor of my life, and where I had before been satisfied with it, with my success as a criminal barrister, with my wide circle of friends, with the pleasant times I had had, I now found it empty and lifeless. And the park would soon be green again! Yet I was to end my life inconspicuously, murdered because I knew too much. I felt a sudden rage. Was I to let life be taken from me just as I had found something that made it so precious?

I had risen to my feet and stood facing Sedel. "You fool!" I said. "Do you think I haven't prepared for this? You have burgled my club to get a statement of mine that I left with the secretary. But do you imagine that that was the only statement?"

He smiled. He had recovered his self-possession. "So, you have another statement? That was to be expected. But I do not think your friend Crisham will pay much attention to it. By describing this tin box as your coffin, I fear I have given you a wrong impression. You will live—for a time. And during the next few weeks you will send Crisham a number of statements. You will accuse various public men of crimes against the State, and each accusation will be more fantastic than the last. By the time he has checked up on a few of

these accusations he will not be inclined to pay much attention to the original statement when it is placed in his hands.
Nor will he be altogether surprised when he hears that you
are an imposter and that the real Kilmartin is dead. You
will be regarded as a madman."

" And who is to sign these false statements?" I asked.

"Why, you, of course."

" You know I shall not," I replied hotly.

"Oh, but I think you will, Mr. Kilmartin." There was a
gleam in his eyes, and the relief, which I had felt at realising
that my death was deferred for the time being, vanished and
my heart sank. The rubber truncheon, the steel-cored whip
and all the other horrors of the concentration camp filled my
mind. I had heard about these things so often. But they
had been something remote, like a flood in China or an
earthquake in South America. They had not touched me. I
tried to think that torture was no longer a weapon used by
civilised nations. I tried to persuade myself that this sort of
thing could not possibly happen in the middle of London. But
I knew it could. I knew that though I was in a well-known
hotel in Piccadilly, I was as far beyond the pale of legal
protection as I should be in Germany itself.

My eyes suddenly met Sedel's and I braced myself. The
little blighter was watching me with a faint smile on his lips.
The gleam was still in his eyes, and in that moment I think I
understood him. Germany is essentially an athletic country,
and this man was no athlete. Physically he was weak. There
is nothing so deadly as a man whose ambition is spurred on
by an inferiority complex. Sedel's absorbing interest in life,
as I saw it then, was power. Not power in the big sense. But
physical power. The power of life and death. The power to
torture. For seven years he had laboured in a hostile country
to build up a position that would give him the power to kill
men. Now he was realising the first fruits of those labours.
And as I looked into those eyes I saw stark bestial cruelty.
The man was a sadist, and I had a horrible fear that his
sadism would take a mental as well as a physical form. He
might even drive me mad.

An awful horror surged through me at that thought. It
centred itself upon the deed-box. I had always had a horror
of being shut up in a place with no means of getting out. It

was a mild form of claustrophobia. It was sheer terror more than anything else that gave me courage. With a sudden movement, I sprang at him, swinging my fist as I came. He was not prepared for this sudden rush. He had no time to use his gun. I am a fairly heavy man, and he caught the full force of the blow on the mouth. I felt his teeth splinter. I swung my left to his stomach and dived for the door.

But the two men in livery cut me off. I turned back and flung myself on Sedel's gun, which he still held in his hand as he sprawled, writhing, across a table. My fingers closed on the steel barrel and I wrenched it from him. Then I turned, and I knew the game was up. I have a very vivid picture of that split second before I passed out. It remains in my mind like a still from a film. I can't remember anyone moving. All I remember is one of the liveried men stooping forward towards me, his right hand half-raised and clutching the soda-water siphon by the neck. Across the knuckles of his hand ran a thin white scar. I also remember quite clearly that on the lapels of his jacket were eagles, swooping on their prey, emblazoned in gold. And then my head seemed to scatter into darkness, and I knew nothing more until I awoke to the gentle movement of a car going slowly.

A great pain in my head came and went, came and went, in agonising rhythmic waves. Like a gentle murmur at the back of my brain I heard the engine of the car, and there were voices, too, but they sounded very far away. For a moment everything went blank again. Then I noticed that the car had stopped. And almost immediately it started again. And alongside it was the pulsating roar of a Diesel-engined vehicle gathering way.

For a time I could not think what had happened. Consciousness kept coming and going with the hammer strokes in my head. For a moment I thought I must have been involved in a street accident, for I had guessed that the Diesel-engined vehicle had been a bus. I could hear faintly the sound of the London streets all about us and I felt certain that I was in an ambulance, being taken to hospital. Then, suddenly, I remembered the blow. It was not the actual blow that I remembered, but the picture I had seen as I turned, the man with his upraised arm, the little white scar and the eagles on his lapels.

And then an awful terror came upon me. Had I been blinded? I could see nothing. Yet I knew it should be day-light. Or, at any rate, there should be a gleam of light in the car. But though I opened my eyes wide, everything was as black as pitch. Men's voices sounded quite close to me, though muffled. I tried to put out my hand to attract their attention. But I could not move. I tried to speak. But some-thing seemed to stifle the words in my throat.

A sudden panic seized me. I cried out. I screamed. I struggled. It was like one of those awful nightmares in which you cannot move. At length I lay still, exhausted. And it was only then that I realised that I was bound and that there was a gag in my mouth. I tried to move my head, but found I could not. And then I remembered the tin box, and for hours it seemed I struggled with a terrible hysteria. But though I eventually calmed myself, I had a horrible fear that I might never be let out. And then I began to develop cramp. I don't know which was worse, the physical pain in my joints or the mental horror of being shut up in that tin box for ever. And the strange thing was that I could not move my arms, legs or head the fraction of an inch. I was fixed to that tin box as though I were a dummy clamped into position.

At length the car stopped and there was much scraping of boots on the floor. The doors were opened just near my head and the familiar sounds of the London streets became suddenly clear. I heard a newsvendor crying the late night final and the murmuring shuffle of countless feet. I guessed that it must be the rush-hour. My box shook violently and I heard the sound of a man's breathing. And then I toppled over on to my side. Instinctively I tried to break my fall. But I could not move my hand. And anyway there was no fall. A second later I was on my head. The tin box grated on the road surface, and then I was righted and laid down on a little trolley. The iron wheels rang as it was pulled up the curb. For a moment we were held up on the pavement. Quite plainly I heard one passer-by saying, " I was just speaking to old Jessop in the House and he told me . . ." The rest was lost. But the word " House " had given me a clue to my whereabouts. And this was confirmed when I heard another voice say, ". . . you were coming. You're

going to Liverpool Street, aren't you? Well, I'm going to
the Bank. Cheerio." I was in the City. " House " meant the
Stock Exchange.

I tried to attract the attention of those countless office
workers, who hurried past my tin coffin to their firesides in
the suburbs. I struggled and screamed. But I made no
audible sound. The wheels rumbled across the pavement and
bumped a step. Then we were crossing stone again, but the
sound was different, and I knew we were inside a building.
Then we stopped, and I heard a thick voice cursing the lift.
When my carriage was manœuvred into it, we went down,
not up—and down a long way, it seemed. Then more stone
passages that had an echoing ring like vaults.

At last came the moment when my box was lifted off the
trolley. The journey was over and I felt an indescribable
longing to see something and to move. " Is he right way
up?" I heard a voice ask. The answer was a grunt.
" Wouldn't do to let him die of apoplexy, would it?" the
voice said. There was a chuckle at that, and then footsteps
sounded on a stone floor. They were going away from me.
They were leaving me. I cried out and struggled. I felt I
should stifle. Then I heard the soft thud of a heavy door
closing, and suddenly I went limp.

The practice of the Spanish inquisitors—and others before
and since them—of walling people up has always had for me
a particular horror, and, like all horrors, a particular fascination. I had often thought about that death and how terrible
it must be. I know now just how terrible it can be. And I
also know that that terror has its limitations. When that
door closed, I really believed I was as near to madness as a
man ever can be without actually going mad. The stillness,
the sense of being deserted, the utter loneliness filled me with
a childish terror. Suppose I were in an old river tideway? I
was in the City and deep underground. Suppose I had been
left here to drown as the tide slowly rose? I could hear small
sounds that I knew instinctively to be rats. But the sound of
the boots on the floor had been the sound of leather on dry
stone.

It was not drowning I feared. And the more my imagination ranged, the more I began to wish that I had been
placed in a tideway. At least it would be a quick death. As

the alternative, I saw myself crouching in that tin box, immovable for days, whilst starvation and the intolerable ache of my limbs drove me mad. I did not fear death then. Death, I knew, would be the release. But I did fear madness. And for hours, it seemed, I struggled to get a grip of myself. At last I succeeded in resigning myself to my fate. I allowed my imagination to picture the worst, to picture my skin sagging on my bones as I hung suspended in the box and to picture the horrible twisted skeleton I should eventually be. And then, when I had allowed myself to come face to face with the ultimate end, with thirst and pain, I felt calm and resigned. My restricted circulation caused me great pain. But, now that I had faced the worst and conquered my fear, I knew I could stand it.

For a time I think I lost consciousness. Whether the pain was too great or whether I slept, I do not know. But, when my brain became active again, I knew that some considerable time had passed. By then my nerves had become dulled to the pain and my brain no longer seemed linked to my body. It was active and quite above the physical. It ranged of its own accord around the problem that had got me in this fix. And in a moment, it had seized upon a few small points and leapt to the wildest conclusion.

And the strange thing was that I knew it was the right conclusion. I felt no elation. My mind was too dulled for that. But I was glad that I had at last pieced the bits together and achieved a pattern. It made Sedel and his gang of secret agents seem less terrifying. Even my own terrible predicament seemed suddenly of little importance.

For the past two days my mind had been fed with scraps and had tried to piece those scraps into a whole. There had been Schmidt and the message I had decoded. There had been the man with the scar on his knuckles who had followed me from David Shiel's studio to my club. There had been Freya and the Cones of Runnel and the boat that had been requisitioned. And then there had been the three Calboyd shareholders—Ronald Dorman, with his sumptuous façade of affluence, John S. Burston, who had been driven over the cliffs below the Belle Toute, and Alfred Cappock. And behind these had been Max Sedel, sleek, well-groomed and efficient, a first-class agent and entirely ruthless.

But none of these mattered. They were the puppets. They were pawns in a game played by a master hand. Behind them loomed the heavy sleepy-eyed figure of Baron Ferdinand Marburg. It was incredible. He was head of the big merchant banking house of Marburg. He was a pillar of the country's financial system. More, he was reputed to be a member of the shadow cabinet. He was a man of tremendous influence and great power—a man, in fact, above suspicion. But, now I had named him, I did not for a moment doubt that I was right.

Sedel had supplied the link in my mind. It was Baron Marburg who had introduced him to journalism. Once having remembered that, everything else fell neatly into place. His membership of the Junior First National. The golden Marburg eagles on the lapels of the man who had hit me in Cappock's suite. And the scraps of conversation I had heard on the pavement outside my prison. Marburgs stood on the corner between Old Broad Street and Threadneedle Street. Two clerks coming out of the bank would part company on the doorstep if one were going to the Bank tube station and the other to Liverpool Street. Moreover, it was just across the road from the Stock Exchange. Then again, the depth we had descended in the lift. No building but a bank would have vaults so deep. Besides, there was the method Sedel had chosen of removing me from the Wendover. A deed-box, even of such large dimensions, would excite no curiosity, being trundled from the bank's own strong room van to the vaults by men in the bank's own livery.

But I couldn't for the moment see what the man had to gain by it. Perhaps it was one of the departmental heads and not Marburg who was implicated? But I discarded that theory at once, for no one but Marburg could have made over a million pounds available to both Burston and Cappock. Perhaps it was money? But I argued that a man who had a world-wide reputation as a financial genius would have no need to play such a dangerous game to make money. There remained only power as the motive. And to this, the answer seemed clear. He had enough power in this country.

But then I remembered something that Peter Venables of the Foreign Office had told me more than a year ago.

Marburg's position as a power in the shadow cabinet had been checked badly when the Government at last swung round to a policy of re-armament. He had strongly opposed it. He had always been a great advocate of close Anglo-German relations and had favoured a secret alliance against the Soviet. He had demanded censorship of the press to prevent the growing virulence of the attacks on Germany. He had not openly favoured Hitler. But he had argued strongly that it was to England's advantage to see Germany all-powerful in Eastern Europe. He had emphasised that a strong Germany was our best safeguard against Bolshevism. But apparently other influences had been at work, especially heavy industry, and his position had been seriously impaired.

Supposing that he had then realised that power—supreme power—was not to be obtained by any one man under a democratic system? He was a dynamic personality, I had been told. I had never talked to him myself. But I had seen him, and I could still remember that powerful, rather stocky figure, with the heavy face and sleepy, heavy-lidded eyes. I had heard him speak at a Guildhall banquet once. His deep baying voice had had fire and eloquence. Above all, he believed in himself—believed in his destiny, perhaps.

Suppose that, having realised the futility of our own democratic system as a ladder to power—even by the back stairs of the shadow cabinet—he had received an offer of supreme power from Germany. Suppose Baron Ferdinand Marburg was Britain's Führer-designate. That would explain everything. I remembered how much to the fore he had been over that Czech gold business, and then earlier there had been much talk of big reconstruction loans by the banking house of Marburg. Unlike some other big international merchant banking houses, the Berlin and Paris houses of Marburg were directly controlled from London. I remembered Schmidt's phrases about a cancer at the heart of England, and what I had then thought to be melodramatic now seemed to be an understatement. I saw that heavy face with the square, powerful jaw and the high forehead, and those sleepy eyes hooded like a hawk. And I knew that that face spelt doom to Britain—that the influence of that one man, if unchecked, was more serious than the loss of several major battles at the front.

And then suddenly the pain in my head returned, and my brain, which had been working with remarkable clarity for a short time, became dulled again. I don't know whether I slept or fell unconscious. At any rate, I knew nothing until I dreamed that my tin box and I were being pitched into the Thames and woke in a cold sweat to find the box being tilted backwards and the scratch of keys against the locks. The next instant my eyes were blinded by a glare of light as the lid swung back.

My bonds were undone and I was released from the clamps that held me secure in the box. I was laid on the cold stone floor and my limbs were so stiff that I could not move them. Then began the agony of returning circulation. I think I cried out with the pain. And when I was not half-screaming with agony I was unconscious.

But the pain gradually lessened and, although the light still hurt my eyes, I was able to take stock of my surroundings. I was sprawled on the floor of what looked like a cellar. It had a vaulted stone roof, black with cobwebs and dirt, and from it, suspended by its flex, hung a naked electric light bulb. The walls, too, were of stone—great square blocks that reminded me of London Wall. And at intervals round the walls hung rusty chains. I could almost imagine that I was in one of the dungeons of the Tower. The place was empty save for the tin box, which stood upright against one wall like an instrument of torture on show. The lid had been pulled back like the door of a small safe, and inside I could see the clamps and straps which had held me in position. It was only then that the relief of being out of it flooded through me. And with that relief came an overwhelming and ghastly fear of being imprisoned in it again. The box seemed to fascinate me, for it was not until a voice said, " I trust you were not too uncomfortable," that I turned my gaze upon the two men who had released me and who were now standing by the half-open door.

One was Sedel and the other was the man with the scar on the back of his hand. It was Sedel who had spoken, and there was something feline about the way he watched me. His lips were swollen and black against the white of his face. Two of his front teeth were missing. But I felt no satisfaction at the damage I had done him. He had me at his mercy and I knew he would repay me a hundredfold for that blow.

He seemed to read my thoughts, for his cracked lips spread into a smile. "That blow of yours was unfortunate, Mr. Kilmartin," he said. "I think you will find that I repay—with a high rate of interest." He came forward, and in his hand he held a sheet of paper. "Will you kindly sign this statement?"

He placed it in my hand. As in a dream I read it through. It was to Crisham, accusing a well-known steel magnate of over-quoting for gun-turrets. It gave details of conversations with works foremen and of estimates obtained from other firms. With weak, shaking fingers I tore the document up, and looked defiantly at Sedel.

But he only smiled. "Yes, I had been expecting that. I have had a number of copies typed." And he pulled another from his pocket. "Now," he said, "are you going to sign?"

"Of course not," I said. But deep within me a horrible fear was growing.

He turned to the other fellow. "Hans," he said, "come and help me get this fool back into his box."

I tried to struggle, but I was as weak as a kitten. In a few minutes I was once again clamped into position inside the box. The door closed and suddenly I was in darkness again. I heard the keys scraping in the locks. I struggled, but I was held as firmly as in any nightmare. And then suddenly I had lost control of myself. Panic seized me. I heard myself sobbing. They had not gagged me this time. And then I was screaming, screaming with uncontrollable fear.

And through my senseless cries I heard Sedel say, "Well, are you going to sign or shall we leave you for the night?"

For the night! At that I stopped screaming. It would be hours and hours. They might never come. They might lose the key or forget about me. "Don't leave me," I sobbed.

"Will you sign?"

"Yes, I'll sign," I cried. "I'll do anything, only let me out of this."

I heard the scrape of the keys again and, as the lid was pulled open, my panic subsided, leaving me weak and disgusted with myself. I signed the document, using the top of the box as a writing-table. I knew it was useless to resist. I could not face that box again. When I had finished, Sedel took the paper and laughed. His hand stretched out and gripped my hair, tilting my head backwards so that I was staring up into his face. " So, you weren't going to sign, eh?" he said, and his eyes gleamed. Then he flung me away from him so that I fell sprawling across the floor. " To-night you are free," he said. " Free to lie here and think about to-morrow. For to-morrow you will go back to your kennel again."

I saw that he meant it. But I had control of myself again now. I rose painfully to my feet. Then I played my last card, hoping against hope that it would prove an ace. He had his back to me and was moving towards the door. " Perhaps you would take me to Baron Marburg," I said.

I had the satisfaction of seeing him swing round on me. His eyes searched mine. " So," he said, " you know all our little secrets." There was a sneer in the way he said this. " You are cleverer than I thought, Mr. Kilmartin. May I ask why you wish to see the Baron?"

" I have a proposition to make to him."

At that he laughed in my face. " A proposition—you! To save yourself from Cappock's deed-box, you will tell the Baron where we can find Schmidt's daughter, perhaps?" He crossed the room to where I stood, rather unsteadily supporting myself against the wall, and he was laughing softly to himself. " Or perhaps you know where Schmidt himself is?"

" So you don't know where Schmidt is?" That pleased me a lot, for I felt that if Schmidt were at liberty and no longer wanted by the police, he might be able to do something.

" No, but I think you may be able to help us there," he replied.

I had complete control of myself again now. " I think it would be best if you took me to Baron Marburg," I said. I spoke calmly, confidently, and I saw at once that my sudden change of mood puzzled him. " Baron Marburg," I went on, " plans to wreck this country and assume the powers of a dictator under the post-war German control. He thinks, I suppose, that because he is the Baron Marburg, he is above suspicion. And whilst he is dreaming of power, he is in imminent danger of losing his life." I felt the thrill I always had when delivering my final address to the jury. " You wonder why he is in imminent danger of his life? Well, I can answer that for you, Sedel. It is because of your bungling. My God, man, do you think you can murder men with impunity in this country as you can in Germany? You killed Burston. And the police know it. You were fool enough to send him straight from a party at your house to his death. Did you never pause to think that that might immediately link you with his death? Why did Burston take the Birling Gap road? And why, when he knew the country so well, did he turn left, instead of right, at the foot of the Belle Toute? You might have got away with it, if the British Secret Service had not been on your track. You knew what Evan Llewellin was? You knew he was a secret agent. You know that Schmidt is no longer wanted for his murder? But do you know why? Because a petty thief saw and described the two men who murdered Llewellin. And now will you take me to your chief?"

I looked him full in the face, and his eyes would not meet mine. But his fear made him venomous. "What's it matter?" he snapped, half to himself. "We have the engine. Soon we shall have Schmidt. As for you," and he suddenly faced me, his eyes glittering, "you will not harm us. The talk of a madman can harm no one. That is what you'll be when I have finished with you. Mad! Do you hear? Mad! To-morrow you go back to your box." And he turned on his heel with his laugh like a soft giggle. His henchman followed him, and the door closed behind them with a dull thud. A key grated in the lock. An instant later the light went out and I was in the dark.

Chapter Seven

LEAD ON, SEWER RAT

SUDDEN DARKNESS is frightening. Few people ever experience the real horrors of darkness. I don't mean the darkness of a room when you are fumbling for the light. I mean the darkness that shuts down on you like blindness and which you have no power to control. The darkness in that vault was complete and utter. There were no windows or ventilation shafts through which even the faintest glimmer of luminosity could penetrate. It closed in around me, and everything was blank. It was as though my eyes had been walled up. And in that darkness I felt stifled, as though I had been buried alive. The mood of sudden inexplicable confidence in which I had addressed Sedel was gone. I remembered only his final words.

He had said I would go mad. And I knew he was right. The mere thought of that foul box made me clench my teeth to control my hysteria. I knew I could not stand it. As I stood in the impenetrable darkness of that vault, I found I was shaking like a leaf. Then the blackness all about me seemed to close in and I found my way to the wall to convince myself that I was not bounded by limitless darkness. The feel of those cold smooth stones was almost comforting. I think I am no more of a coward than the next man and darkness did not usually hold any terrors for me. But I had never known darkness such as this. It was black and with no change in shade anywhere. It pressed down relentlessly on my wide, staring eyeballs as I searched it.

And then I suddenly remembered my fountain-pen torch. I kept it in the breast pocket of my jacket for use in the black-out. It was still there, and in an instant its pale light flooded the vault. There was my coffin, shining black against the dungeon grey of the walls. I crossed to the vault door and tried it. It was an old iron-studded affair, and, though I shook it with all my strength, it held as firm as though it were part of the wall. And then, as I leant against it, I noticed a plate of food lying on the floor. Evidently Sedel had brought it and in the heat of the moment had forgotten to draw my attention to it. There was a roll and some ham. I seized upon it hungrily.

I have never eaten a more peculiar meal. I sat cross-legged on the floor of that vault with the plate on my lap. The monogram JL printed on the plate filled my heart with longing for the commonplace humdrum world somewhere above me. Yesterday, maybe, this plate had been in use in a Lyon's teashop. Now the last meal of a doomed man was being eaten off it. I have not often enjoyed a meal so much, for I was hungry. They had provided me with a knife and fork. The only thing I lacked was water. And my need of it grew. It was not until I had swallowed the last mouthful of ham that I realised how salt it had been. And then a new horror dawned on me and I realised just what a fiend Sedel was. Besides the horror of that box, I was to know the agony of thirst. I pushed the empty plate from me and, climbing to my feet, searched frantically round the vault. But the walls were blocks of solid stone about a foot high by two feet long, and the iron-studded door was quite immovable. I searched the floor and played the light of my torch on the roof, but I knew there was no hope of escape. And then I suddenly had a fear that my torch would give out. I switched it off and found the darkness bearable since, by the pressure of my finger on the pen clip, I could light my cell. And so, in a mood of utter despair, I settled myself against the wall farthest from the box and tried to sleep. Sleep did not come easily. After a while I fancy I dozed off. But almost instantly, it seemed, I was awake. And I knew I was not alone. My nerves were all to pieces and I opened my mouth to scream. But I think I was too petrified to make the necessary effort. Something was moving on the other side of the vault. Then came the sound of metal against crockery. It had touched my plate. And then my fingers closed about the torch.

In the sudden light I found myself staring across the room at the largest rat I think I had ever seen. It was dark and sleek, with eyes that gleamed redly. It bared its teeth at the light. Then suddenly it dived across the cell and vanished into a corner. I lay for a moment, staring at the empty vault, wondering whether my eyes had played me a trick. But then I remembered that I had heard rats scampering about the floor when I had been inside the tin box. The rat had left behind it a faint unpleasant smell. My mind struggled for a moment to account for the smell. And then I realised suddenly that what I had seen had been a sewer rat. And I almost retched at the thought. There could be no doubt about it. No rat but a sewer rat would be so large and vilely sleek.

Then my mind suddenly remembered a story told me by a City journalist. He had described it as true. The directors of the Bank of England had, some years ago, received an anonymous letter, stating that the writer could gain access to the vaults of the bank at any time. And, when they had taken no notice, the fellow had written again, asking them to meet him in the vaults on a given night. And when they went down there, the fellow appeared through the floor from an old sewer. They had paid him the better part of a thousand pounds for his trouble. Supposing the sewers ran close to this vault? The rats came and went. And where the rats could go, perhaps a man could.

I scrambled hurriedly to my feet and crossed over to the corner where the rat had disappeared. Sure enough, there, between two blocks of stone that did not fit very well, was a hole about the size of a Jaffa orange. I went down on my hands and knees and thrust my torch into it. But I could see nothing. Beyond the stone blocks the hole seemed to widen out. But I could smell. Faintly came a warm fetid stench— the stench of a sewer.

I was really excited now. Perhaps this was more than a rat hole? Perhaps behind the solid-seeming wall was a passage-way leading to the sewers? As I rose to my feet, I brushed against one of the rusty chains and it clinked against the stone. The sight of that chain stirred a chord in my memory. And then suddenly I could have cried aloud in my excitement. For I had remembered that to the right of the main entrance door of Marburgs was one of the little blue plaques put up by the City Corporation. I had forgotten the details, but I did remember that it informed a forgetful world that here, on this site, many years ago, stood a prison. And this was one of the old cells. To these chains prisoners had once been fettered. And these deep cells had remained behind the façade of civilisation that Marburgs had raised between Old Broad Street and Threadneedle Street. What more likely than that there had been a passage from the old prison to the ancient sewers of the city? Perhaps it had been used as a convenient method of getting rid of men who had died here? Perhaps it had been a secret means of communication between the prison and the river? I played my torch on the stonework, rubbing away the dirt and feeling the cold blocks with the tips of my fingers. And it seemed to me that the stones here were less rough, as though they had been built in later. I became convinced of this when I noticed that the blocks were shorter on one side, as though they had been specially cut to fit into the space that had originally been the entrance to a passage. The edges, too, were rougher.

I glanced at my watch. It was nearly midnight. Sedel would not arrive before eight at the very earliest. That gave me eight hours. But I knew it was a long job I had before me and I set to work feverishly. My only implement was the knife with which I had eaten my meal. God! how I blessed that knife! I could almost forgive Sedel his fiendish trick of supplying me with salt ham and nothing to drink.

I started on the block of stone to the right of the rat hole. It was hard, back-breaking work. The mortar was only about a quarter of an inch thick between the blocks and much harder than the stuff that builders use now. Moreover, I had to work largely in the dark, for the light from my torch already had a yellow tinge and I knew it would not last much longer. I was in a sweat of fear lest it would give out altogether, for I dreaded the thought of wandering in an ancient sewer in complete darkness.

But I was happy. Heavens, how happy I was to have something to do other than to lie and think about that damned tin box and Sedel's sneering look as hysteria took me by the throat! After a time, of course, the blade of the knife snapped, but, except for the fact that I could not work so deep, the broken blade proved the more serviceable implement. I don't think that I ever worked with such a terrible urgency. My back and muscles ached until I could have cried out with the pain, and the sweat poured off me. But I did not pause. I dared not pause. The work was so slow. And all the time I smelt faintly that musty decayed stench of an ancient sewer.

For two hours I sawed and hammered and scraped, until at last I could bury my knife to the handle all round the block of stone. But the blade was now only some four inches long and the depth of these blocks was near on a foot. I lay on my back and battered away at the stone with my feet. I kept on with this until at length I lay flat on the stone floor, exhausted. The stone had not budged a fraction. I glanced at my watch again. Half-past two! I got dazedly to my feet and stood breathing heavily and staring at that wall, as

though I would walk through it like Alice through the
looking-glass.

Then I knew what I must do, and I set to work on the
block of stone immediately above the one I had been working on. I must loosen the mortar as deep as I could round
every block, working upwards. It was a Herculean task and,
looking back on it, I cannot understand how I found the
strength to do it. Those blocks were not one on top of the
other. No, each row interlocked, so that every other row I
had to loosen two of them.

It was past seven in the morning before I had finished.
And during those last hours I had been working like an
automaton. I was dazed with fatigue, and only fear kept me
at it. I just had to do it, and so I went dazedly on. And
when at last it was done, I leant against the wall and went
fast asleep. The next I knew it was five to eight and I was
lying in a heap on the floor. I climbed stiffly to my feet. I
was covered with fine mortar dust from head to foot, and my
soul cried out for water. But though it had lost me a valuable
hour, that short rest made all the difference in the world.
Without it, I doubt whether I should have been able to do
what I had to do. I flexed my muscles to get the stiffness out
of them. Then I threw my weight against the wall.

I don't know how many times I did this. But I was aching
with the force of my contact with the stone before I ceased.
It had not yielded an inch. It was then that a horrible doubt
began to assail my mind. Suppose there was no passage?
Suppose the rat hole just opened out because behind the
stone was earth? In a panic I bent down and looked into
it again. But there was no sign of earth. In despair I seized
upon the deed-box. Having bent the fork round my torch, so
that it remained alight without my holding it, I lifted the box
endways in my arms and, using it as a battering ram, charged
the wall. The din of the metal striking the stone was terrific.
By now I had worked myself into a frenzy of fear that was
very near to panic. At any moment Sedel might arrive.
After having been allowed the hope of escape, I could not
bear the thought of that tin coffin.

Again and again I charged that wall, always driving the
corner of the box against one particular block of stone. And

when I was staggering with weariness, I noted with a leap of joy that the two blocks below it had given about an inch at the point where they met each other. The light of the torch was becoming so feeble that as often as not I had been driving the corner of the box against these, instead of against the stone above. The discovery gave me strength. A few more charges and I saw that the blocks above and below were caving in. Again and again I charged that wall, making a din like a blacksmith's forge. And after every blow I found the blocks had given ground. At first it was only an inch. Then it was two or three, and at last as much as six, with all the blocks to the floor moved slightly inwards.

By this time it was past nine. Every minute I expected the electric light to be switched on and the key to grate in the lock. But the terrible urgency gave me strength, and though my limbs ached with tiredness, I yet found the strength to go on battering against that wall with the deed-box. And at last, on a rush, I felt the box follow through slightly. The blow was followed almost immediately by the sound of a heavy stone striking against stone. I drew back. There, at breast height, was a gap where one of the blocks had been forced through. The two above it were sagging slightly. I pushed them with my hand, thrusting at them with the whole weight of my body. And at each thrust they gave slightly, pivoting outwards and away from each other. And then suddenly one of them fell, clattering on to stone. A moment later I had pushed the other out. The smell of the sewers was stronger now. It seemed to fill the whole cell. I thrust furiously at the stones below. A few minutes and another had fallen out. There was now a gap like a window in a ruined castle. I got my torch and peered through.

I think, if I had not been so utterly weary, I should have danced a reel and whooped aloud at what I saw. In the dull yellow light, I saw stone steps leading downwards to darkness beyond which my torch's feeble light could not penetrate. The loosened blocks gave me a footing and, in an instant, I had thrust my legs through the gap. I lowered myself gently on the other side, and by hanging with one hand and playing my torch on the stone steps below, I was able to drop on them without hurting myself.

For a second I hesitated, wondering whether to try to

replace the blocks of stone I had dislodged to make the gap. But the size of the blocks was such that I doubted whether, in my weak state, I should be able to lift them into position. In any case, I thought that the time I should spend in rebuilding the wall would be greater than the check it would give to the pursuit. So I turned and hurried down the steps.

The air in that old stairway was warm and damp. The smell of the sewers was strong in my nostrils now, but at the same time the staleness of the atmosphere showed that there was little or no ventilation. It was then that I first began to wonder whether I should ever be able to get out of the place. In my dread of that cell and that horrible box, my discovery of a means of escape had been enough. I had not thought beyond the actual escape from that cell. Only now did I begin to wonder what lay ahead.

The steps soon ceased and I found myself hurrying along a stone passageway that sloped steadily downwards. The walls were dripping with moisture, and here and there were white and yellow fungus growths. The passage was constructed of smaller blocks of stone than those in my cell and the roof was arched and only five feet high, so that I had to stoop. The floor was flagged and in places broken up. Once I came across a small fall and could see the earth behind the stone. I walked hurriedly, the echo of my footsteps sounding behind as well as in front, so that several times I thought I was being followed. Now and then a rat scampered away from me. And always I was peering ahead of me, for besides the weakness of my torch, there seemed a kind of mist in the place.

Suddenly my passage came out into a broader one, running at right angles. Left or right? I hesitated. I sensed rather than actually saw that the slope of this was to the right, and I chose that direction. There was no doubt about it. This was an old sewer. And I thought that the downward slope would lead me to the river, for what few sewers there were in the old London carried the sewage straight to the Thames.

I was able to walk upright now. The rounded tunnel had long since ceased to function as a sewer. But as I ploughed down the centre of the runway, the water was over my ankles. The walls were running with water, and every now and then, beyond the dim circle of light cast by my torch, I heard the sound of a rat in the water.

I seemed to plough through that ancient sewer for hours. Yet it could have been only a few minutes. The uncanny sounds of the place frayed my nerves. I was gradually overcome by one terrible fear—that my torch would give out before I reached daylight. My brain dwelt with a horrible fascination on all the most unpleasant stories I had read of men who had died, stark raving mad, because they had not been able to find their way out of some underground labyrinth. There were the Catacombs, old Cornish tin mines and strange caves from which there was no escape. My brain dwelt on these, until I found myself almost running down that old culvert.

And then suddenly I stopped. The sewer ended. Facing me was a blank wall. But it was not of stone. It was brick, and it curved away from me. For a moment a sensation of complete despair overtook me. And then I had taken heart again. Those bricks gave me hope. Bricks meant a more modern construction, probably sewers now in use. And that curved construction was not made to bear localised pressure from the outside. I raised my foot and brought the heel of my shoe down against the bricks. I repeated this several times. But the leather of my shoes was so sodden with water that I did more injury to the shoes than to the brickwork.

So I turned back and went in search of a stone. I was fortunate. About fifty yards back there was a gap in the arch of the roof, and feeling about in the water, I found a big stone that had fallen. Those fifty yards back to the brickwork seemed a long way. The stone was heavy and very slimy. But at last I got there. Using this as a hammer, I soon had the satisfaction of feeling the bricks give. I knocked out several of the bricks and heard them fall with a splash. More followed at the next blow. I shone my torch through the gap. Below me was a slow-flowing turgid stream. And on the side nearest me ran a narrow slippery-looking pathway, something like a towpath. Few people can ever have been as glad as I was to see a sewer.

As I raised the stone to widen the gap in the brickwork, I heard an unfamiliar sound. I paused and half turned. It came echoing down the old sewer along which I had just come. It was the sound of voices. They sounded strange in that peculiar setting—strange and fearful. I turned and attacked the brickwork like a maniac. The hunt was up and I knew I had little chance if they came up with me.

Three strong blows and the brickwork had crumbled away sufficiently for me to tumble through the gap. I slipped on the slimy path and sprawled half into the actual runway of the sewer. I scrambled to my feet, wet to the knees. Fortunately I still held my torch, and in its feeble glimmer I hurried, almost running, along the narrow pathway of the sewer, following the flow of the water.

Unlike the old sewer, this was full of sound. The murmur of the slow-flowing sewage water was everywhere. And ahead of me rats in their thousands, it seemed, scampered and plopped into the water. And the place stank most foully. But unpleasant though it was, it had the friendliness of something associated with man. It had none of the haunting lostness of the unused culvert from which I had just come. And then I caught my first glimpse of daylight. What a blessed sight that was! And how unattainable! It came from one of the ventilation shafts. I paused for a moment beneath it. There was a circular hole in the roof and far above me I saw a little circle of very white light. It was like looking up the shaft of a deep well. And down that shaft came a friendly sound—the sound of a London bus. For a moment it was quite distinct. Then it was gone, merged into the gentle murmur of traffic in the roadway far above and in the nearer sound of moving water.

I was just starting forward again, when a sound made me turn. It was the sound of voices, distant, but clear as in a speaking tube. Behind me flashed the light of torches. They must have been nearly a quarter of a mile away, for the sewer ran straight as a die. For a second I was riveted to the spot. Not by fear, but by my first glimpse along the sewer. The curve of the walls showed black and glistening and the tunnel seemed to narrow down to those pinpoints of light. The shape of the sewer was that of an egg. The roof was nicely rounded, like the tubes of the Underground, but the walls came sharply inwards as they fell and finished almost in a point. And constructed out of the wall nearest me was the little platform on which I was standing. To the right of that platform, the water moved sluggishly towards me, black and unpleasant. The Styx itself could not have looked more grim. And between me and those pinpoints of light were rats—thousands of them.

Like a fool, I had turned with my torch still alight. In an instant, I heard the faint echo of " There he is." That broke the spell. I turned and ran. But I was hampered by the dimness of my torch and I could sense my followers closing up on me. Every fifty yards or so I passed beneath a ventilation shaft, and occasionally I heard the murmur of the street above. And behind me was the ever-present sound of running feet, hollow and distorted by the echo. I passed several subsidiary sewers. These were much smaller than the main sewer and had no platform along which to walk. I dared not turn off up any of these, because my pursuers could see my movements and I feared being trapped in a dead end. That same fear prevented me from hiding in any of the exit shafts I passed. These were dark openings in the wall of the sewer that led to a brick shaft. As I ran past them, the light of my torch showed dimly the lower rungs of an iron ladder. These were the exits for the sewer men and led to the pavement above. But I knew that, without the iron key with which to unlock the metal trapdoor at the top, it would only lead to my capture.

By now I must have run more than a mile along that main sewer. I was almost dropping with fatigue and was rapidly losing the will to go on. I felt my capture was inevitable and I wanted to give in. At the same time I was spurred automatically on by the fear that was in my heart. My torch was very dim now. But that no longer worried me. The sewers seemed a friendly place. My imagination no longer dwelt upon the horror of wandering alone and in darkness in this evil-smelling rat-infested, subterranean rabbit warren. All my thoughts were centred upon that box again. Anything was better than that. And at every step I felt my pursuers gaining on me.

The horror of it was that I knew my strength would soon give out. I had had no sleep. I had laboured as I had not laboured in years throughout the night, and now I was running for my life. I could not keep it up for ever. I knew enough about London's sewers to know that the main sewers run down to the Barking flats. There the sewage is separated, the water is purified and run out into the Thames and the sludge is carried out in barges to be dumped out by the Nore lightship. And Barking was miles away!

I had reached the conclusion that the only thing to do was to hide in one of the exit shafts and hope for the best, when I noticed that the sewer was bearing away to the right. The bend proved quite a sharp one, doubtless following the roadway above. I followed it round, and when the walls straightened out again, I glanced back over my shoulder. All was dark behind me. My pursuers were lost round the bend. I increased my pace, breathing heavily. I had developed a painful stitch and I knew I was at the end of my tether.

Then I saw what I wanted. The black circle of a tributary sewer showing in the wall to my right. There was no pathway along it. The water ran steadily out from the tunnel dark and filthy. I did not hesitate. I stepped down into that tunnel and splashed up it. The sewage was about a foot and a half deep. But it did not worry me. With a last burst of energy, I surged through it, glancing every now and then over my shoulder for the glow of light that would tell me that the chase had reached the entrance. When I saw that glow outlining the circular opening of my sewer, I switched off my torch and slowed up so that I made no sound as I pushed steadily on through the sewage water.

I saw the flash of their torches as they passed the entrance and went on down the main sewer, and I breathed a sigh of relief. But that relief was short-lived, for within a minute the beam of a powerful torch was shone along the sewer. Impeded by the water and my weak condition, my progress had been slow, so that I was still no more than a hundred yards from the entrance. A shout echoed eerily along the tunnel, and a second later there was a loud report and a bullet sang past me, hit the wall ahead and went singing up the sewer.

But the light of the torches had showed me a bend in the tunnel ahead. The sound of that bullet whistling up that narrow tunnel gave me fresh strength. I splashed furiously on. Another shot was fired, but I think the bullet must have hit the water behind me, for it never reached me. A few moments later and I had rounded the bend. I could have cried out for joy then, for the sewer forked. I took the right-hand branch, for I saw there was a bend in it.

My pursuers no longer had the advantage of their torches, for it was impossible to push ahead through the water at anything but a slow rate. It was up to my knees. Moreover, I was able to save my torch, for the sewer was a circular pipe and I could feel the middle with my feet. I could touch the wall, too, on either side. And as I staggered on a faint luminosity grew behind me until I could actually see the sweating concrete of the tunnel on either side of me. My pursuers had guessed which fork I had taken.

I could have sat down and cried like a child for weariness and despair. The tunnel ran straight before me and, at any moment, they would sight me and I should be under fire again.

And then I had my first real bit of luck. I saw a square opening in the tunnel on my left. I peered into it as I passed and saw daylight shining upon an iron ladder. Quite distinctly I heard a voice say, " Mind where you're treading, Bert." I stopped, and down that ladder appeared the heavy waders of a sewer man. I had an overwhelming urge to reach the light of day. But I suppose a sixth sense held me back. In an instant my brain took up the argument of my instinct. I should not be able to get up before the pursuit was upon me. I knew I must look a terrible sight. Apart from the mess my clothes were in, I was unshaven and hollow-eyed. At best I should be taken to a police station, and if Marburgs charged me as one of their clerks with some petty crime, I might have considerable difficulty in clearing myself. And the engine was due to leave London in two nights' time.

All this flashed through my mind as the man's waders came slowly into view. I knew instantly that I dared not risk it. I hurried on up the sewer, making as little noise as possible. And then it began to bend. I think I must have been round that bend before the chase came into the straight behind me. And then the sound of voices echoed and re-echoed along the tunnel. The best that I could have hoped for had happened. The sewer men had stepped out into the tunnel to find out who was coming along the sewer. The long altercation faded away behind me. The sewer forked again. Then

I came to a ventilation shaft, the top of which was scarcely
ten feet above my head. I could see wheels crossing over it
and the roar of traffic was practically continuous. I guessed
I must be somewhere near the river now, for I had turned
right from the main sewer, which must have been leading in
the direction of Barking, and I was now clearly in a low-
lying part of London. The number of tributary sewers—
little more than pipes—became increasingly numerous, so that
I guessed I was in a district of congested, narrow streets. The
concrete circular walls of the sewer in which I was walking
had now given place to stone, and I realised that this must
be one of the old sewers still in use. The rats, too, seemed
more numerous here. My legs were perpetually brushing
against them.

I was beginning to wonder how I was to get out. I had
hoped, once I had shaken off my pursuers, to climb one of
the exit shafts, and by shouting and beating on the cast-iron
trapdoor at the top to attract the attention of a passer-by.
But there seemed to be no exit shafts to this sewer.

I think it was the fear that I might have to retrace my steps
and risk the possibility of capture if I were ever to get out,
that made me pause before a patch of bricks. The bricks
formed a large square, like the entrance to a passage, in the
left-hand wall of the sewer. I peered at them closely in the
dull glimmer of my fading torch. One or two near the top
were missing and the mortar was crumbling badly. I pulled
two or three away and, pushing my torch into the gap, I
gazed through. There seemed to be a sort of passageway
with walls of stone that reminded me of the old sewer I had
got into from the Marburg vaults. But it was not that so
much as the air that decided me. The atmosphere in the old
tunnel was cool and almost fresh by comparison with the
warm stench to which I had become accustomed.

The bricks presented little difficulty. They came away
quite easily, and in a short space of time I had made a hole
big enough to climb through. There was no doubt about it.
This was an old sewer. And it led, I felt certain, in the
direction of the river. This seemed to be confirmed by the
fact that it sloped gently in the direction in which I was
going. But progress was slow. My torch was reduced to
such a feeble glimmer that it made no impression upon the

darkness unless thrust very close to the floor. The culvert was in a very bad state of repair. Probably it had not been used for more than a century.

Soon my torch gave out completely. I went forward, feeling my way, my hands stretched out on either side to touch the wet slimy stone of the walls. The darkness was the darkness of the vaults from which I had escaped. It pressed down against my eyes. I was filled with a terrible lassitude and I was hungry, and above all thirsty. But I kept doggedly on because the air on my face was fresh and I knew there must be an opening somewhere.

Often I looked at the luminous dial of my watch—not to see the time, but to see its friendly little face shining at me in the darkness. I was determined not to use a match until it was absolutely necessary, for the box in my pocket was half empty. For hours and hours I groped my way along that culvert. There were no ventilation shafts. I could see nothing, only the Stygian blackness. But the warm stench of the sewers was behind me, and for that I was thankful.

I had entered the culvert shortly after ten. I think it was about one o'clock that I slipped and lay on the stones, exhausted. I slept fitfully for a while. And when at last I had recovered strength enough to climb to my feet, I found it was three o'clock. I was soaked to the skin, for there was a certain amount of water in the culvert, and I was shivering with cold.

Nevertheless, the sleep had done me good. But with my recovered strength I found my brain no longer dulled. And my imagination, always a little too vivid, pictured myself groping along that tunnel unendingly till I died. Once I nearly panicked. Only the dial of my wrist-watch saved me. It was a friendly face and gave me courage. The culvert twisted and turned and my feet were sore and bruised with stumbling against the blocks of broken stone that had fallen from the roof. My one great fear was that I should bear away from the open air on a branch of the culvert. But always I had the satisfaction of feeling cool air on my face. As long as I felt that cool air in front of me, I knew I should find strength to go on. Pains were beginning to shoot through my belly, pains of hunger. But they were nothing to the thirst, which swelled my tongue and clove it to the roof of my mouth. And all the time I was slopping through water, which I still had sense enough not to touch.

Suddenly the walls on either side of me opened out. I lost contact with them. I stopped and pulled out my box of matches. But I found them sodden by the water in which I had lain asleep. I went back a few steps, found the left-hand wall and began to follow it. Almost immediately it fell away again and I had to turn sharp left to keep in touch with it. Before I had gone more than a few paces I realised that I was no longer facing into cool air, and faint, but quite distinguishable, I smelt the sewers again. I knew then that I had come to a point at which two of these old sewers met. I retraced my steps, found my own sewer, and began following the right-hand wall. The same thing happened. After that, I turned my face towards the cool air and moved slowly, blindly forward, feeling my way with my feet. Soon my hands which were outstretched in front of me touched the wet cold surface of a stone wall. I followed it and found that I was still facing the cool air.

After a time, I stopped and, facing directly away from this wall, went forward a few paces. The ground sloped away to water. I stumbled against a stone and found my feet sinking into mud. Then the ground rose again and I came up against another wall. I knew then that I was in a much wider sewer, and my spirits rose.

It was now nearly four. If I did not reach the entrance soon, darkness would have fallen. I knew it would be folly to attempt to get out into the Thames, presuming that that was where the sewer led, in the dark. And I had no desire to spend the night in the place. Where I had fallen and slept there had been hardly any rats. But here there seemed to be thousands of them. The sound of their movement was everywhere, like the soughing of a wind up the sewer.

Soon I encountered slimy weed on the wall along which I was feeling my way. Then my feet began to slither and squelch on a thin layer of mud, which extended close up to the wall. I knew then that I must be nearing the Thames, and a new fear assailed me. Until that moment I had had no thought of what the exit of the sewer into the river would be like. I had just been intent on reaching that exit—nothing else. The mud got deeper until it was pulling at my sodden shoes. Then I found I was floundering through a few inches of water. I had a sudden awful fear that the sewer might come out into the river underwater. Or supposing the water came right up the sewer at high tide? Should I be able to find my way back faster than the water flowed up the culvert? It was an unpleasant thought. But I went doggedly on, encouraged by the cool air on my face, which could now be described as almost a breeze.

Soon I was in nearly a foot of water. I glanced at my watch. It was nearly a quarter to five. And then I noticed a peculiar thing. That friendly little face was not as bright as it had been. I peered closely at the watch. But there was no doubt about it. The luminosity was dulled. I stared around me at the darkness. Was it my imagination, or had it lightened? Was there a tinge of grey in the inky blackness?

I stumbled hurriedly on, the wall curving away to the right. Soon I was left in no doubt at all. The darkness was lifting. Ahead of me I could begin to make out vaguely the bend of the sewer. A little farther and the darkness had become definitely grey. Soon I could see the walls, all weedgrown and slimy. And then the sewer itself took shape —a sixteen-foot wide arched culvert made of great stone blocks, beneath which a sheet of water stretched from wall to wall.

The relief of seeing daylight filtering through into that disused tunnel! I went forward at an increased rate, my hunger and thirst and weariness forgotten in my joy at the sight of that grey light. The sewer bore away to the left, and as I rounded the bend, the water now over my knees, I saw the actual opening into the river. There before me was an arch of daylight that almost hurt my eyes. And across that arched sewer exit was a lattice-work of iron bars, like a portcullis.

It was the last straw. I think I should have burst into tears if I had not been so buoyed up by the sight of that grey half-circle of daylight. Beyond it, I could see some sort of wharf. The great wooden piles were wrapped in green weed, and around them the river slopped. There was a wooden ladder, too, its rungs rotting, but giving promise of a way to safety, if only I could get through those iron bars. They reached right to the arched roof of the sewer. But there was a cross-bar near the water level. I could stand on that and perhaps by shouting I should be able to attract attention to my plight.

I went forward resolutely. The iron grille was only about fifty yards from me. The water rose to my waist. It was bitterly cold and there was a scum of oil floating on its dark surface. At each step my feet sank deeper into mud. I had soon lost both my shoes, but I did not mind, for it lightened my feet. When the water was up to my chest, I launched out, using a long sweeping breast stroke and ducking my head at each thrust of my arms. I made good pace and I was within a few yards of the bars before my muscles had grown tired with the weight of my waterlogged clothes.

Four more strokes and I was clutching a bar near the centre. But the cross-bar, which from a distance of fifty yards had seemed so near the water level, was over three feet above my head. In my exhausted condition, I knew I could never draw myself up to it. I looked back. The darkness of that tunnel, full of inky water, appalled me. I could not face the prospect of going back. Besides, I was doubtful whether I could make it.

Twenty yards beyond the grille the water slopped tantalisingly against the lower rungs of the ladder to the wharf. I thought if I clung to the bars for a time, the incoming tide might lift me to the cross bar. But then, out beyond the green timbers of the wharf, I saw a barge drifting slowly downstream, and I knew then that the tide was still on the ebb. The centre of the river was whipped into brown waves by the tide and the wind, and beyond was a drab line of wharves and cranes. How homely and safe they seemed! I had many times looked at such a scene from the security of London Bridge, and I longed to be back there, treading its firm pavements.

My left hand suddenly slipped on the rust-coated bar. I quickly took a fresh grip. The cold was beginning to tell on me. Soon my hands would be numb and I should have to let go and attempt to get back into the sewer. And perhaps I should never have the strength to swim out to the grille again. I had to do something. I began to shout. I shouted till my throat was rough. My calls echoed back at me from the sewer. The big stone archway rang with my cries. But no one came. I began to scream. The panic feeling of a drowning man had seized me. But it was Saturday. No one was about. And when no one came or answered, blank despair suddenly fell upon me. I was suddenly silent, clutching the cold bars with my hands and looking out upon the river with my chin just above the water. And with my silence, came a mental calm, and I knew that I must either go back or find a means of going forward. And whichever I did, I should have to do it quickly.

There was only one possible chance of going forward. I took a deep breath, shut my mouth and then, with my hands on the bars, pushed myself under the water. It seemed a long way that I went down, and all the time my feet were against the bars. My lungs felt as though they would burst. But one more thrust of my arms and my feet were no longer touching the bars. I felt about, but there were no bars where my feet were. Another thrust and they sank into mud. I let go my hold of the bars and struggled to the surface, where I gulped in fresh air in great mouthfuls.

I rested for a moment, clutching the bars again. I reckoned there was a gap of about two feet, or perhaps a little more, between the end of the bars and the mud. But it was a long dive and there was the mud. I had an awful fear of being caught in that mud. And then there might be spikes sticking out on the other side, which would prevent me from rising.

It was a long time before I could pluck up the necessary courage. But with every minute I was getting colder. And so, suddenly, like a diver taking his first plunge of the year, I took a deep breath and began thrusting myself down hand over hand. It was done before I had time to think about it. In no time, it seemed, my feet were clear of the bars. I thrust myself sideways, pulling my body down with my hands, like a monkey crawling across the face of his cage. I felt the pointed end of a bar. The water was singing in my ears. I thrust myself farther down. I felt my body press against mud that yielded and bubbled unpleasantly. I had the point of a bar in the palm of my hand. I thrust myself under it. For a moment my foot became entangled with the points of the bars. My lungs now felt as though they must burst my chest apart. I wrenched my foot clear, and in the

same movement, thrust myself upwards, letting go my hold
on the bars.

I thought I should never reach the surface. But I did, and
as I panted for breath, I found the tide carrying me slowly
towards the wharf. It was perhaps as well, for I was very
weak now. But I had sense enough to realise that the tide
might grow stronger and sweep me past the ladder if I did
not fend for myself. I summoned my last remaining energy,
and with a few desperate strokes, reached the ladder and
hung there, gasping and half crying.

I never thought a ladder twenty feet high could seem so
far. My clothes, sodden with water, added to my weight,
and my exhausted muscles, now relaxed in the relief of
safety, would scarcely pull me from one rung to the next.

Chapter Eight

IN WAPPING

When I hauled myself up on to that wharf I was met by
the full force of a bitter east wind. My skin was blue and I
was shivering from cold and exhaustion. That wind seemed
to blow right through my sodden clothes direct on to my
naked flesh. I looked around me. Behind, across a huddle
of cranes and masts and funnels, I saw the misty outline of
Tower Bridge. Ahead stretched the river, bending away to
the Lower Pool, the brown waters flecked with little tufts of
white as the wind whipped chilly at the wave caps. The
wharf was deserted.

Wretched with cold, I crossed the uneven planks, leaving a
trail of water behind me. At the back of the wharf rose the
grimy mass of a warehouse. The air was full of the smell of
malt and cinnamon and sacks ; a queer, musty, but exciting
conglomeration of scents. The entrances to the warehouse
were barred with worn wooden doors. The place looked like
some old barracks. But between it and the next warehouse
were steps leading up from the river. By climbing down over
some old barrels, I reached these steps. They led up to a

narrow street lined with warehouses on the river side. On the other side, the buildings were much lower, mainly shops and lodging houses. During working hours it would be fantastically congested with lorries and carts, but now it was quiet and practically deserted. A dirty cast-iron street sign told me that this was Wapping High Street. Anything less like a high street I have never seen. But I found a little eating place called Alf's Dining Rooms and went in. There was no one there. But at the tinkle of the door bell an old woman came out from the back quarters. When she saw me, she stopped and stared, her mouth agape. I am not surprised. I must have presented a sorry spectacle, standing there, the water dripping from my clothes, which stank ruthlessly in the warmth of that eating-house.

My teeth chattering. I explained to her that I had fallen into the river. I was too dulled by cold and fatigue to tell her my wants. I did not even tell her that I had any money. "It's a cold day for falling in the river," was all she said, and led me through into the kitchen at the back. She shooed a big full-bosomed girl from her pastry-making and sent her upstairs for blankets. Then she told me to strip. I was too far gone to feel any sense of discomfort at her presence. In front of the blazing range I stood and towelled myself down. The warmth and the friction soon restored my circulation.

In the midst of this an old man dressed in a seaman's cap and jersey came in. He stopped at the sight of me, standing nude before the fire. Then he took his pipe out of his mouth and spat in the coal bucket. "'Ullo, ma," he said. "See yer've got company, like."

I hastened to explain. But he held up his hand. "Now why bother to explain," he said. "Nobody explains things around 'ere, see. They just 'appens. You fell in the river. Orl right. But what I says is the river 'as acquired a fruitier scent than when I last smelt it. So you keep yer explanations to them as wants 'em, me lad."

There was nothing I could say to that. If I told him the truth, he would never believe me. And if I made up a lie, he wouldn't believe that either. We just left it at that. I wrapped myself in the blankets that the girl had brought down and, sitting like an Indian in front of the fire, I ran through my sodden garments, removing anything of value that remained in the pockets. Fortunately my wallet was still there. In it were three wet pound notes. And I found two half-crowns and several coppers in the pocket of my trousers.

I looked across at the old man, who had sat himself down on a chair. " Have you got any old clothes you'd be willing to sell me?" I asked. I pointed to the pound notes in the wallet. " I expect they'll dry all right, won't they?"

" Blimey!" he said. " Where did yer get those?" Then he picked himself up. " Orl right, me lad. Never mind where they comes from. They'll dry orl right. But if it's orl the same to you, I'll take those two half-crowns. And in exchange you can 'ave a pair of my old trousers and a sweater."

He disappeared upstairs. The old woman came and picked up my clothes. " You'd better throw those away," I said. " They're in a filthy state."

I saw her gnarled hands fingering the cloth. " Throw them away!" she said. " Not likely I won't. It'll all come out in the wash. I can see you 'aven't 'ad anything to do with children."

And with that, she disappeared with the clothes, leaving me alone with the girl, who had returned to her pastry. I had been conscious of her eyes on me ever since she had returned to find me standing in front of the fire with nothing but a towel round me. " You do look funny in that blanket," was her opening line.

It was not the best she could have chosen, for I was already conscious enough of my appearance. I looked at her. Her figure was big and clumsy, and she had dark rather sullen features. Beneath her tousled hair was a rather fine pair of brown eyes. She was smiling at me. " Tell me wot reely 'appened," she said. " Did yer get much?"

At that I laughed. " Nothing, I'm afraid," I said. " You see, I raided a big City bank, and they caught me and shoved me in the vaults. But I broke out into a sewer. I've been chased all day through the sewers by four big men in top hats. They all had beards, too," I added as an afterthought.

" Oo, I don't believe yer. Yer teasing." And she laughed, a husky, rich sound. " 'Ere, that blanket's slippin' orf yer. Wait a minute. I'll tuck yer up."

But, as she was wiping the flour off her hands, the old woman came back and she returned sullenly to her pastry. was not sorry, for a great lethargy was stealing over me, and I was not in the mood to cope with such a wench. A few minutes later the old man came down with trousers, a tattered old vest, a thick blue woollen jersey and a pair of socks carefully darned. He watched over me as I put them on. The jersey was a little on the high side, but who was I to complain, having come straight from the sewers?

The problem of footwear still remained. But the old man who, now that I was clad in his cast-offs, seemed to take a fatherly interest in me, said he knew of a good second-hand clothes dealer in Wapping High. So, a little later, when the notes in my wallet had dried, I entrusted him with one to go and buy me a pair of shoes, size nine, and some sort of a coat. I told him to see to it that there was enough left over to buy himself some tobacco. But I had to assure him repeatedly that the note was genuine before he would agree to run the errand. In the meantime I had a wash and a meal of cold meat and bread and pickles. With it I was given some of the strongest tea I have ever tasted from a big black pot on the hob. It was bitter with tannin, yet I drank three cups, and liked it.

When the old man returned, he brought with him a pair of black boots, ex-service, I guessed, and a tattered old coat of dark-blue serge. He evidently noticed my surprise when he proffered me boots instead of shoes, for he said, " Boots is what you'd be wearing in them clothes. Besides, they were reel cheap—only five bob the pair. And you was quite correct—them notes was orl right."

I was loath to leave the warmth of that fire. But I had much to do. So I thanked them for their kindness and went out into Wapping High Street. My immediate need was a call box. I made my way west along the narrow street. It was still practically deserted, the gaunt grimy faces of the warehouses barred and lifeless. Only round the pubs was there any sign of life. I crossed the bridge over the Hermitage entrance to London Docks and, skirting the blank castle-like walls of St. Katherine Docks, I made my way to Tower Hill, where I found a call box. I was thankful to go inside and shut the door. My tattered coat and woollen jersey seemed no protection against the biting wind, and I was deathly tired. I lifted the receiver, inserted two pennies and dialled Whitehall 1212. I was put straight through to Crisham.

" Is that you, Kilmartin?" His voice was terse and I was surprised at his use of my surname.

" Listen, Desmond," I said, " do you know who controls Calboyds? Is it Baron Marburg?"

" Well, what of it?" he demanded. " I suppose he has been over-quoting for the sale of Diesel engines to the Government?"

" So they've sent you that statement accusing Terstall of over-quoting for gun turrets, have they?" I asked.

" Yes. Who signed that statement?"

" I did," I said. " But I was forced to. Their idea was to make me sign a number of absurd statements, so that when, after my death, you were handed my original statement, which dealt with Calboyds, you wouldn't believe a word of it."

" Look here," he said, " did you ring me up yesterday?"

" Yes, of course I did. Why?"

" And on the previous day?"

" Yes—why?"

" You said you were coming along to see me yesterday."

" Yes, but I couldn't. I went straight from that call box to the Wendover Hotel. I wanted to frighten Cappock—he's one of the big Calboyd shareholders—into an admission. But they were waiting for me there. They packed me up in a deed-box and took me along to Marburgs' Bank in Thread-needle Street."

" Who is they?"

" Max Sedel for one. He's the fellow at whose house John Burston is supposed to have got drunk enough to drive him-self over the cliffs at Beachy Head. Actually he was mur-dered by Sedel. Sedel, for your information, is a Nazi agent."

" You'd better come along to the Yard and have a talk with me," Crisham suggested.

" That's what I want to do," I said. " But I want you to know what the position is first, just in case I don't reach the Yard. I escaped from the vaults of Marburgs by way of the sewers. I've been all day getting out of them with the pack at my heels. I tell you, Desmond, this Marburg business is the biggest thing that has happened in this war, so far. Do you know what Baron Marburg is? He's Führer-designate of Britain. And if Germany gets that engine that your police were fool enough to let out of their grasp, it's good-bye to air supremacy with Calboyds making obsolete Diesel engines for the Government."

"Just what are you talking about?" His voice sounded exasperated. Then a moment later it was suddenly conciliatory. "Look here, old man, you'd better tell me the whole thing from the beginning."

He had never addressed me as "old man" before. I was puzzled. I knew the man well enough to know that it was a mode of address he only used when wheedling a suspect. "You've got the guts of it," I said. "I'm coming up to the Yard right away to talk to you. And don't breath a word of this to anyone until I've seen you."

"Wait a minute," he said. "I've got to dash out almost immediately. Just let me have the story from the beginning."

"What the devil has got into you?" I said. "Can't you understand the importance of what I'm telling you? You stay right where you are till I get there."

"Stop!" he said. "They might get you on the way. I'll have a squad car sent round for you."

I think it was that mention of a squad car that touched some sixth sense in my brain. Then reason took up the argument of instinct. One minute he had not seemed to understand what I was talking about and the next he was offering me a squad car for protection. One minute he had been terse, and the next conciliatory. I replaced the receiver and left the call box. As I crossed the road towards the Mint, I saw steam rising from a man-hole cover in the roadway. It was the ventilation shaft of a sewer smoking in the raw air. Involuntarily I shuddered. But a few hours ago I had been in those sewers. Perhaps I had passed along beneath Royal Mint Street itself.

I had barely reached the other side of the road, when I saw a big black roadster coming fast down Tower Bridge approach, weaving its way in and out of the traffic. It drew up by the curb opposite the call box and three policemen

jumped out. I was on the point of crossing the road to it,
thinking that Crisham had been as good as his word and sent
a car along to take me to the Yard, when I realised that
three policemen were not necessary to invite the friend of an
inspector along to Scotland Yard. Anyway, it had not come
from the direction of the Yard. And there was no mistaking
the manner in which they closed in on that call box. They
were there to make an arrest.

It was with a horrible sinking sensation in my stomach
that I mingled with the crowd on the pavement. The pur-
posefulness of those policemen could mean only one thing.
The other side had got in first. They had smirched my reputation so successfully that even Crisham, whom I regarded
as a friend, believed them. I think, perhaps, if I had been
feeling fresh, I should have jumped into a taxi and driven
straight to the Yard. I don't know. It is difficult to tell what
one would do in any particular instance had the circumstances been slightly different.

My mood was definitely a defeatist one. I was frightened
of the power I was up against. Perhaps I exaggerated that
power. At least, I was afraid at the time that I might not be
able to convince even Crisham of my sincerity. It was asking
a good deal of a policeman to expect him to believe that a
man of Marburg's standing was a Nazi. Policemen have too
great a sense of propriety readily to accept accusations of
treason against well-known banking figures. They stand for
the *status quo*, and I knew that even if I were not suspect, I
should find it well-nigh impossible to convince Crisham of
the truth.

It was in a state of complete frustration that I walked
towards the Minories. I felt impotent against this power that
was able to range the police, as well as its own agents, against
me. I was puzzled to know how they had managed it. Then
I saw the placard. FAMOUS K.C.'s DEATH RIDDLE. I stopped.
I knew, instinctively, that here was the answer. I bought a
copy of the *Record*.

There it was in a banner head right across the front page.
MYSTERY OF FAMOUS K.C.—ANDREW KILMARTIN KILLED IN
CAR SMASH—IMPOSTOR RINGS UP YARD. That final head
explained Crisham's attitude and the arrival of the squad car
so clearly. I glanced quickly through the story. Apparently

the wreckage of a car had been discovered at a lonely par
of the coast near Bude called Strangler's Beach. The car
had been hired at Launceston late on Thursday and had
been discovered by a shepherd on the Friday at the foot of
a four-hundred-foot cliff. The body had been identified that
morning as mine.

The subtlety of it was terrifying. As the story pointed out
I had left my rooms in the Temple on Tuesday for a short
holiday in the West Country. My normal haunts had not
seen me since. And then at the bottom of the page was a
cross head—MYSTERY OF YARD PHONE CALLS. Doubtless
Sedel, with his knowledge of Fleet Street, had provided that
part of the story.

It had all been planned prior to their picking me up at
the Wendover. But even now that I had escaped, their plans
stood them in good stead. I dared not go to the police, for
by the time I had proved my identity, the engine might have
left the country. And even if I went straight to Crisham or
to the Chief Commissioner, whom I knew slightly, and
showed them, by my knowledge of what had passed at certain private conversations I had had with them, that I was
not an impostor, would they believe what I had to say about
Marburg, or even what I could tell them about Calboyds?
They might believe my story of the sewers, but for the
rest, they would shake their heads and say that the experience
had upset me and that what I needed was a rest. That statement I had signed the previous night had done its work.
The suggestion of mental derangement had been sown. And
that seed would still be there, even when Crisham knew that
it was not an impostor who had phoned him. Whatever I did,
I faced a blank wall, because of the time factor. According
to Sedel, the engine was due to leave in three days' time now.
That meant Monday. Two days in which first to prove my
identity and then prove that one of the biggest banking
figures in the country was a Nazi.

The impossibility of it swept over me, and suddenly I
knew how deadly tired I was. I peered back across the
cobbled roadway. The police car was still there and behind
it loomed the grey, imposing bulk of the Tower. Presumably
they were making inquiries. I turned at right angles and

hurried down Royal Mint Street. Exhaustion made that
hunted sensation strong in me, and almost in a daze I made
my way back, through the squalid streets that skirt the docks,
to Alf's Dining Rooms. I had no plan. All I knew was that
I must get some rest. They had thought me a criminal and
had helped me. I felt I should be safe with them.

It was half-past six when I dragged myself wearily into
the eating-house. It was almost dark. One or two customers
were seated at the tables, eating. They glanced up at my
entrance, but without curiosity. I saw them in a kind of
haze. I was suddenly very near collapse. The girl, with her
hair tidied and a clean apron, was serving. I went through
into the kitchen. Neither the old man nor his wife showed
any sign of surprise at my return. And when I asked if they
had a room to spare, where I could rest the night, the old
woman took me upstairs to a little room with an iron bed-
stead and a lace-trimmed window that looked out across a
huddle of chimney pots to the river. She placed a board of
three-ply over the window before switching on the light.

I don't remember taking off my clothes or removing the
board from the window. All I remember is the momentary
joy of the cold sheets against my tired body and the restful-
ness of a bed.

And then daylight was flooding in through the window and
there was the sound of movement in the house. I climbed out
of bed. The events of the previous day seemed like a nightmare. But the stiffness of my joints bore witness to their
reality. And then I saw the sun was high over the river and
I looked at my watch. It was eleven-thirty. I remembered
then how much I had to do.

I washed myself quickly in cold water and hurried into my
clothes. Down in the kitchen I found the old woman just
beginning the day's cooking. It was Sunday and the joint
was standing floured upon the table. Her husband was sitting by the fire, his feet in a pair of old carpet slippers and
a dirty clay pipe in his mouth. He was reading the *News of
the Globe*. He looked up as I came in, peering at me over
the top of a pair of steel-rimmed spectacles. But he made no
comment, so I said, " You should have woken me up."

But the old woman smiled and shook her head. " A nice lie
in is what yer needed," she said.

"That's right," the old man nodded. "A nice lie in. That's wot I tells the missis."

The old woman put the joint in the oven and then set about getting my breakfast. And all the time the old man was reading out scraps of news from the paper. I sat by the fire and tried to think out my next move. The events of the past two days seemed strangely remote. But I knew that I had made progress. I had discovered that Max Sedel was a Nazi agent, and that he had a number of agents working under him. I had discovered that he was closely connected with the dummy Calboyd shareholders, who controlled, presumably through the directors nominated by them, the policy of Calboyds. I was reasonably certain that he had murdered one of these shareholders. Above all, I had found out who controlled these dummy shareholders. But had I? I had been so certain about it when in that vault. But now I was not certain. It seemed so utterly fantastic. True, Sedel had not denied it. In fact, he had said, "So you know all our little secrets." But then he might have been just leading me on. And if I myself were not certain, then how could I expect to convince the authorities. It seemed so absurd that a man like Marburg should be a traitor to the country of his adoption. What had he to gain out of it? I had suggested to myself power. But money was power. And, as a capitalist, why should the man work for the downfall of England, which was the stronghold of capitalism?

Then my breakfast was brought to me and for a while I forgot my problems in the joys of bacon and eggs. But when I had taken the edge off my appetite, my mind returned to the problem. Now that I was fed, my mind seemed more inclined to deal with realities. I found myself dismissing the problem of Marburg and concentrating on the question of the engine. Marburg could wait. The engine could not. But though I racked my brains till my head ached, I could not see how I was to prevent it from leaving the country. Quite apart from the time I should inevitably waste in convincing some responsible person of my identity, I did not know where the engine was or how they intended to smuggle it out of the country.

And then there occurred one of those incredible strokes of luck that make life so incomprehensible. My mind, browsing

over my problems, occasionally caught isolated scraps of the
news that the old man was reading out to his wife. And
suddenly my mind fastened on the name of Marburg. I
looked up from my bread and marmalade. "What did you
say?" I asked.

"Eh?" The old man looked quite startled, for it was the
first word I had uttered since I had been given my breakfast,
and I had spoken somewhat peremptorily.

"What was that bit you were reading out about Marburg?" I asked.

"D'yer mean this about the bankers sending a boat-load
of munitions to Finland? A feller called Marburg organised
it, so the paper says. They're 'olding a service on board this
afternoon. There you are. Read it for yourself." And he
handed me a page of the paper.

I seized it and spread it out on the table beside my plate.
A sudden wild hope made the blood beat in my temples. I
found the story. It was headed—BANKER SENDS MUNITIONS
TO FINLAND. My eye ran rapidly down the column. "The
fight for democracy. . . . Moral obligation to help. . . .
Service of dedication to be held at 3 p.m. this afternoon on
board the *Thirlmere*, which is lying at the Wilson's Wren
Wharf. . . Baron Ferdinand Marburg, who raised the fund,
will be present at the simple little ceremony. Many bankers
and industrialists who subscribed will also be present. . . .
Finland's gratitude for this generous gesture was expressed
yesterday by. . . . The precious cargo is valued at close on
£100,000." Ah, here it was! "The cargo consists of 25 of
the latest British fighter planes . . . tanks . . . hand-grenades
. . . anti-tank guns . . . and——" So I had been right!
"And one of the latest Calboyd naval torpedo craft as supplied to the Royal Navy."

I sat back in my chair. The audacity of the scheme took
my breath away. I could not but feel admiration for the
fellow. It was so perfect. Elementary, of course. It was one
of the first things I had been taught when I went into the
Intelligence over twenty-five years ago. A clever agent
always puts himself in the most obvious place. But there are
ways and ways of carrying out that fundamental precept.
Marburg chose to do it in the grand manner. And for the
first time since I had left the Wendover Hotel in a deed-box,

I felt elated. Sedel I knew for a secret agent who would stop at nothing. To me he was a rat whom I would avoid like the plague. I hate brute force. I always have done. Probably because as a barrister my weapon has always been my brain. Marburg I could understand. He fought with my weapons. And I could have laughed with the sheer excitement of it.

It may seem strange that I no longer had any doubts about Marburg. But that column was like a sign from heaven. The whole thing fitted too well. What a way to take an engine out of the country! Put it in a torpedo boat and ship it out of the country, together with a stack of other munitions for Finland, with the Government's blessing, a dedication service and—— I glanced down the column again. Yes, there it was. " The *Thirlmere* will have a British naval escort as far as Norwegian territorial waters." Perfect! And all those lovely munitions, paid for by Britain's bankers and industrialists—where were they bound for?

In my mind's eye I saw the British naval escort of two destroyers, perhaps, swing in a wide arc as they turned for home. And the *Thirlmere*, instead of keeping inside territorial waters, would turn away to the south as soon as they were out of sight. And then over the horizon would come German warships. Not only would Marburg be delivering to Germany an engine that would give her superiority in the air, but with it, as a kind of garnish, a shipload of munitions.

And what the devil was I to do about it? The thought had a dampening effect on my spirits. Somehow the *Thirlmere* had to be prevented from reaching Germany. But how?

I turned to the old man, who was now reading the history of a divorce case to his wife. " I'd like to attend this service," I said, interrupting him. " But I suppose the wharf will be closed to the public?"

He took off his glasses and peered at me out of his pale blue eyes. " Well, wot d'yer think? D'yer expect them to invite every bloody communist in the East End to their little do? Anyway, there's plenty more places in the world besides Finland. Wot yer want to do—volunteer? Bloody poor look out, if yer asks me. So don't say Alf 'Iggins didn't warn yer.

Russia's all right looked at from a distance. But you keep yer distance, me lad. That's wot I says."

"I wasn't aiming to go to Finland," I said. "Though, come to think of it, it is an idea. No, I just thought it'd be a pleasant way of spending Sunday afternoon, that's all."

"Wot, listening to a service?"

"Well, there'd be some interesting people there. And it's not every day you see a shipload of munitions dedicated to the service of God on the banks of the Thames."

"Yer right there. But then money does strange things, me lad. Reckon a banker can get most things dedicated to God if that's the way 'e wants it." Then suddenly he leaned a little forward. "Who d'yer want to win—Finland or Russia?" he demanded.

I looked at him sharply, wondering what he was getting at. "I hope the Finns manage to hold out," I replied. "I don't expect them to win."

At that he snorted. "So, you're not a Red. I might have known it. Nobody interesting ever comes round this blasted street—just sailors and petty thieves and fellers who fall in the river." This last with a sidelong glance at me. Then he turned to his wife. "And I was just beginning to think, Ma, that 'e aimed to blow this 'ere ship up, dedication and all."

"Blow her up," I said, half to myself. That wasn't at all a bad idea. She was carrying hand grenades. If I could stow away on board or something and get at those hand grenades. It would be a quick death. "Yes," I said aloud, "I'd like to fight for Finland. I'd like to get on to the *Thirlmere*."

"Then you must be a bleeding fool," the old man snapped. "D'yer want to go and sign yer death warrant just to get out of the country? God Almighty! Don't yer know there are ways of lying low?"

"Oh, I know," I said. "Still, I'd like a bit of a change and some excitement. Anyway, I'd like to have a look at the *Thirlmere* while this ceremony is on. I suppose you don't happen to know of any way I could get on to Wilson's Wren Wharf?"

"Wilson's Wren Wharf, is it?" He peered at me again. "Wot's it worth to you?"

I hesitated. I had under a pound left. "Five bob," I said. "I'd make it more, only I'm getting a bit short."

" That's orl right. Why should you worry because it's only five bob. Five bob is five bob, ain't it. I wouldn't take yer money, only it means rowing yer across the river, and that's hard work for a Sunday. Wot d'you say, Ma—shall we go across and 'ave a dekko? The missis likes a little trip on the river after the Sunday joint, when it's a fine day like it is now, don't ye, Ma?" The old woman nodded, but said nothing.

" But how do we get on to the wharf?" I asked.

" We don't," was the reply. " Wilson's Wren Wharf is down in the Lower Pool. Next to it is the Percivale Banana Company's Wharf. It's closed now, but Bill Fevvers, wot looks after it for 'em, 'e's a chum of mine."

I thanked him as he returned to his divorce case. Whilst finishing my bread and marmalade, I read carefully through the *Thirlmere* story and found one point which seemed to me important. The Government had recently announced that Britons were to be allowed to volunteer for Finland. Apparently a batch of ten—the first volunteers from Britain—were leaving on the *Thirlmere*. They were acting as a guard. It occurred to me that if they had been chosen by Marburg, they would prove very useful, presuming that the captain and crew of the *Thirlmere* were just plain seamen.

And then, as I sat thinking out my first move, I noticed a brief story headed—ARMS WORKS MANAGER MISSING. It was the name Calboyd in the opening sentence that caught my eye. Mr. Sefton Raikes, works manager of the Calboyd Diesel Company, had apparently left the works on Thursday evening as usual by car and had not been seen since. A section of the canal had been dragged without success and the whole length of road between the works and his home had been thoroughly searched. Both the car and its owner had simply disappeared. And then followed a significant paragraph. " Anxiety is being felt by those who were closely associated with him in his work. It is believed that he was opposed to the policy of the directors. His plans for the production of a special type of Diesel engine had been repeatedly overridden by the board. His assistant, Mr. West, has told the police that he had been depressed and very worried during the past few weeks."

Thursday evening! My thoughts had immediately switched to a lonely beach somewhere near Bude, where the wreckage of a car had been found on Friday. It seemed too improbable that there should be any connection. Yet a body, which certainly was not mine, had been found in that car. It had to be someone's body, and if Raikes had been giving trouble, they would be killing two birds with one stone. But that implied that there was something like revolt brewing among the technical staff at Calboyds. I got up in some excitement. 'Could I have the City page a minute?' I asked.

The old man, who was now sitting with the paper on his knee, staring into the fire, looked round and then handed me the whole paper. I ran through it quickly and found the page I wanted. I could have shouted for joy, for there, right across the top of the page, was the headline—ARE CALBOYD SHARES TOO HIGH? And below, I read—" Calboyds received a sharp jolt on Friday. Throughout the week these shares had been steadily rising to a peak of 52s. 6d. On Friday they opened at this figure, but by midday they had reacted 1s. By the 3 o'clock close they had slumped to 45s. to the accompaniment of ugly rumours about the prospects of the expected Government contract." There followed a discussion of the merits of the shares with information about the expected contract. And then came this sentence: " The fall in the shares is being attributed in some quarters to the disappearance of Mr. Sefton Raikes, the works manager. It is said that there have been considerable differences between the company's executive and the board. There are apparently some grounds for this rumour and until the matter has been cleared up, I should advise investors to keep clear of these shares."

I put the paper down on the table. My mind was made up. The first thing to do was to get hold of David. That wire he had sent from Oldham must have meant something. He may even have talked to Raikes on the eve of his disappearance. If he had discovered something concrete about Calboyds, we might even be able to write up a really hot story about the company. There was Jim Fisher of the *Evening Record*. I knew him. He'd jump at it, if he thought there was a chance of getting away with it without a big libel suit. I went upstairs and got my old coat. "What time will you be ready to go over to the wharf?" I asked the old man when I returned to the kitchen.

"Better say 'alf-past two," he grunted sleepily. "We'll just catch the tide before she turns."

"Right," I said. "I'll be back at two-thirty." And I hurried through the empty dining-room and out into Wapping High. The sun was shining, but the air was raw, with a cold wind that swept in gusts across the dusty cobbles. I made straight for Tower Hill. Thence down Eastcheap to Cannon Street, where I picked up a bus which took me to Charing Cross. And as I slid through the empty Sunday streets of London with the warm sunshine on my neck, I found myself thinking of Freya and wondering whether she had been worried at my absence. It was a silly thought, but I remembered her lovely face puckered as she smiled at me over her glass on our evening out together, and I thought how nice it would be to have her anxious for me.

At Charing Cross station I felt myself far enough from Wapping to go into a call box. I dialled TERminus 6795, and almost immediately there was a gabble of barely intelligible English over the wire. I asked for David, but was told that he was not in. I asked for Freya and was told she, too, "no home." In desperation I asked for Mrs. Lawrence. "Och, it's you, is it, Mr. Kilmartin? Wherever have ye been? The young lady was fair worrit to death when ye didna come home."

"I'm sorry," I said. "I was—er—unavoidably detained. Are Mr. Shiel and Miss Smith both out?"

"Aye, and I'm worrit aboot them myself. Young Mr. Shiel, he got back on Saturday morning at about seven. He'd travelled all night, and he was that excited, Mr. Kilmartin. But then he found that you hadn't come home, and he and the young lady left hurriedly in a taxi. They looked terrible anxious. They didna come back last night and I havena seen them since."

"Did they say where they were going?"

"No. But they were in an awful hurry."

"All right. Don't you worry, Mrs. Lawrence. I'll find them." I rang off. For a moment after I had replaced the receiver I just stood there in a daze. I was thinking of

Freya, and there was a horrible clutching fear at my heart.
It was then that I realised consciously for the first time that
I was in love with her. The realisation of it did me good. I
had never allowed myself any illusions. I allowed myself
none now. When a confirmed bachelor of forty-two finds
himself in love with a girl of twenty-six—yes, subconsciously
I had even made a note of her age, based on what Schmidt
had told me—there is only one thing for him to do, and that
is to realise his folly and face up to it. I faced up to it
then and the knowledge that I was being a fool cleared my
brain.

There could only be one explanation of their failure to
return. If trouble were brewing up at Oldham, the probability
was that Sedel had men up there. One of them must have
recognised David and followed him back to London. What
he and Freya had dashed off for in such a hurry, I did not
know. Perhaps they had gone to see Crisham? No, that
was hardly likely, for it was on Saturday evening that I had
spoken to Crisham over the phone and he had given no
indication that he had seen them. But whatever they had
been up to, they had not returned to the digs. Either they
had discovered that they were being followed and had gone
somewhere else for the night, or they had been picked up
by Sedel's gang. And of the two possibilities, I feared the
latter, for I thought it possible that David might have made
straight for his godfather, Sir Geoffrey Carr. Sedel would
not like that. I looked up the number in the telephone directory, but when I got through, his butler informed me that
Sir Geoffrey was out.

I hesitated. If there were trouble at Calboyds and if
David had seen Carr, then things might be coming to a head.
But I knew enough about the workings of the official mind
to know that, even if David had seen his godfather and had
been able to convince him of the seriousness of the situation,
there was little likelihood of action being taken before the
Thirlmere sailed. In any case, David knew nothing about
either Marburg or the *Thirlmere*. He would not be able to
tell them where to find the engine. It was up to me. And I
decided upon the bold course. I rang Jim Fisher. At first he
was dubious of my identity. But when I repeated in some
detail conversations we had had at various times and I had

tossed him the bait of a good story, he seemed convinced and
agreed to see me.

I must admit that, as I took the bus up Kingsway to Russell
Square, I was sorry that Fisher was not the editor of a daily
paper. On the other hand, evening paper editors, especially
now that sales had fallen off so badly, are always more
inclined to take chances. Anyway, he was the only editor I
knew well. He opened the door of his flat to me himself.
His small restless eyes took in every detail of my appearance.
Then he suddenly grinned and held out his hand. " Glad to
see you, Andrew," he said.

" So you agree to my identity?" I said, as I shook his hand.

He gave me a quick glance. " Of course," he said. " Anyone who was trying to impersonate you wouldn't be fool
enough to come along in that fantastic rigout. Have a
whisky? And now let's hear your story."

So I let him have it as briefly as possible. When I had
finished he looked glum. " My God!" he said morosely.
" What a story! Man, there's enough there to provide a
splash for every day of the week. If we could use it," he
added dourly.

" Good God, Jim!" I said. " At least you can have a crack
at Calboyds."

" Aye, that's what young Shiel wanted me to do."

" Shiel!" I cried. " Why, he's the fellow I mentioned, who
had gone up to have a look at Calboyds."

" Aye. Well, he's come down with a fine tale. If the
blighter had given it to me exclusive, I might have done
something about it. But he told me he was giving it to every
editor he knew in the Street."

" Had he got a girl with him?" I asked eagerly.

" No." He glanced at me. " Why, has he got the Schmidt
girl in tow?"

" Evidently not," I said, a trifle sharply. " Anyway, what's
his story?"

" There's trouble brewing up at the Calboyd works. Apparently the board has been unlucky enough to pick execu-
tives who think more of their country than they do of their
firm. Anyway, under the leadership of this fellow Raikes,
who is missing, they went in a deputation to the directors two

weeks ago. Apparently one of them has produced an engine
that gives a good deal better performance than the much-
vaunted Dragon, which is the one chosen by the Air Ministry
for mass production. The deputation pointed out that the
Dragon was not the best Diesel engine the country could
produce. It seems that not only is there this engine, which
one of their own number has designed, but they recently
tested, without the knowledge of the directors, an engine
taken from a new type of German bomber, and found it
definitely superior to the Dragon. They suggested that the
board should offer the Air Ministry a new and superior
engine. The suggestion was refused on the grounds that it
would all take time and that what they were interested in was
getting the contract. Since then Raikes has disappeared and
the whole of the technical staff is in a ferment."

"Will any of this get into print?" I asked.

"Oh, yes, I think so." He crossed over to his desk and
came back with a telegram. "As soon as Shiel had given me
his story, I sent one of our men straight off to Oldham.
Here's his initial report."

He handed me the telegram. It read: INFORMATION OKAY
STOP TECHNICAL STAFF MET TO-DAY THREATEN STRIKE
STOP NO NEWS RAIKES STOP FULL STORY FOLLOWING—
MELLERS.

"How many papers will print the story to-morrow morning?" I asked.

"Every one that David Shiel has been to. It just can't be
hushed up. Most of the others, too, will have something
from their Manchester correspondents following the fall in
Calboyd shares on Friday."

"Fine!" I said. I was filled with a sudden sense of elation.
If pressure were brought to bear by the press, it was just
possible that the Government might be forced to act.
"Listen," I said. "You'll want a follow-up to that story.
Why not use some of what I've told you?"

"See here, Andrew," Fisher said, "there is a limit. Calboyds is one thing, but Marburg is quite another. I haven't
doubted you, which is more than most men would have
done. Your story is fantastic enough to be true. But I'm
not running my head into a noose. This engine you speak of

may be all Schmidt says it is. On the other hand, it may not. You yourself don't know. You haven't tested it. I don't know. And I'm certainly not going to pretend I do."

"I quite understand how you feel about Marburg," I said. "As for the engine, I agree with you—I haven't the faintest idea what its performance really is. All I know is that Nazi agents find it worth their while to go out after him. And that's good enough for me." I leaned towards him. "What's your splash to-morrow? If the dailies are going to run Calboyds, you've got to have some sort of a follow-up, if you're to sell your paper. I suggest you send a man to Bude. Get a detailed description of the missing Raikes, and I've got a hunch that he'll be able to identify the body that is supposed to be mine. If he can, then there's your story. Trouble at Calboyds—Raikes, the ringleader, killed—Body mistaken for that of Andrew Kilmartin—— Then my story. You can churn the stuff out in relays all through the day."

"If this body proves to be Raikes's," he murmured doubtfully.

"Even if it doesn't, you've still got my story. I was news yesterday." I saw his hesitation. "Look here, Fisher," I said. "I brought you this story because I know you. If you don't want it, say so. I haven't any too much time to spare. And if you don't want it, maybe the *Globe* would take it."

"Wait a minute, wait a minute. Who said I didn't want it? I'm only just chewing over it, old boy." Suddenly he seemed to make up his mind. He took a notebook from his desk and seated himself in an easy-chair by the fire. "All right, let's have it in detail, roughly as you think it ought to appear. Only don't go too fast because my shorthand isn't what it used to be."

I glanced at my watch. It was past one. "Perhaps if I could have a few sandwiches or something," I said. "I've got to get over to the *Thirlmere* service. I'm meeting an old fellow down at Wapping at two-thirty who is going to row me across to the neighbouring wharf."

Fisher rang the bell by the fireplace. "Well, I can help you there," he said. "I've got an invitation card. I wasn't sending anyone, so there it is, if you want it. You're about my height. I can rig you out in a suit." The door opened and a manservant appeared. "Light lunch for two at about one-thirty, Parkes. And put out some clothes of mine suitable for this gentleman to wear as a representative of the press. Now," he said, as the manservant closed the door, "go ahead."

Chapter Nine

THE MUNITION SHIP "THIRLMERE"

WILSON'S WREN Wharf is on the south side of the river, in Rortherhithe. My taxi set me down in a narrow, dusty street lined with warehouses. On a week-day, I had no doubt, the street would have been full of the movement of wagons and vans as the hand-cranes loaded the contents of the warehouses for transport. But now the cranes were folded back against the blackened brick of the buildings, which ran, uniform in height and appearance, the whole length of the street. In the bright wintry sunshine the place presented an appearance of desolation that the gleaming line of parked cars only served to accentuate.

It was just on three as I walked through the archway beneath one of the warehouses and caught my first glimpse of the *Thirlmere*, her superstructure and funnels towering over the concrete wharf. Iron-barred gates guarded the entrance to the wharf and here my pass was scrutinised. There were several policemen standing about, but I could see no one who was likely to recognise me. I was passed through in the wake of a party of three, whom I judged by their conversation at the gates to be industrialists. All were dressed in sporting clothes—probably they had spent the morning playing golf. Dressed as I was in an old tweed suit of Fisher's, this was to my advantage, and, as I crossed the wharf, I closed the distance, so that, as I climbed the gangway to the deck of the *Thirlmere*, I was close behind them. It was well that I did so. At the head of the gangway two volunteers for Finland stood guard with fixed bayonets. They were dressed in mufti, but wore armlets. As I stepped on to the deck of the ship, my eyes, which I had kept lowered,

noticed the hand of the left-hand guard as it held his rifle.
Across the knuckles ran a thin white scar. For a second my
heart leapt to my throat. I expected to hear the rattle of the
rifle being raised and the sound of a challenge. Then I was
walking along the deck in the wake of the three industrialists,
who were talking audibly of Russia, and I knew that my
fears had been groundless. Dressed in brown tweeds with a
virulent yellow tie and a green pork-pie hat, it was hardly to
be expected that a fellow who had seen me only three times
in his life, and always in the sober garb of my profession,
should recognise me. Besides, when I had shaved, I had
left my upper lip. My beard is of the fast-growing variety,
and though I had only been without a shave for just over
fifty hours, my moustache was already quite a healthy one.
At the same time, I had allowed myself rather long side pieces
and had acquired a pair of glasses.

The *Thirlmere* was a Norwegian ship designed specifically
for the transport of locomotives and railway rolling stock.
Doubtless she had been chosen for this particular job because
she was a handy vessel for a difficult cargo. But I fancied
there was another reason also. She had the necessary winch
gear for loading and unloading under her own steam locomotives weighing many tons. If necessary, she would be
able to unload the Calboyd torpedo boat at sea. I could see
no sign of this boat as I came on board. But I noticed that a
cradle had been rigged up at the after end of the big well
deck, and presumed that the boat had still to come aboard.
Flat against the poop stood the great girder to which
rolling stock was slung, and beneath it, on the well deck, eight
tanks were parked, shoulder to shoulder, and lashed down
with thick wire hawsers. They were coated thick with grease
to protect them against the salt spray. About a dozen more
stood on the wharf. Presumably they had been left until after
the service, so that there was room to hold the ceremony in
the well deck.

It was in this deep well deck that the crowd was gathering,
facing for'ard towards the bridge. Before mingling with it, I
glanced quickly towards the neighbouring wharf. Two black
figures were seated on the base of one of the cranes and an
empty rowing boat bobbed at the foot of a wooden ladder.
I felt a twinge of conscience. Beyond the Percivale Banana

Company's wharf the river curved away towards Limehouse Reach, a broad expanse of sluggish water lined with empty wharves. No traffic moved and few ships were berthed along the huddled banks. Only barges jostled each other as they strained to the turning tide.

My gaze turned to the bridge of the *Thirlmere*. On it stood two clergymen in their white surplices and several frock-coated gentlemen, among whom I recognised Sir James Calboyd, a young-looking elderly man, with a very shiny top hat over his silvery hair and a rather ostentatious monocle. Directly beneath the bridge the choir stood facing us, and a little to one side an elderly man sat bowed over a harmonium. Glancing round amongst the crowd, which was a queer mixture of morning-dress and sports clothes, I caught sight of Sedel's short puffy figure. He was standing amongst a group of frock-coated individuals, but I saw that, though he was talking most of the time, his little eyes were darting here and there amongst the crowd. I moved as far away from him as I could. I fancied that if my eyes at any time met his, my disguise would be pierced at once. I had barely taken up my new position when the old man at the harmonium came to life. Then Baron Ferdinand Marburg, accompanied by the Finnish minister, came out on to the bridge. As he reached the front of it, he removed his hat. His sleek, well-groomed hair gleamed in the sunlight. At once the buzz of conversation ceased. All eyes were fixed upon that massive, black-coated figure. Cameras clicked and the faint whirr of the news cameras could be heard. In that instant Marburg dominated the whole scene. That great head with its thick black eyebrows and square jaw was striking enough beneath the sleek black hair. But, as ever, it was the eyes that drew the gaze of everyone. For one moment those deep-set sockets were alive, as he took in the scene before him, and then the heavy eyelids had hooded them and that powerful face might have been cut in stone for all the life that showed in it.

Then the service started. It did not take long. A stirring hymn, a few prayers for Finland, and finally the dedication. And when all the deadly cargo of that ship had been dedicated to the service of God, Marburg addressed the assembly. I cannot remember what he said. In print it would not, I fancy, seem inspired. In fact, what he said was probably quite banal. It was the man himself who held that crowd spellbound. Not because his eloquence gripped them, not because he wrung tears of pity from them on Finland's behalf, but because of the power he radiated. His great sombre voice boomed out across the bows of that ill-fated ship, even and monotonous, but with a terrible sense of the power of the speaker. I remember only one sentence. " I am going to Finland myself on this ship," he said, " to see how desperate things are and what must be done." And the impression left was that the Russian forces would melt away at the speaker's arrival.

And when he had finished, there was a deathly silence. It was broken by the usual British enthusiasm for cheers. And so they cheered Baron Ferdinand Marburg on his way to Germany, and I stood there silent, wondering what the hell I was going to do about it.

Two things I had discovered since I had come on board. The first was that the volunteers were, as I had suspected, Marburg's own picked men. The second was that Marburg was sailing with the *Thirlmere*. That could only mean one of two things—either this was his planned exit, or it meant that his position was getting precarious. I hoped it was the latter, for then something might result from my visit to Fisher. Apart from using the statement I had given him as the basis for a story, he had promised to have copies made straight away. One was to be sent to the Chief Commissioner and another to the Air Minister himself. " If all this is true," Fisher had said, " there are bound to be some loose threads somewhere. There always are in any big move of this sort. No one knows anything about it, until someone turns up to give the show away, and then all the little pieces fall into place. And the loose threads, the pieces of the jig-saw, will either be in the hands of the police or in the hands of the Intelligence." That had seemed the best I could do. Fisher was Scot enough to be obstinate once he got an idea into his head. I had not made the mistake of trying to plead the truth of my statement as though I needed to defend it. I had just told it simply to him and left him to judge its truth.

But, as I stood on that crowded well deck, looking up at the impassive mask-like features of Marburg, I wondered whether there was not something else I could do. I felt the

need for action. I felt the need to go to someone in authority
—the Chief Commissioner, for instance, or a member of the
Cabinet—and get them to act. But I knew that, because I
could convince a man like Fisher, it did not necessarily mean
that I could convince a Cabinet minister or a policeman.
Fisher was a newspaper man. In him the will to believe was
there, for it was a story. But anyone in authority would be
unwilling to believe something that placed upon his already
overweighted shoulders further responsibility. And though
I felt the need for action, I knew that it was best left to
Fisher. The best I could hope for myself would be that they
would believe me. Action was another matter, and would
only be reluctantly taken after everything had been checked
and re-checked. But Fisher, with a powerful newspaper
behind him, could demand action and, because of the threat
of publicity, might be able to get it. I had left him in a state
of growing excitement. "It's terrific, Kilmartin," he had
said, as he handed me the ten pound notes I had asked for.
"I'll get on to Sir John Kelf—he's our proprietor, you know.
He'll start things moving and we'll get action in no time."

I could only hope he was right. In just over twenty-four
hours the *Thirlmere* would be steaming down the Thames.
It seemed short enough time in which to get action. True,
the *Thirlmere* would have a naval escort as far as Norwegian
territorial waters. That gave them another twelve hours, or
perhaps a little more, in which to make up their minds. In
all they had, perhaps, a little over thirty-six hours. Even as
I arrived at this conclusion, the Finnish minister closed his
speech amidst tumultuous cheers and Lord Waign began
to speak on behalf of the British Government. And thirty-
six hours seemed short enough. I had no illusions on the
matter. The chances of Government action were remote, even
though Fisher and Sir John Kelf used every endeavour to
obtain at least the detention of the *Thirlmere* and an inquiry.
The Government had given their blessing to this enterprise.
And Marburg and his friends could pull strings. What,
against these weighty considerations, was the fantastic statement of a K.C., however famous, who had first been reported
dead and who, though now miraculously come to life, had
nevertheless sent a ridiculous statement to the Yard only two
days ago.

It was in a state of utter depression that, at the end of the ceremony, I wandered aft with the rest of the gathering. The captain, at the close of the affair, had given everyone the freedom of the decks, but had announced in broken English that, in view of the fact that this was a munitions ship, he had orders to allow no one below decks.

I found myself examining the powerful winch gear with a little sharp-featured man. His restless eyes met mine. "You press?" he asked. I nodded. "What do you think of this for a bloody silly business? Every editor in the Street is yelling his head off for pro-Finnish stuff. And now when a story with a big British angle breaks, everything is frightfully hush-hush. 'MacPherson,' my news editor says to me, 'there's a grand story here.' Grand story be damned! A lot of pious publicity-seeking drivel from Marburg. A lot more drivel from yon Finn. And we're not allowed below decks. How the hell do they expect one to get a good background story? I want to see for myself what they've got."

I did not think he was being reasonable and said so. "You can't expect them to allow a crowd like this to wander all over the ship. But Marburg knows the value of publicity. If several of us applied to him to-morrow for permission to look round, I expect we'd get it."

At that he gave a short laugh. "What the devil's the good of a permit to-morrow, when the ship sails to-night?"

We were walking round the stern of the ship and I checked in my stride. "Sailing to-night?" I asked.

"Yes. Can't you see they've got steam up? All they're waiting for is the torpedo boat. I happen to understand Norwegian and I heard the captain discussing the sailing with his mate. They leave with the ebb."

I felt a sudden void in my stomach. Why the change of plan? The answer seemed plain enough, but it brought me little joy. Things might not be going too well for them. In the circumstances they might well consider that my escape made it essential to get under way as soon as possible. But because they advanced their sailing date by twenty-four hours, it did not mean that Government action was imminent. In less than six hours the tide would be on the ebb and the *Thirlmere* would be outward bound. Within a little more than twenty hours the ship would reach Germany. I could not believe that Fisher and Kelf would get Government action on a Sunday evening. And by dawn to-morrow the *Thirlmere* would be pounding her way towards Norwegian territorial waters. By midday she would be shot of her naval escort. The void in my stomach was caused by the knowledge that if I wanted action I should have to provide it myself. I had a vivid picture of myself standing over the hold with a hand grenade in my hand, threatening to toss it amongst the cargo of high explosives, and I was wondering whether I should ever be able to summon up the courage to drop it if my bluff were called.

My companion had been talking and I suddenly caught the drift of his conversation. "There she is coming up the river now," he was saying. "Perhaps we'll see something interesting after all. It's the first time old Petersen has shipped a boat on board one of his ships. Have you ever seen them loading up with locomotives?" I shook my head. We had climbed the iron ladder to the poop and I was peering past one of the lifeboats to see the sharp bows of a torpedo boat creaming the water brown as she ran smoothly up the centre of the river. "It's an extraordinary sight," he went on. "The whole ship cants as the winch gear swings it on board. They shove the locomotives down in the hold. It's specially constructed for that purpose. Then for the rolling stock, rails are run lengthways across the whole of this well deck and the carriages or trucks are lashed to its rails. By Jove! there's someone going down into the hold. There, just below the bridge. See that little iron trapdoor?" I was just in time to see the head and shoulders of one of the crew disappearing below the level of the brief fo'c'sle deck.

At the time I took little notice of this incident, for the torpedo boat was rapidly approaching the *Thirlmere* and it was there my interest lay. The crowd, which had already thinned out, was lining the bulwarks of the well deck, peering down the river. The torpedo boat came up fast with the tide, swung in a wide circle and nosed up alongside the *Thirlmere*, the propeller creaming the water at her stern as she maintained way against the flow of the tide. Ropes were flung and she was made fast. The engine, quietly running, had a familiar sound, and I remembered the white-painted *Sea Spray* chugging out from Porthgwarra. It seemed incredible

to think that this was the same engine. In place of the white
friendly lines of the *Sea Spray* was the dull grey menacing
hull of this small warship. Over the pointed bows showed
the muzzle of a small gun, and on either side of the short
mast were multiple anti-aircraft pom-poms. Astern was the
depth charge apparatus, and doubtless below the level of the
water would be a torpedo tube.

In appearance, the boat was a warship. And as I stood
there in the cold sunlight I had a feeling of admiration for
the man who had planned this method of removing a secret
Diesel engine from the country. Looking at that devilish little
craft, bristling with armaments, no one would give any
attention to its engine. The boat was a Calboyd product and
would, of course, be fitted with a Calboyd Dragon engine.
Who was there to realise that that engine spelt disaster for
one or other of two warring nations! Well, there was myself.
And I was helpless. Should I stand up here on the poop and
tell the press that installed in that boat was an engine that
revolutionised aero engine production? Should I tell them
that the *Thirlmere* was not bound for Finland at all, but for
Germany, and that the volunteers were in reality Nazi
agents? I could just imagine the laughter that would greet
this denunciation, and the good-humoured comments as those
same agents marched me ashore. Or there might be angry
cries as the crowd denounced me for a communist. No, it
was useless. I should achieve nothing that way. The stage
had been too well set. Denunciations would only recoil upon
the head of the denunciator.

Sailors had now climbed on to the poop and with a clatter
the steam winches came to life. Slowly the great steel girder
used for lifting locomotives and rolling stock was swung
clear of the deck. Cloth-bound rope slings were attached to
each end and the girder was swung out over the side of the
Thirlmere and lowered until it was only a few feet above
the boat, whose mast had been lowered.

For a time I became absorbed in the efforts of the crew
of the boat to get the slings into position beneath the keel. I
think it was the sound of a camera that made me turn.
Almost directly behind me, one of the news-cameramen was
taking shots of the man operating the steam winch. He was
squatting on his heels, his broad back bent over his camera,

which was lodged on a bollard. I was just turning away to see how the men on board the torpedo boat had progressed with their task, when he rose to his feet. Something about his figure made me hesitate. Then, as he picked up his camera and turned to find a new vantage point, I knew who he was.

"David!" I exclaimed.

He started and then stared at me as though I were a ghost. For a moment both of us were too surprised to speak. "Good God!" he said. "It really is you, isn't it?"

"It certainly is," I replied. "What are you doing here? And what's the news, David? Where's Freya? There's a whole heap of questions I want to ask you."

"And there's a whole heap I want to ask you," he said. His eyes glanced furtively in the direction of the bridge. "I'm going to take shots from the stern," he added, bending to adjust the mechanism of his camera. "If the coast is clear, drop down and have a few words in a minute. They're keeping an eye on me."

I turned back and resumed my interest in the settling of the slings under the torpedo boat. They had managed to get the for'ard sling in position now. But I barely took in the scene below. My whole mind was concentrated on the fact of David's presence. I heard him climb down the ladder on to the after deck. I glanced towards the bridge and caught my breath. Sedel was standing on the fo'c'sle. He was by himself and he seemed to be staring straight at me. I looked down again at the figures moving in the boat below. Had Sedel seen us talking? Was David really suspect, and if so, why was the fool on board the *Thirlmere* at all? These and many other questions raced through my mind, and I was conscious all the time of my companion's curiosity. But he had the self-control not to ask questions.

A seaman on the afterdeck suddenly raised his hand and the steam winches broke into clattering activity. The torpedo boat, now slung firmly below the girder, rose slowly from the water. Soon its decks were level with the poop on which we were standing and I could see its keel, with the water dripping from it. I glanced for'ard. Sedel had disappeared. Everyone's attention seemed riveted on the torpedo boat. I climbed down on to the afterdeck and joined David, who was taking shots of the boat's stern as it rose above the deck level.

He did not pause in his work or look up. "Thank God you're all right, Andrew," he said. "When I saw that story in the evening papers yesterday I thought they must have got you."

"So they did," I said. "But I escaped."

"Well, they're after me, too," he said. "That's why you mustn't be seen talking to me. I've been under observation ever since I came on board."

"Then why the devil did you come?"

"I wanted to find out what had happened to Freya. And I'm going to find out before I leave this ship, if I have to break every bone in Marburg's great carcass."

"Freya," I cried, with a sudden horrible fear. "They haven't got Freya, have they?"

"Afraid so," he said laconically.

I was on the point of cursing him. But he seemed to sense my condemnation, for he said, "I'm sorry, Andrew. I ought to have been more careful. I think they trailed me down from Calboyds. I arrived back at Guilford Street about nine yesterday morning with a pretty hot story, to find Freya in a terrible state of emotional turmoil. You were missing, and she had discovered her father was still alive. There had been a message for Olwyn in the personal column of the *Daily Telegraph* that morning. He had suggested a meeting place in Billingsgate, of all places, and we had just time to make the appointment. Yes, it was genuine, all right. I've never seen two people so overjoyed at seeing each other again. Freya told the old boy about your disappearance. He was very upset. He gave us the low-down on the whole thing then. Do you realise who is behind this business, Andrew?"

"For goodness' sake come to the point, David," I said. "What's happened to Freya?"

"But this is the point, old boy. The man behind this business is Baron Marburg, the banker."

"I know that," I said, losing my patience. "This munitions for Finland story is a ramp and there, in that boat, is Schmidt's precious engine. But what's happened to Freya?"

"I'm sorry, Andrew." He was apologetic. "I don't know. We left old Schmidt in Fish Street shortly after eleven yes-

erday morning. I left Freya to pick up an '18' bus and
ook the District to Westminster. That's the last I saw of
er. She never reached Guilford Street."

" And you went to see your godfather?"

"Correct. And the old boy listened open-mouthed."

" And pigeon-holed your story as soon as the door was
losed?"

David hesitated. " No, I don't think so. He certainly
idn't believe me when I brought Marburg's name into it.
Schmidt could give no very convincing evidence. But I think
e believed what I told him about Calboyds and about the
tealing of the engine, and I fancy he'll try and do some-
hing. But I am afraid he found my accusations about the
Thirlmere business as difficult to swallow as those about
Marburg."

" But you don't think anything will be done in time?" I
aid.

" Afraid not. At best they'll be slow to reach a decision.
But the other side is getting rattled. They've advanced the
ailing schedule by twenty-four hours, and Marburg himself
as suddenly decided to sail with the ship."

" And you come galloping like Saint George right into
he dragon's mouth," I said. " Man, what dam'-fool game
re you playing? Are you aiming to try and blow the ship
p, or what?"

" No—to rescue Freya," was the reply.

My heart leapt. " Is she on board?"

" Yes, she was brought on board in a tank in the early
ours of the morning."

" In a tank!" I exploded. " Why in a tank?"

" Well, it's unobtrusive, isn't it? One of the tanks was
riven on board by a volunteer and she was inside it."

" But how do you know?"

" Her father told me. He's got a berth as something in the
galley. Knows a Jewish export firm that has a pull with
he captain. That's an incredible little man, Andrew. He
ooks so shabby and nondescript, until you meet his eyes.
Where do you think he went to earth? At the Calboyd Power
Boat yard at Tilbury. Got a job as a fitter."

" But why didn't he come and see me on the Monday?" I
asked.

T.T.H.   F

" The chase was getting too hot. He had no more information to give you, and he thought that if he disappeared, you'd be more inclined to treat the matter seriously and do what you could. He didn't know, of course, that most of the information had been pinched from us. Another thing, he thought that sooner or later the *Sea Spray* would be discovered at Porthgwarra, and he guessed they'd bring it up to the Calboyd works. When that happened, he wanted to be on the spot, in order either to destroy it, or to get it away. Do you know he nearly succeeded? The night after it arrived, he started a fire in a corner of the works. The police guard on the *Sea Spray* came ashore and he went aboard. As soon as he had started down river, Sedel's men were after him in a power boat. Unfortunately, he knew nothing about the special valve Freya had put in, and he couldn't open the engine out. He hadn't a chance, so he ran her full tilt into a pier and sank her. He only just managed . . ." David's eyes suddenly became riveted on the far side of the poop. " We're being watched," he whispered.

I glanced round. One of the volunteers was coming down on to the after deck. I became interested in the lower.ng of the torpedo boat amidships and climbed back over the poop. David had given me plenty to think about. And the focus of all my thoughts was Freya. Why had she been captured? And why had she been brought aboard the *Thirlmere*? Did they want her as a hostage? Or—and then I knew the reason. She was the bait. They were taking his engine to Germany. But what was the good of that if the man who knew the formula of the special alloy and who had designed it was still in England? Not only had they got Schmidt on board, whether they knew it or not, but they had got the only other two people who could really testify that an engine of outstanding performance had passed into German hands. I paused in the midst of clambering over the maze of winch machinery. My journalist friend was no longer standing against the deck rail of the poop. And down on the well deck the crowd was gathered about the torpedo boat which was being lowered on to its cradle. I was just on the point of descending to the well deck, when I heard a dull thud behind me from the after deck. Almost simultaneously there was a low cry, and this was followed by the sound of

metal striking metal. I was very close to the deck rail here
and instinctively I leaned over the side, thinking someone
might have fallen overboard. I was just in time to see what
looked like a square bright lump of metal fall into the water
with a splash. The ripples were already beginning to fade
before I realised that what I had seen fall into the water was
news-camera.

In an instant I had leapt across the huddle of machinery
and was staring down at an empty after deck.

David was nowhere to be seen. I had no illusions as to
what had happened. I remembered the volunteer who had
been hovering on the starboard side of the fo'c'sle. Doubtless
he had been waiting his chance.

Then I became conscious of shouts from the neighbouring
dock, and I could have laughed. The agent had bided his
time and when David had actually been knocked out, there
had been no one on the after deck and the man had doubtless
thought, with some reason, that anyone overlooking the ship
from the other side of the Thames would not notice the
blow even if they did see a man collapse. But he had forgotten Alf Higgins sitting quietly with his missis on the
Percivale Banana Company's wharf. The old man had
advanced to the barrier dividing the two docks and was
calling for the police and yelling at the top of his voice that a
man had been assaulted on the after deck.

Not desiring to be picked out as a possible witness, I turned
and climbed down to the well deck, where I mingled with the
crowd, which was now lining the starboard bulwarks and
peering down at the wharf. A few minutes later Alf Higgins
was brought on board by two policemen. The captain was
summoned and he went aft to make inquiries. In a minute
he was back again to say that it was quite correct, one of the
camera-men had fainted. "He is in the fo'c'sle," he told the
police. "The ship's doctor, he is attending to him."

This, however, did not content Alf Higgins, who swore
that he had seen the man struck by one of the crew. Where-
upon, one of the policemen, a sergeant, went aft to investi-
gate. A few minutes later he returned to announce that he
had seen the gent and that he was suffering from a slight
stroke. When the old man insisted that he had seen the
fellow assaulted, the policemen gently took him by the arms

and marched him down the gangway, the sergeant suggesting that he had been on the booze.

"It was Shiel, wasn't it?" said a voice at my elbow.

I started, and turned to find the journalist, MacPherson just behind me. "Yes," I said. "How did you know?"

"He used to do a certain amount of photographic work for the *Globe*," was the reply. Then the fellow added, "Seems funny that he should have a stroke. I shouldn't have thought Shiel was the sort of man to suffer from strokes."

"He isn't," I said. "He was knocked out by one of these volunteers."

"But what the hell for?"

"Ah," I said. "If I told you, I don't think you'd believe me."

"You could try me," he suggested with a grin.

"I will, on one condition," I said.

"What's that?"

"That you go straight from here to Sir Geoffrey Carr of the Home Office. David Shiel is his godson. Explain what has happened and tell him that David is a prisoner on board the *Thirlmere*. Only if you're to do any good you must run Carr to earth within three hours—that is before the ship sails. Will you do that?"

"Yes, I'll do that. Now what's the story that I won't believe if told?"

I hesitated, wondering how he would take it. I had no desire to make him incredulous. If he found Carr before the *Thirlmere* sailed it was just possible that the ship might be delayed whilst the police searched it. "This ship isn't going to Finland," I said. "As soon as it is in Norwegian territorial waters and no longer has a British naval escort watching over it, the volunteers will take control and the ship will alter course for Germany."

MacPherson was staring at me. "But why?" he demanded.

"Because the volunteers are all Nazis. Because that fellow Sedel is a Nazi. Because Marburg himself is a Nazi. But above all, because inside that torpedo boat is not a Calboyd Dragon engine, but an engine made of a new alloy which is being spirited out of this country to Germany."

"It's fantastic," he said.

I laughed. I must have sounded a trifle bitter. "I told you you wouldn't believe me," I said.

He looked straight at me for a moment, his eyes meeting and holding mine. Suddenly he said, "On the contrary I do believe you. The whole thing is much too fantastic not to be true. Can I have any more details?"

"Well, I don't know," I said, suddenly remembering that the *Globe* was the *Record*'s great rival. "You see, I've been working on the matter for Fisher of the *Record*. I think I've said enough. I'll give you a tip, though. The *Record* will be running this to-morrow. I've told you what I have because my desire for Government action to prevent the ship reaching Germany comes before my desire to get a scoop for the *Record*."

"Okay, pal. Thanks for the tip. And I'll see that Carr hears about David Shiel."

I watched him disappear down the gangway with a feeling that at least I was maintaining the initiative. That pleased me, for in other respects the outlook was grim enough. The crowd was beginning to drift away now that there was nothing of interest to hold them. I hesitated. If I remained on board much longer I should become conspicuous. On the other hand, once I passed out through the gates of the wharf, I should never get back to the *Thirlmere* unless it was with a squad of police and a search warrant. And there was David unconscious in the poop and Freya somewhere else on board. I could not just walk off the ship and leave them to their fate. It wasn't as though I could do anything, either in Whitehall or at the Yard. I had to leave that to Fisher and myself in any case.

It did not take me long to make up my mind. I must maintain the initiative and I decided to tackle Marburg. Looking back on it, I cannot imagine what I expected to achieve. I had not prepared my brief. I was going to face him and leave it to the inspiration of the moment to decide what I was going to say. With this intention, I climbed the iron deck ladder to the fo'c'sle. I then crossed to the port side, which seemed the easiest approach to the bridge. In doing so, I passed the trapdoor leading to the hold. It was open, a small square hole in the deck plates, with barely room for a

man to squeeze through. A rifle stood against the supe
structure of the bridge. Presumably one of the voluntee
guarding this entrance to the hold had found it necessary
go down. I hesitated, peering down it. All I could see w.
the top of an iron ladder. The rest was blackness.

I glanced quickly about me. No one appeared to be ove
looking the fo'c'sle. Quickly I dropped to the deck an
lowered my feet into the opening A second later they four
the rungs of the ladder and I had disappeared below th
level of the deck. I paused for a moment, to discover wheth
my movements had been noticed. But there was no outcr
and I began to clamber quietly down. Somewhere below, n
doubt, was the guard. As I clambered down dirty rung aft
dirty rung, I kept on peering below, expecting to see the lig
of a torch. But all was dark, and the smell of stale oil wa
very strong.

Suddenly a light flashed below me. Then the framewor
of the ladder began to shake as someone began to climb. Th
guard! My heart leapt to my throat. For a second I was
a panic. The man had only to glance upward to see me
silhouette against the square light of the trapdoor. If
climbed back to the deck, he was sure to see me and
remembered what had happened to David. If I faced hir
the odds were about even—he probably had a revolver, bu
I had the advantage of being uppermost on the ladder. B
even if I were able to kick him from his hold before he fire
his absence would be noticed. All these thoughts race
through my mind in an instant, and at the same moment
leant away from the ladder and thrust out my hand. Ther
was wood there, cases by the feel of it. Ammunition case
probably.

At that thought I began to climb quietly upwards, on
hand outstretched, feeling the cases. The ship was suppose
to be carrying more tanks than those I had seen on the we
deck and the wharf. If they were stowed in the hold on to
of the ammunition. . . . I had climbed to the height of fiv
cases when suddenly my hand encountered a void. I fe
about. There was nothing within reach. I had been righ
The hold was not stowed to the deck plates with ammunitio
boxes. I turned, put my hands on the last of the cases an
drew my feet from the ladder.

A second later the guard climbed past where I lay on top of the cases. Then the trapdoor closed with a clang and I was in complete darkness. I felt about me with my hands. The cases presented a level surface running back from the ladder. I rose to my feet, and though I had moved carefully, I nearly brained myself against a piece of jutting metal. For a moment I crouched on my knees, nursing my head in agony. Then I pulled out a small torch I had borrowed from Fisher.

No wonder I had hurt my head. I had struck it on the caterpillar tractors of a large tank. In the pale light of the torch the monstrous machine reared above me to the deck-plates. Next to it was another, and beyond that I made out a third. I crawled between them and then rose to my feet. The clumsy-looking monsters were ranged five abreast across the hold and attached by steel hawsers to girders which ran below the deck plates. There were ten of them altogether, and behind them were Spitfires with their wings stacked against the side of the hold.

Freya had been brought aboard in a tank. She might have been left in it. It was the safest place to hide a prisoner. I remembered my own experience of being trussed up in a steel container and made haste to locate her. It took me some time to visit each one, tapping against its steel plates and calling out her name.

When I had contacted every one without result, I came to the conclusion that either she was not there, or else she was bound and gagged so firmly that she could not even tap in reply. Perhaps she was unconscious. At the thought I felt a sudden surge of anger through my veins—not at Marburg, but at Sedel. The man was a fiend, and I could well believe the pleasure it would give him to hurt a woman.

I realised then that if Freya were in one of those tanks, the only way I could discover her was by getting into each one. That was a lengthy job, and before starting on it, I decided to go down the ladder and see what was at the bottom of it. The guard must have had some reason for going down there. As I swung myself on to the ladder, there was a sudden tremendous noise overhead. It grew louder until it was pounding on the deck plates above my head. It continued for a moment and then ceased. It was some

moments before I realised what is was. They were bringing
the tanks from the wharf on board.

I began to descend the ladder just as the next one came
on board. The ladder was set in a kind of recess in the
bulkhead, so that with the munition cases flush with the
bulkhead proper, it descended what was virtually a small
square well. At the bottom I found a massive steel door. It
required all my strength to slide this back. When at length
I got through, I found myself facing more munition cases.
Presumably this was No. 1 hold. There was no ladder here,
but a rope hung down the wall of cases that faced me. I
glanced up. The cases were stacked to within little more
than a foot of the deck plates.

I went back into the main hold and, after closing the
bulkhead door, climbed back up the ladder. I felt certain
there was no hold aft. The space beyond the after bulkhead
would be taken up by the engine-room. There was only one
thing to do. I should have to search each of those tanks,
and the planes, if necessary.

Chapter Ten

OFF OUR COURSE

BY THE time I had finished examining those tanks the *Thirlmere* was under way. It was past eight now and I was
hungry, dirty and dispirited. I had found no trace of Freya.
Presumably she had been removed to another h ding place.
It had not been easy to make the search thorough, for in
some cases the hatches were difficult to open and some were
tucked under steel girders so that I had scarcely been able
to squeeze myself inside. However, I had managed to search
thoroughly every tank, and now I sat on the back of the
one nearest the ladder and wondered what the next move
was.

The hold was very hot and everything seemed to pulse to
the rhythmic throb of the engines. Shortly after eight-thirty
we hove to for a while. The silence seemed uncanny. But it
only lasted for about a quarter of an hour. I did not know

it at the time, but the *Thirlmere* had stopped for the River
Police. MacPherson of the *Globe* had kept his word, and off
Gravesend the police made a hurried search of the ship for
David Shiel. On Baron Marburg's assurance that David had
left as soon as he had recovered—an assurance that was
corroborated by the evidence of three of the volunteers, who
swore they had seen him go down the gangway—the police
left.

The next stop was at about nine-thirty off the Nore. This
was for the purpose of picking up our escort, a destroyer of
the Dover patrol. Thereafter the engines pounded away
unceasingly, the whole ship vibrating as she forged ahead at
her full ten knots.

I had made up my mind to wait until the early hours of
the morning, and then to go up on deck and try to contact
Schmidt. Events, however, were rather taken out of my
hands. Shortly after ten the trapdoor was opened and a man
with a flashlight descended. In one hand he carried what
looked like a mess tin. I was certain of this when the light
of his torch suddenly flashed full on it and showed me the
handle of a spoon or fork sticking out of it.

He climbed down to the bottom of the ladder and, peering
from the top of the munition cases, I saw him pass through
the door into No. 1 hold. He was gone about ten minutes.
When he returned, he still had the mess tin, but by the
way the spoon in it rattled, I gathered it was now empty. As
he passed me, I saw he wore the armlet of a volunteer. It
was with a beating heart that I swung myself on to the ladder
as soon as the trapdoor was shut. At the bottom I pulled
open the bulkhead door and passed into the for'ard hold.
The rope, I noticed, was not hanging in quite the same position as I had seen it before. After closing the bulkhead door
behind me and fixing my torch to one of the buttons of
my jacket, I swung myself up on the rope.

The gap between the top of the munition cases and the
deck plates was bigger than it had seemed from the bottom
of the hold. In all there must have been the better part of
three feet clearance. I went forward on hands and knees.
Every now and then I had to duck for a steel girder. At last
the beam of my torch showed me the for'ard end of the hold.
There was no sign of Freya or of any case that might con-

tain her. Yet I was certain she was here somewhere. Well
there was only one place she could be and that was in one
of the cases across which I was crawling. I examined the
one I was kneeling on. It was iron-bound, and fitted flush
to the next. The probability was that when I found the right
one I should only have to lift the lid. A lock would have
showed.

I must have spent the better part of an hour crawling over
those cases, and at length I lay down on my back from sheer
exhaustion. My shoulders ached with crouching in that
cramped position and my knees were sore. I had tapped and
pulled at the tops of countless cases. I had called her name.
All in vain. And now I had only about ten feet to go to the
for'ard end of the hold. And I had a feeling that those ten
feet would yield no more than the rest. I was conscious, too,
of the fact that I should by now be thinking of how to
contact Schmidt and David, and what we were going to do to
prevent the ship reaching Germany.

I decided to finish my search of the hold as quickly as
possible and then try my luck on deck. I had half risen to
my feet, when a grating sound checked me. The bulkhead
door was being slid back. I looked wildly about me. There
was no cover on those cases. I scrambled quickly to a position against the for'ard bulkhead. I slid along it to the
corner, and waited, breathing hard.

But though the glow of a torch showed above the top of
the cases, the rope was not pulled taut and no one appeared
to be climbing to my hiding-place. The soft murmur of a
voice reached me. I crawled across the munition cases.
Suddenly I recognised the voice and stiffened. It was Sedel's.
I went on until I could actually peer over the top of the cases.
Sedel and one of the volunteers were standing at the bottom
of the well formed by the cases and the recess of the bulkhead. The volunteer held a hurricane lantern and its light
cast fantastic shadows of their heads on the steel plates of
the bulkhead.

But though my eyes took in the details of the scene in that
one quick glance, what they centred on was the side of one
of the cases opposite the bulkhead door. This had been let
down like a flap. Sedel was speaking. His voice was soft and

I only caught a phrase here and there. I heard the word
" bait " followed by that effeminate titter of his. ". . . the
boy friend," he said. " Your father " was mentioned, then
I heard my own name. He laughed again and said rather
louder, " I just thought you'd like to know that everything
has gone off according to plan, Miss Schmidt. Close her up
now, Hans. Pleasant dreams. We shall be in the Reich
to-morrow."

There was the bang of the case being closed and then the
light disappeared and the bulkhead door grated as it was
closed.

I waited for more than ten minutes before venturing
down. The first thing I did was to go over to the bulkhead
door. Inch by inch, so that it made hardly a sound, I pressed
it back. As soon as there was room I squeezed through. The
trapdoor was closed. All was dark in the main hold. The
only sound was the slapping of the water against the sides
of the ship and the incessant throbbing of the engines. I
stood there a while, listening and wondering whether this was
perhaps a trap. Supposing they knew I had not left the ship?
Supposing they had not gone out by the trapdoor, but were
hiding up there among the tanks?

Well, I had to risk that. I slid the bulkhead door back
again and switched on my torch. It did not take me long to
locate the dummy case. I had marked it carefully and,
searching across the surface, I found tiny holes at the corners.
The thing was bolted on the inside and the bolts were
operated, I discovered, by a large screw in the centre. Fortunately I had a sixpence on me and the groove of the screw
was big enough for me to turn it with this.

I lowered the flap. Freya's eyes were open, but she could
not move her head. A canvas gag was stretched tightly
across her mouth and fixed on each side of her head to the
bottom of the case. Her arms and legs were bound to
wooden supports in much the same way as mine had been
strapped to the clamps in the deed-box. I told her who I was
as I set to work on the gag. I don't think she believed me,
for her first words to me when I had removed the gag were,
" Will you shine the torch on your face?" I did so. " Then
you really are Andrew Kilmartin," she said, and smiled. It

was only then that I realised that she must have seen the evening papers the day before and had thought me dead. I said no more then, for her eyes were closed.

It took me some time to untie all the knots. But at length she was free and I picked her up in my arms and lifted her out of her cramped quarters. Quickly I worked at her hands and legs to restore the circulation. Every moment I was afraid someone would come through from the main hold and discover me in the act of releasing her.

It must have been a quarter of an hour before she was able to move her limbs freely enough to be able to attempt the ladder. I closed up the case and slid back the bulkhead door. We passed through, and closing the door behind us, began the ascent of the ladder. How she managed it, I don't know. She had been in that dummy munition case for well over twelve hours and her limbs were stiff and very painful. Yet I dared not delay longer than was absolutely necessary. I sent her up first, myself following very close so that she could rest her weight on my shoulder. Even so it was a struggle and once or twice I was certain we must both fall.

At length we were safe among the tanks. I think she fainted with the reaction then. She lay very still for a while, whilst I chafed her limbs. After some time she stirred and sat up. I felt her hand on mine. " It really is you, isn't it?" she asked. " I didn't dream that?"

" You thought I was dead?" I asked.

" Yes," she said. " It was all over the papers on . . . What's to-day?"

I glanced at my watch. " We're ten minutes into Monday," I said.

" And on the *Thirlmere* headed for Germany?"

" Yes," I said. " We should reach Norwegian territorial waters about ten in the morning."

" Have they got the boat on board?"

" Yes. And your father is on board, too."

" I know. That man Sedel told me just before you let me out. Franzie thought he was being so clever, and they knew all the time. Sedel said they also had David."

" I'm afraid so," I said. And then added, " He came on board quite openly for the dedication ceremony as a camera-

man. Your father had told him they had brought you on
board in a tank and he came to rescue you."

" I know." She spoke dispiritedly. " I was the bait. Sedel
told me that. How well their scheme has worked—Franzie,
David, and you, too! Why did you come on board?"

" I was determined to prevent the engine from getting out
of the country somehow," I said.

" Ah," she said. " I'm glad it was not on account of me."

" I did not know you were on board until I met David,"
I explained. Then I told her how I had escaped from the
vaults of Marburg's and of my flight through the sewers.
" You see," I finished, " I just had to square up accounts
somehow."

She pressed my hand and in the darkness I sensed that she
was smiling. " The obstinate Scot in you, Andrew." And
she gave a gurgle of laughter. " Franzie insists that your
obstinacy is the key to your whole character."

I was glad of the darkness. The blood had rushed to my
cheeks at her use of my Christian name, and I should have
hated her to notice it. " How did you fall into their
clutches?" I asked.

Apparently she had picked up an " 18 " bus and got out
at Guilford Street. They had been waiting for her outside
the digs. There had been a black saloon car at the kerb and
a uniformed chauffeur had come up to her just as she was
getting out her key. He was in Bart's livery. Would she
come at once to the hospital? Mr. Kilmartin had been
brought there and was asking for her. He had been badly
cut up in a car smash. She had hesitated. It was the old
dodge and she was suspicious. Then he played his trump
card. He showed her the evening paper. He had relied on her
not reading the story through and discovering where the
accident was supposed to have taken place. When she
pointed out that I was supposed to be dead, he told her that
the journalists were a little premature, that was all. Then
she had got into the car. And of course they had to stop and
pick up a famous surgeon from his home in Gray's Inn.
Chloroform had done the rest. She did not know anything
about being brought on board in a tank. The first thing
she had remembered was the cramped feeling of that case.

After telling me this, she asked me whether anyone had been able to communicate with the authorities. I told her how far I had got. When I had finished, she said, " But you are not hopeful?"

" Frankly, no," I said. " But we can't be sure."

" Then if we are going to try anything on our own, we had best wait till we reach Norwegian territorial waters?"

" If we can," I agreed. " But don't forget, even supposing they are prepared to let you have a quiet night, they will be down in the morning."

" How silly of me—of course." She was on the point of putting another question when she stopped. There was a sudden empty feeling in the pit of my stomach. I did not need the rush of cold air to tell me what the sound was that had stopped Freya. The trapdoor had been thrown back.

Then there was a soft thud as it closed again and an instant later a torch was switched on. Freya and I had slid behind the nearest tank. Peering round its gun turret, I saw that two men were descending the ladder. I did not know what to do. Naturally my first thought was that it was Sedel and his companion returning to question Freya about something. And once they discovered that she was no longer there, the hunt would be up. We had no weapons. The position was hopeless.

But the men, instead of climbing to the bottom of the ladder, dropped off it on to the cases. My heart was in my mouth as I thrust Freya farther into the shadow of the tank, for they were coming straight towards us.

Then the beam of the torch swung upward and I saw the face of the second man. It was in profile as the first one, who was much shorter, indicating the tank behind which we were hiding. " You see, they have two-pounders like the ones on deck," said the little man. " We can test down here."

In the instant that I had recognised the big man to whom the words were addressed, Freya had let go of my hand and rushed forward. " Franzie!" she cried, and flung herself into the arms of the smaller of the two men.

" Quite a gathering of the clans," I said, as I stepped forward. The torch was shone on my face. Then Schmidt put

Freya to one side and took my hand. "It's you, Kilmartin, is it?" he said, and I had a feeling he was going to embrace me. But he restrained himself and said quietly, "I was so afraid they had got you."

"Andrew has been chased through the sewers," Freya explained in a rush of words. "Then he got on board as a pressman and has just rescued me from an empty munition case in which they'd imprisoned me. All wonderfully melodramatic. But how did you get down here? Only a little while ago Sedel told me that he knew you were on board."

Schmidt took off his glasses and polished them vigorously. His big dark eyes were brilliant in the torchlight. "There are certain advantages in being employed in the galley. The volunteers mess together. They are all sound asleep now. So, I fancy, are Sedel and his chief of staff. I took them coffee after they had returned from visiting Freya."

"He's an absolute wizard," David said. "Drugged the lot of them. Then he came and let me out of the chain locker in which they'd imprisoned me. Now we take control of the ship."

"You go too fast, Mr. Shiel," put in Schmidt. "We can only make our preparations to take over the ship. We can go to our action stations, but we cannot go into action until we have dropped our escort."

"But with those pseudo-volunteers all unconscious it would be so easy," David insisted. "Just tie them up, take their guns and have the ship turned back."

"You seem to have forgotten our escort," Schmidt said quietly. "My dear Mr. Shiel, we cannot show our hand until they have shown theirs. That is, of course, unless Mr. Kilmartin can assure me that the British Government is by now convinced that this ship is bound for Germany." He turned to me. "You have made attempts to convince the authorities, yes?"

I nodded. "Frankly, I am not very hopeful," I said.

He put his glasses on again. "Then my plan is best," he said. "We must give them the rope necessary to hang themselves. They will wake up in the morning to find everything just as it was the night before, except that myself and the two prisoners will have disappeared. I doubt whether they will have time to make a thorough search of the ship, for it will be getting late by then. They will say good-bye to their escort and, when she has passed out of sight, they will go through with their plan to take control of the ship. The course will be set for Germany."

" And where are we?" asked Freya.

"Inside one of the tanks on the deck. Here "—he waved his hand round the hold—" we have ammunition of several kinds. Ammunition for machine-guns. Ammunition for these two-pounders. We take a stock of ammunition up to our tank and then we have command of the ship." He looked at me. " You agree?" he asked.

I nodded. It really seemed most ingenious. " It's essential that they show their hand first," I said. " It will be clear proof and that's the only way to convince the British Government."

" Good! Then let us get to work."

Schmidt had done his reconnaissance work well. He could distinguish the markings on the cases, and with the aid of tools from one of the tanks we soon had a case of machine-gun and a case of two-pounder ammunition opened. The cases were bound with light metal bands and these David broke by inserting a large screwdriver and twisting. At one moment, whilst we were standing by watching him break open a case, Schmidt took my arm. " I am overjoyed to find you here," he said. " I cannot thank you enough."

I laughed. " I should thank you," I said. " You have given me back my youth." My eyes as I spoke were fixed on Freya. She looked tired, but that did not mar the beauty of her features. She was watching David with his broad powerful shoulders bent to the task of breaking the metal bands.

When both cases were open, Schmidt took us over to the nearest tank and we climbed in. Briefly he explained to the three of us the workings of the machine-gun and the two-pounder. As soon as he was satisfied that we knew how to work both guns in an emergency, we climbed out again and set about the task of removing the necessary quantity of ammunition on deck. David had brought two sacks with him and into each of these we dropped as much as one man could carry. Schmidt and I were to do the donkey work. David was to act as escort and effectively silence any opposition, if we were unlucky enough to meet any. It must be

emembered that, though the volunteers were presumably all
drugged, the crew were still awake. "There's a watch on the
bridge," Schmidt told us, as we began to climb the ladder.
"But he should be looking in front of him."

David led the way, with myself, then Schmidt, and Freya
bringing up the rear. The trapdoor was pushed quietly
back, making a square of white light. I followed David on to
the fo'c'sle to find the whole ship bathed in brilliant moonlight. Involuntarily I paused. It was a wonderful sight after
the darkness of the hold. The moon was almost full and
hung low over the sea, so that a path of dancing light showed
to the horizon. And in the midst of that silver path was the
black outline of our escort. The *Thirlmere* herself was
brilliantly lit, every object clear-cut and accentuated by the
darkness of the shadow it cast. Beside the open trapdoor one
of the volunteers lay dozing. It was bitterly cold after the
warmth of the hold.

No one was in sight and David led the way quickly to the
well deck, where we were at once swallowed up in the shadow
of the high bulwarks. Schmidt had chosen one of the central
tanks next to the torpedo boat. His choice, I discovered
later, had been governed by its field of fire, which was
excellent. It was so placed that from it we could rake the
whole of the fo'c'sle and cover the one entrance to the hold.

The most dangerous job, so far as discovery was concerned, was getting into the tank. This could only be done
through its two small hatches. Freya went first, and we spent
several uncomfortable seconds as, lying flat on the moonlit
surface of the tank, she pulled open one of the hatches and
slipped inside. Apparently no one had seen her. She closed
the hatch and opened up the driver's protecting flap. Fortunately this was in shadow and we passed the ammunition
through without fear of discovery. Then the three of us went
back to the hold. This time we closed up the cases after fill-
ing the sacks with ammunition, and when we emerged on to
the fo'c'sle again, we put back the trapdoor. We made the
well deck without incident. But then David noticed the figure
of the man on watch standing on the edge of the bridge. He
was gazing in the direction of the destroyer. At length he
turned and very deliberately stared the length of the ship.

I felt he must see us. But he moved towards the other end
of the bridge and disappeared from view behind the chart
room. We hesitated a moment and then crossed the patch
of moonlight into the shelter of the tanks. After passing the
second load of ammunition to Freya, we climbed in through
the driver's flap, closing it behind us.

Schmidt had had the foresight to provide sandwiches. I
appreciated this, for I was by now extremely hungry. The
quarters were cramped and uncomfortable, though the tank
had been designed to hold a crew of four. Freya was marvellous. She was suffering both physically and mentally from
her long imprisonment in the munition case. Fresh from
my experience of Sedel's deed-box, I understood how she felt.
She was in great need of strenuous exercise to free her
cramped muscles, and she was suffering from a sense of
claustrophobia.

The moonlight filtered in through the gun vents, casting
thin white beams across the dark interior of the tank.
Schmidt had taken up his post in the gun turret, whilst David
was in the driver's seat. Placed opposite Freya as I was, it
was not long before I noticed that she was suffering from
violent shivers every now and then. It was the sense of being
closed up, and at length I leaned forward and gave her arm
an encouraging squeeze. She turned and I saw that her face
was very pale and that she was biting her lips. She took my
hand then and held it tight. It seemed to help her, for after
a time her grip relaxed and she fell asleep with her head
against the butt of a machine-gun.

We had divided the night up into three watches of two
hours each. David took the first watch. I relieved him at
four in the morning, having slept fitfully. When he woke me,
I found that Freya's hand was still in mine. Her head was
bowed over the gun and her muscles were relaxed. My arm
was cramped, but I dared not let go her hand for fear of
waking her. Schmidt took over at six.

I woke him by tapping against his legs, which extended
below the turret. The moon had set and it was very dark
inside the tank, so that I had to feel for them. I was by
then becoming very tired of my position. Nevertheless, I
slept soundly, and the next thing I knew was that someone

was shaking me. It was Freya, and as I opened my mouth
to speak, she put her hand over it. It felt warm and soft
against my lips. Shafts of sunlight threaded into the interior
of the tank, which was now quite light. The ship was alive
about us. Orders were being shouted and there was the
clatter of boots on the steel deck plates.

"It's past nine," she whispered in my ear. "And they've
discovered that we're missing. They're searching the hold."

I sat up and looked through my gun sights. I could see
the whole of the for'ard part of the ship. The grey superstructure of the bridge shone in the morning sunshine. And
beyond was blue sky sweeping down to the shimmering green
of the sea. There was not a cloud to be seen and the sun
was already high in the sky on the port bow. The position of
the sun told me that we were still headed for the Kattegat.
Presumably we had not yet dropped our escort. The trapdoor to the hold was open and I saw one of the volunteers
come out. He climbed the ladder to the bridge and was met
by Sedel. He shouted something and Sedel cursed.

Schmidt came down from his perch in the gun turret. His
unshaven chin accentuated the pallor of his face. But though
he looked tired, almost ill, his eyes were as alive as ever.
He had a word with David, who climbed quietly out of
the driver's seat and joined us in the body of the tank.

"Freya, you will pass up the ammunition when required,"
Schmidt said in a low voice. "Mr. Shiel, you will take over
this gun, and Mr. Kilmartin, you will stay where you are. If
they begin searching these tanks before the escort is dropped,
we shall have to show our hand. That will be unfortunate.
But I do not think they will. It is now nine-forty-five and
they are due to part from the escort at any moment . Then
they will take control of the ship. The Norwegians will be
taken for'ard. When I am certain that all the volunteers are
either in the fo'c'sle or on the bridge, I shall open fire. I
shall blow away each end of the bridge, and you will both
fire a few bursts with your machine-guns in order to test
the accuracy of your aim. Under no circumstances must any
of the volunteers be allowed to reach the well deck alive. Our
only danger is if we are taken in the rear. We shall have
nothing to fear from the crew, only from the volunteers.

The only way they can get aft is by means of the well deck.
It is your business, with the machine-guns, to see they do not
leave the fo'c'sle. We have plenty of ammunition."

I cannot begin to describe the impression Schmidt created.
It was strange to see this shabby little Jew, unshaven and
filthy with oil, issuing precise and elaborate orders for action.
And yet it was not incongruous. It was in the character of the
man. I remembered the impression I had had of him in my
office, a hunted, frightened man, fleeing from justice. Physically he still gave that impression of weakness. Yet there was
neither weakness nor indecision in his black eyes. He gave
us our orders as though he were arranging the mechanism
of a machine. He brought to a scene of action the cool, clear
brain of an engineer, and at zero hour he made his disposi-
tions and explained his plan as though he were in a laboratory
about to conduct an important experiment.

When he had finished, he climbed back into the turret. I
was completely awake now, and I waited, my mind alert and
my eyes fixed on my field of vision, with only the slightest
void in my stomach to indicate that we were about to go into
action.

There was much coming and going on the fo'c'sle. Sedel
was constantly issuing orders, and once Marburg himself
appeared, his features as expressionless as ever. It was
strange to be bottled up in that tank on such a beautiful
morning. Stranger still to imagine the burst of action that
would break out in this ship as soon as the escort had been
dropped. Everything was so bright and fresh, with promise
of summer in the warmth of the sunshine. I thought of the
battle of the River Plate. Fought in conditions of bright
sunlight, the combatants must have felt much as I did at the
thought of fighting on a day that was so obviously made for
pleasure.

My thoughts were interrupted by the sight of all the men
I could see on the fo'c'sle standing motionless, gazing to port.
I guessed that the escort was closing with the *Thirlmere*,
before she came into my field of vision. Very sleek and
beautiful, and rather deadly she looked, with the bow wave
creaming white against her grey hull. She came up fast to
within a stone's throw. I could see the gold braid on the
commander's cap as he hailed us through cupped hands.

I could not hear what he said. But after receiving a reply from our bridge, the destroyer sheered off and swung away from us in a great arc. The captain had come to the port side of the bridge and stood watching the destroyer as she fell astern of us. His figure, rigid against the cloudless blue of the sky, was joined by two others—Marburg and Sedel.

Five, ten minutes—I don't know how long they stayed there watching the departure of their escort. Time meant nothing to me at that moment. A minute seemed a lifetime.

Then suddenly Sedel raised his hand to his lips. A whistle shrilled out, loud and insistent above the throb of the engines. The captain turned towards him and then his eyes fell to the thing in Sedel's hands. Almost involuntarily his hands rose above his head. Then suddenly he swung his right at Sedel's chin. But the German had anticipated the blow. He stepped back, quickly, precisely, and then deliberately fired two shots. The captain never recovered from his lunge, but plunged straight on and fetched up, sprawled across the railings of the bridge. Then slowly his body slipped from sight, his cap tilted drunkenly over his eyes.

Zero hour! The thing had been planned and I could imagine the precision with which it was executed. The wireless operator would look up as the door of his cabin opened. If he resisted, he would be ruthlessly shot down like the captain. If not. . . . Already they were herding the members of the crew on the fo'c'sle. Several passed under guard along the well deck within a few feet of us. They were searched and bundled into one of the fo'c'sle cabins. Only the engine-room crew were left. Presumably a guard had been placed over them. Meantime, the ship had changed course and the sun was now on the starboard bow.

The minutes ticked slowly by. I thought Schmidt would never give the word to go into action. But I understood the reason for his delay. The farther we got off our course in the direction of Germany, the clearer the proof of guilt. There was a great deal of movement on the fo'c'sle. In the bustle of the ship's capture I had endeavoured to keep check on the number of volunteers now for'ard. As far as I could tell there were eight, besides Sedel and Marburg. That left only two unaccounted for, and they would presumably be looking after the engine-room.

A man came hurrying down from the bridge with a small bundle under his arm. He stopped at the foot of the mast and looped it to a halyard. Then he hauled the bundle up and the Nazi swastika flag was broken out at the masthead. There was a great cheer from the fo'c'sle at this. And then there was the sound of orders being issued and a moment later two of the men came hurrying down from the bridge. They went straight to the trapdoor leading to the hold.

" Get them covered," I heard Schmidt say. My hand closed round the trigger of my gun. The cold feel of the steel was somehow comfortingly impersonal. I held the two of them in my sights. " Fire!" came Schmidt's voice. I heard the rat-a-tat-tat of David's gun as I pressed my trigger. The gun chattered in my hand. Both men were thrown against the side of the deck housing with the force of the twofold burst of fire.

Then the whole tank rocked and my ear drums sang as Schmidt fired the gun. Through the narrow aperture of my sights I saw the whole of the port side of the bridge, where the captain had so recently been shot, explode. The flash of the explosion seemed a part of this detonation above my head. The whole side of the bridge burst into fragments. Then the structure subsided gently until it hung draped against the more solidly constructed deck housing. A second explosion followed almost immediately. This time the shot was fired at the starboard side of the bridge, but only the extreme edge of it was carried away.

There followed a complete and startled silence, so that above the throb of the engines I heard a gull screaming imprecations at the disturbance. Then, as though some vitalising force had suddenly brought the ship to life again, it echoed with shouts and the running of feet. Two men swung themselves down the broken superstructure of the bridge, heavy service revolvers swinging from their lanyards.

" Give them a few warning bursts," Schmidt ordered.

We did so, and the two of them dived for cover. The hatch of the gun turret clanged above my head as Schmidt threw it open. " I wish to speak to Baron Marburg," he shouted.

No one answered him.

" Unless he comes forward in ten seconds," Schmidt called out, " I shall put another shell into the bridge."

I could hear him counting softly to himself. The now derelict-seeming superstructure of the bridge was lifeless. Eight—nine—ten. Once again the tank bucked to the kick of the gun. This time the whole of the starboard end of the bridge collapsed into a mass of twisted wreckage.

"Do you want me to demolish the whole forward part of the ship bit by bit?" Schmidt called out.

But Marburg had already made his appearance. He was at the port end of the bridge, his heavy body in silhouette against the sun. "Who are you and what do you want?" The question was put in a cold dispassionate voice. I think at that moment I admired the man. I could well imagine the shock that burst of fire must have been to him, when everything had appeared to be going according to plan. Yet there was no tremor in his voice. He might have been addressing a board meeting.

"My name is Franz Schmidt," came the reply from above my head. "I think you may remember it in connection with a new type of Diesel engine. As you will realise, we control this ship. We have plenty of ammunition and we can quite easily blast the whole of the upper works of the ship away. As a last resort, of course, we have the means of blowing the ship up."

"What do you want?" As he asked this question Marburg glanced over his shoulder as though to speak to someone. Then he added, "I understand the strength of your position. Do you want us to put back to England?"

"There is no need for that," Schmidt replied. "I want you to send the crew down into the well deck. They are to come down one by one, and remember that I know them all by sight."

"Very well, I will do that." Marburg disappeared. We waited anxiously. I was afraid that they would try driving the crew in front of them as a shield. I knew we could not afford to be squeamish, but my whole being revolted at the idea of shooting innocent neutrals down in cold blood, however imperative the reason.

"Keep the approaches to the well deck covered," came Schmidt's voice.

I, too, had seen the movement of a man's head that had prompted the warning. The next instant four of the volun-

teers dashed forward, two from either side of the deck houses.
Their intention was to jump on to the well deck. But they
hadn't a chance. Before they had covered the few feet of
open deck they fell, riddled with bullets. And to add point
to their death Schmidt fired another round at the bridge,
demolishing a further section on the port side.

" Now perhaps you will send the prisoners singly into the
well deck?"

After a few moments the first of the crew appeared.
Schmidt spoke rapidly in Norwegian. The man came down
to the well deck and stopped at a point where he was covered
by our guns. He was followed by eight others. Schmidt then
spoke for several minutes. Though I did not understand a
word of what he was saying, I guessed that he was explaining
the situation to them and giving them instructions. At length
he dismissed them.

They immediately made their way aft. Three of them had
taken guns from the dead Germans. I learned later that one
of them was killed in a fight with the two engine-room
guards. Both of the Germans were killed. A moment later
the donkey engine came to life.

My task of keeping watch on the for'ard part of the ship
prevented me from seeing what was happening aft. But I
knew well enough what Schmidt's intention was. He was
getting the torpedo boat unshipped. The work took more
than a quarter of an hour. By the time he announced that it
was completed and the boat lowered over the side, I had
sighted what I instantly knew Marburg had sighted when
he had spoken with us from the bridge. Beyond the broken
superstructure I made out the sharp black bows of a destroyer. The huge wave at her bow told of engines running
at full speed. Close behind her came a second.

Schmidt dropped into the interior of the tank. He had
seen the danger. " We have only just time," he said. " Freya,
get out as quickly as you can. Get the engine started. You,"
he said to me, " and Shiel will follow. Take a drum of
ammunition each. They fit the guns on the boat. I'll keep the
bridge occupied."

" No, you go," I said. " Let me stay."

" There's no time for argument," was the curt reply.

I realised that his decision was final. Freya was already

clambering out. I followed her, with David close at my
heels. The first thing I noticed as I jumped on to the deck
was the gap left by the torpedo boat. The great derrick boom
was swung over the side of the ship. I slipped down at the
rear of the tank just as a bullet ricocheted off the armour
plating. An instant later the whole vehicle shook as Schmidt
fired straight into the centre of the bridge.

No more shots were fired after that. We slid down a rope
ladder into the boat. Freya went aft to get the engine going,
whilst David and I manned the machine-guns. Close above
our heads hung the great girder on which the boat had been
lowered. The moments seemed like hours. And every minute
the two destroyers were coming closer. I could see the
swastika flags quite clearly now.

Suddenly there was a roar overhead and a large plane swept
by black against the sun. I looked round the packed boat.
It hardly seemed as though we had a chance. As soon as we
were clear of the *Thirlmere* we should be under fire from
the destroyers. And now there was this plane. An instant
later the engine came to life. Still we waited. Then came
the sound of three shots, clear and distinct above the noise
of the engine. I looked up just as Schmidt swung himself over
the side and slid on to the deck. At the same moment the
engine roared again and we began to move, swinging away
from the side of the *Thirlmere*.

I glanced back to see Freya, her hair blowing free in the
gathering wind of our movement, holding the wheel, her
face splodged with grease and a smile on her lips. Behind
her towered the bulk of the *Thirlmere*. Figures were moving
on the broken bridge structure. A rifle cracked and then
another. I swung my gun on to these tiny targets and
opened fire.

When next I glanced back, Freya had handed the wheel to
her father and was moving towards the engine hatch. She
caught my eyes as she disappeared. There was the light of
battle in her eyes and she lifted a small object that hung
from a chain round her neck. For an instant I did not understand the significance of her gesture. Then I realised that this
was the key to the special valve. For the first time the
Schmidt Diesel engine was to show its paces.

A few minutes later the boat seemed to leap forward in

the water, and the high-pitched drone of the engine almost drowned the clatter of my gun. The bows rose high out of the water and the spray swept from them in two great curves that glinted in the sunlight with rainbow tints. In an instant it seemed we were out of range.

As soon as I joined Schmidt in the deckhouse I knew that he was wounded. His left arm hung limp from the shoulder and a dark stain showed just above the elbow. But he refused to hand the wheel to anyone. " It's only a scratch," he yelled at me, and his face was a white mask in which his eyes glowed feverishly like coals.

Above the roar of the engine the distant boom of a gun sounded—then another and another. Three great fountains of water shot up ahead of us. Schmidt swung the wheel over and the boat skidded round on her stern. Behind us I could see the bow waves of the two destroyers white and menacing. The hunt was up and I could not believe that we could possibly escape from those sharp-nosed sea hounds. Boom, boom, boom! More fountains of spray, this time only fifty yards on the port bow. Again the boat skidded in a great curve as the wheel went hard over. The water creamed in our wake, a huge half circle of foam-flecked sea. The day was perfect.

Then suddenly a shadow swept like a huge bird across the sea, and down across our stern came the plane. Schmidt swung the boat away to port again. The aircraft swept past only fifty feet above our heads. David had swung his gun on to it. But he did not fire, for as she climbed steeply up into the azure blue of the sky, the sun glinted on her wings, showing us the triple circles of the Royal Air Force against the drab grey and green of her camouflage paint.

More shells, this time astern. Over went the wheel again. With shaded eyes I watched the flight of the aircraft. She had circled in a great bank and was now headed back towards the destroyer. I watched her, fascinated. She had climbed to about a thousand feet. But instead of attacking the German destroyers, she skirted them and swept on to the *Thirlmere*, now no more than a drab grey toy ship far astern.

When she was no more than a speck in the sky, the size of a gull, the plane dived. She swept over the *Thirlmere*. Six tiny dots slipped from beneath her. She must have straddled the ship nicely, for an instant later the *Thirlmere* seemed to burst into a thousand fragments. Even at that distance the roar of the explosion was shatteringly loud. For a while a pall of smoke hung like a cloud over the spot where the *Thirlmere* had been. When it cleared away, the sea beyond the two German destroyers was clear to the horizon.

A moment later the clatter of the destroyers' pom-poms sounded as the aircraft dived to the attack of our pursuers. But already we were drawing away from them at a tremendous pace, the whole boat shuddering under our feet as though at any moment the engine must shake loose from its mountings. And hull down on the horizon ahead we saw two ships. They grew rapidly larger and Schmidt swung our own boat away to port with the intention of skirting them. But David, who had found a pair of glasses in the control room, reported that they were flying the white ensign. It was, in fact, the *Thirlmere*'s late escort in company with another destroyer. We closed with them shortly before noon and the enemy destroyers then sheered off. Just before twelve-thirty we were joined by three Avro Ansons of the Coastal Command.

Freya came up the companionway from the engine-room a little later. Her wide grey eyes were alight with excitement. She went for'ard towards her father who was still at the wheel. As she came abreast of where I stood beside my gun, she paused and looked up into my face. "I'm so happy," she said. And then suddenly my heart was jumping at the touch of her hand on mine. "We owe so much to you," she added. "I want you to know . . ."

But her words were drowned in the clamour of the pom-poms on the destroyers. Three black specks swept down at us out of the sun. The roar of them rose to a scream that drowned the thunder of the guns. Huge spouts of water rose all round us. There was no doubt that we and not the destroyers were the target. Suddenly they were no longer black specks but huge winged objects in silhouette against the blue sky as they swept up out of their dive. Three more followed. More spouts of water. The deck was soaked with spray so that the water ran green in the scuppers. They were Heinkels and down behind them came the three Ansons. One of the Heinkels failed to pull out of its dive and hit the

water with a crack of broken metal within a hundred yards
of us.

And when that first dive was over and we remained miraculously unhit, I found my arm was about Freya and she
was clinging to my coat as though for protection from the
rain of high explosive. I did not move, and we stood there
watching the Avros scrapping with the Heinkels a thousand
feet above us in the blue. A squadron of Hurricanes appeared suddenly from the west. The Heinkels broke and with
their noses down made off into the sun. The Hurricanes
circled above us, and the rest of the way to Harwich we had
an escort of fighters. Twice enemy aircraft were sighted, but
each time they made off.

The aircraft that had destroyed the *Thirlmere* was not able
to press home her attack on the German destroyers owing
to shortage of bombs. She circled lazily round us like a great
buzzard as our little procession made for home. Half an
hour later she was joined by three more machines of the
Coastal Command.

At the time, I remember, I said to Schmidt, " The Government seem determined to make amends." I thought the procession unnecessary. But shortly before one, a flight of a
dozen Heinkels swept down out of the sun. We were left in
no doubt as to the object of their visit, for they avoided
the destroyers and dived in formation straight down upon our
own little craft. One again Schmidt's engine showed its
paces. The boat skidded to starboard and seemed to crane
right up out of the water as we closed with the nearest
destroyer for the protection of her guns.

The Heinkel formation was broken up by the skill and
daring of our own pilots before the attack could be pressed
home. Nevertheless, we seemed to be surrounded by spouts
of water. One of these was so close that solid water fell on
to us, soaking us all to the skin. The rattle of machine-gun
fire could be heard even above the racket of the destroyers'
guns. The action lasted about a quarter of an hour. The
enemy was at length driven off with the loss of two machines.
We lost one.

Shortly after this, no less than twenty-five aircraft of the
Coastal Command joined us. It was borne in on me then
that the authorities were suddenly taking the whole thing

very seriously. Twice before we reached port enemy aircraft
were sighted, but no attack was made.

At Harwich we were met by Sir Geoffrey Carr and Air
Marshal Sir Jervis Mayle. Fisher was also there, and it was
he who explained to me why the authorities had finally
decided to act.

Fisher himself had pressed them to detain and search the
Thirlmere, but without success. Sir John Kelf had seen the
Prime Minister. But the *Thirlmere* was the toy of big
financial interests and no member of the Cabinet was willing
to take action on such flimsy evidence. But by Sunday evening Fisher and his proprietor had created sufficient stir in
Whitehall for individual inquiries to be made by at least
two Cabinet ministers. M.I.5 contributed an interesting
document on the peculiar circumstances of Llewellin's death,
linking up with the activities of Sedel. Then there was the
trouble at the Calboyd Works at Oldham. Fisher's local man
reported that the body found at Strangler's Beach corres-
ponded with the description of the missing Calboyd works
manager. The Yard's contribution came from Crisham, who
was able to produce the statement I had left with my bank.
On top of it all came MacPherson's story of David Shiel's
capture on the *Thirlmere*.

Even then no action was taken. But the First Lord decided
to keep an eye on the *Thirlmere* after she had parted from
her escort. As soon as the aircraft reported that the munition
ship had changed course and was making for Germany, the
escort destroyer, together with another, was ordered to
capture the *Thirlmere* by boarding.

" Kelf was with the First Lord at the time," Fisher said,
" and things were apparently pretty tense. Mayle was there
with a report from A.I. about the relative speed of secret
German Diesels. Combined with the sudden revelation of
the attitude of the technical staff at Calboyds, this report
had scared him a good deal. From that moment he'd put all
his hopes on the engine that was supposed to be on the
Thirlmere. Kelf says he was almost out of his mind when
the message came through that two German destroyers were
closing with the *Thirlmere*. Then, of course, came the news
of your getaway. Actual wording of the message was:
' Torpedo boat left *Thirlmere* stop Making tremendous speed

due West.' The order was then given to sink the *Thirlmere*. You know the rest. The quality of that engine was largely measured by the lengths to which Germany had gone to obtain it."

Fisher was right there. It had needed German initiative to bring the invention of an Austrian Jew to the notice of the Air Ministry. The importance of that invention is best judged by results.

THE END

HAMMOND INNES

"His work stands in a class by itself." *V. S. Pritchett*

Atlantic Fury
"For sheer physical authenticity and power of sustained and vivid imagery . . . stands almost *sans pareil* in seagoing literature. This powerful, storm-wracked, rock-hard novel demands to be judged by Conradian standards." *Peter Green, Bookman*

Wreckers Must Breathe
A tale of espionage, violence and the claustrophobic stress of life under the sea. "Hammond Innes deals magnificently with disaster." *Observer*

The White South
"I can still hear the roar of the ice as the great bergs close in upon those stranded men of the whaling fleet." *Daphne du Maurier*

Maddon's Rock
"As grim and thrilling as you could wish . . . Hammond Innes certainly knows how to describe storms at sea." *Oxford Mail*

The Strode Venturer
"Yes! A rip-roarer!—those action sequences at which he is so brilliant, the equatorial heat, the bubbling seabed, an outworn ship and a drunken skipper—Splendid!" *Richard Lister, Evening Standard*

Dead and Alive
The disappearance of a girl in the chaos of post-war Europe leads to a dangerous expedition among men who deal in violence and death. "Hammond Innes has an ability to make anything he touches excitingly readable." *Dennis Wheatley*

All available in Fontana Books

HAMMOND INNES

"Hammond Innes is a writer who is a master of his craft —he earns my enjoyment as much as my respect." *John Connell*

The Angry Mountain
"Begins under the evil shadow of terrorism in Czecho-slovakia . . . reaches a magnificent climax on the slopes of Vesuvius in full eruption." *Sunday Times*

The Land God Gave to Cain
"It is set along and beyond the construction camps of a great railway being driven yard by yard into the wastes of the Labrador . . . A first-class story, a highly authentic background—Hammond Innes scores on both counts." *Richard Lister, Evening Standard*

Air Bridge
"Hammond Innes is in the forefront of modern writers of the straightforward action story. He achieves a masterly sense of urgency as the story rises to the climax." *Daily Telegraph*

The Blue Ice
A desperate man searches for precious metals among the desolate mountains of Norway. "The description of the long, lonely ski trek is a masterpiece." *Manchester Evening News*

The Wreck of the Mary Deare
"The ship and the sea that batters it emerge as dramatis personae in their own right." *Peter Quennell, Daily Mail* "People say people can't write stories any more. Tell that to Hammond Innes!" *John Metcalfe, Sunday Times*

The Doomed Oasis
A searing story of present-day Arabia. "The writing shines as vivid and sharp as the desert sun." *Gavin Lyall*

All available in Fontana Books